Gods, Cija, face it, write it down, put it on your page, can a nightmare break through into waking life and *that* into—into vivid supra-life, something reaching out to destroy, something out there intent on me, drawing ever nearer, reached its concentration out to *me* all the time from the other side—nearer and nearer, no longer whispers as in the City, here in the kind laughing Court that leaves me quite alone at night while I lie sweating and rigid, small and unknowledgeable and terrified and utterly alone, while it draws steadily nearer night by night, knocking, not stealthily but calmly, little groups of knocks on the wall separating it from reality—quite ready to flow through—reaching all ready and eager to reach for *me*—its long goal—and it may *be tonight,*

THE ATLAN SAGA
by Jane Gaskell:

THE SERPENT
THE DRAGON
ATLAN
THE CITY
SOME SUMMER LANDS

THE ATLAN SAGA: 2
THE DRAGON

JANE GASKELL

DAW BOOKS, INC.
DONALD A. WOLLHEIM, PUBLISHER

1633 Broadway, New York, NY 10019

And on earth shall be monsters, a generation
of dragons of men, and likewise of serpents.
Clement, Apocalyptic Fragment

First DAW Printing, March 1985

1 2 3 4 5 6 7 8 9

PRINTED IN U.S.A.

— I —

THE BED IN
SOUTHERN CITY

SMAHIL lifted me on to the saddle and solicitously bundled
his wet coat round me. He mounted and, cradling me
before him, rode down the steep path.

His arms were very tender. We had not spoken a word.
I wondered if he were embarrassed. I felt drowsy and
innocent. I had one hand on his black lapel, and felt
rocked like a child. I knew that I am at least as safe with
Smahil as no other woman can ever be.

I looked up at him.

His face, which he had cleansed, seemed to hold an
intense gravity. His lips were closed, his flaxen hair, dark-
ened by the teeming rain, was plastered in thick lank
strips to his head. He peered down at me. The bulkiness
of the coat had slipped a little. He tucked it round me
again, his muscles hard and warm through the sodden
shirt. I was held closer as he kissed my hair again and
again.

'You belong to me at last.'

The bird's claws rang no longer on the stony path of the
hill, but on the roadway.

'This is not the way to HQ,' I roused myself presently to
murmur.

He laughed contentedly.

'I shall always be sure of you while you are such a child.'

We turned down an alley with high, grimy brick walls. At first I accepted the rebuke, thinking this was a short cut I didn't know of, but when we came to turnings he consistently took the wrong one. We began to meet people, scurrying along through the puddles with their cloaks held over their heads, and I was glad that the leather wrapped me, for what shreds of my shirt remained clung transparently to my flesh.

'Where are you going, Smahil?' 'Home,' he replied, his lips against my hair.

Presently a row of high, narrow, grey-gabled houses rose out of the rain. We clattered into a courtyard, about a quarter of the size of the one at headquarters. It was quite deserted, but birds and horses could be glimpsed in the boxes which lined it. Ours picked its way splay-clawed across the puddled cobbles, big splashing puddles in which were droppings, manure, a lot of straw and fruit peels and cores. Smahil carried me to the ground and led the bird into a stall. I stood shivering in the dry, straw-filled gloom while he unsaddled.

'But, Smahil, this bird isn't even yours.'

He rubbed it down perfunctorily.

'I'll send the inn-woman's son back with it when the rain's over. Well, come into the house.'

We emerged into the rain and then into a gloomy passage, paved and walled with cracked, grubby white tiles. The effect was both antiseptic and squalid, and I was grateful for Smahil's presence. At regular intervals there were windows, without shutters, which admitted both the chill, fluctuating, grey light and spatterings of rain. There were pools on the tiles before them.

At the end of the passage was a wooden staircase.

Smahil took my hand and led me up it; it wound into real darkness and some of the treads were rickety. The whole contraption creaked and rattled mournfully at our use.

There were doors opening off from its side, darker oblongs in the darkness, one would have to be familiar with them to see them without peering, and Smahil opened one of these. To step easily from the stair to the narrow wooden doorstep required skill, particularly as the doorstep was rounded, but almost at once I found myself in a reasonably large room. Smahil shut the door behind us.

'Well?'

He faced me, his thumbs in his belt.

'I *should* be glad of a towel and—a change of clothes? —before I go home—'

'You are home.'

. . . 'But, Smahil—'

'You are home.'

He pushed me gently into a chair, and began to pull off my boots. He removed my shirt, and put his arms round me to undo my belt.

'No . . .'

Rain rattled against some window I could not see, perhaps behind one of the wall hangings. Smahil laughed softly. My belt fell, but there were his arms instead. He ripped off my soaked tights, tearing them. My skin appeared lavender in the dimness of the room. I shivered.

With a large, coarse towel he scrubbed a warmth glowing into me.

'Cija, my Cija—'

He lifted me, caressing me, and carried me over to a kind of broad cupboard door which he opened with his foot. There were several around the room. Inside the cupboard was a wide, soft bed covered with a pelt of some kind on which he laid me. He shut the door and we were alone in the cupboard bed, its privacy freshened by a breeze bearing raindrops through the little window in the wall-side. Smahil flung aside his shirt, belt and trousers and gripped me violently against him.

*   *   *

Three other young officers share this room with Smahil. I
met them when they came off duty that evening. I was
wearing some clothes which Smahil happened to have
here, a plunge-necked jacket shimmering with gold threads
and buttoning with gold dragons, a stiff, short, gold skid
over transparent trousers.

'I'm sure Terez would prefer your other mistresses not
to wear them.'

'Nonsense, you look so beautiful! Oh, Gods, how tired I
am of gold in gold, eternally conscious in every fibre of
nothing but its own hard flamboyance, like the mythical
coin-floor of the Northern king—You point the difference—
You have always pointed every difference. Damn you,
Cija, you *are* mine now.'

I reminded him that he is harbouring the murderess.

'You are never going back to that monster's headquarters,'
he said.

'You're very melodramatic—'

'Because you're no longer the child whose body drives
me insane, from whom I want never to be separated, and
who behaves as if I were an interesting rock she passed
one day and thought about never again except when it
made her—because I know something about our Mighty
General which it would be more than my life's worth even
to think of too often—because I know if he ever remembered his hostage Cija he'd have her at once—'

'Do you think I—' I cried.

'Yes, I do think you—' he mimicked. He kissed me
hungrily. He is never particularly gentle. He really dis-
likes me, I'm sure.

I see little of the other three who are usually on duty
and with whom generally we do not even eat. Even when
they bring home girls they only disappear with them into
their shut-beds. I have seen such beds in the houses of the
wealthier peasants, they obviate the need for a separate
bedroom, but these are carved, and wide. The young

leaders are quite ordinary young men, not even particularly pleasant, though perhaps I'd see a nicer side of their personalities if they thought me more than Smahil's strumpet. Occasionally it happens that one of them is off duty while Smahil is away, though mostly I am alone all day; the army is working its officers and men hard. And when they are off duty, it's usual for them to do anything but stay in their billet. But once when I was playing chess with Anad—I *thought* he was playing very off-handedly—he suddenly seized my hand as I was making a move, and dragged me across the board; the men clattered to the floor and rolled. 'All right, little Queen,' he said wittily. He gripped me as I lay on the board and kissed me.

'Anad!' I said angrily. 'Stop this at once!' and I hit the side of his head as hard as I could with the flat of my hand. I was surprised when I didn't hear his ears ring. Before anything else could develop, Smahil walked in, stripping off his cloak. He saw the situation, bounded at Anad and buffeted him back and forwards across the head. Anad stood for it at first, then decided he wouldn't, and with a roar kicked Smahil's feet from the floor. They rolled over together cursing curses unfit for a lady's ears. I threw a bowl of water over them, withered flowers and all; Smahil rose and marched me off to bed, and nothing untoward has happened since. Besides, I think they all realise by now that I am a very nice girl, which I am when nothing's bothering me.

Smahil hires the inn-woman to bring up meals; she is an indifferent cook and will sniff haughtily at me. Also, the things are usually cold after being brought up all those stairs, and the cutlery and plates are dirty.

Sometimes nowadays he takes me out to a nearby tavern. We sit in an alcove sticky and smelly with lamp-smoke, and Smahil keeps up a sneering patter with me and glares at any man who looks at me. These visits are only possible since he bought me some clothes. 'These are rather squalid outings,' I remark calmly one day, more in sympathy than in rancour. Immediately he snarls sneeringly at me. 'Regretting the days of your kitchen-sloven innocence, sliming yourself in grease to prevent our beloved fighting-monster getting food-poisoning?' Or some such thing. 'Talking of food-poisoning—' I said hotly one day.

'It's all I can afford on my pay,' he pointed out. 'Aren't you being a little demanding, doxy darling, considering that I now have to feed two mouths—and buy you clothes to make you presentable.' He always likes to mention the fact I belong to him, he seems full of resentment for the time when I kept holding him at arm's length or forcibly rejecting him. Apparently we were not such good friends as I thought in those days. 'You should have kept the clothes Terez threw at you,' he finished, then pushed his plate across the table and kissed me. He can never stop touching and kissing me nowadays, and it is true, Smahil and I call fiercely to each other, flesh to flesh, bone to bone, youth to fierce youth.

Wanted by the law, no longer with a place in the Northern headquarters, I am offered a home and protection which I must take: Smahil is not the good gay playmate I had once got into the habit of thinking him, but it is true we are violently young together, his lithe hardness makes me tremble and it is the one stable thing I have to cling to in a rather squalid little world of loneliness, chilly dreariness, cold, dirt and the corroding tongue of someone who resents the hold I have over his body and the long time for which I denied him even that hold. Physically he seems to have a core of fire.

Terez came uninvited to see him one evening. I was sitting alone, listlessly staring into the empty fireplace, empty that is except for cobwebs. I have nothing to read, I can't remember reading properly since the days I raided the library of my tower; books used to be passed backwards and forwards between the hostages and the young leaders and waiting-girls of the Beauty's household, but they were all either coquettisly pornographic, or endless lovesick poetry.

Sometimes I sew on buttons and cobble tears in Smahil's shirts, though I loathe sewing, but that doesn't take up much time—and I can't be writing in my Diary all the time. And I'm rather nervous of walking alone about these streets.

So there I was, pouting at nothing, when the door opened and in walked this superb vision in gold.

She had been magnificent in the headquarters' kitchen; now she was overpowering. She stood in the middle of the room, stared at me, and said abruptly: 'Do you know—the lord Smahil? A fair gentleman, is he in the house?'

My mind ranged quickly over the three uncouth young officers. Which did she guess I belonged to?

I rose, smiled and said, 'He'll be in soon. Do sit down. Would you like some kind of refreshment while you're waiting?'

She looked surprised, but sank into a rickety chair and loosened her flimsy wrap.

'It's a nice day outside,' I remarked.

'Yes. The sun is shining,' she vouchsafed, slightly off balance.

She stretched out her legs in front of her, tapped on the chair arm, completely ignored me.

Now I was wearing her own transparent trousers, the only women's trousers in the place, incompetent as they were. And over that one of Smahil's black officer's-shirts, which are long enough to serve the gentlemen as night-shirts when not tucked in their breeches. I found the gold jacket and skirt too bright and stiff. Curiously enough, the combination made quite a smart effect if you didn't look too closely at the skirt: so I felt perfectly at my ease with her, and was sitting relaxed when Smahil came in.

She immediately jumped to her feet. I went on filing my nails.

Terez embraced him, her bell-shaped skirt swinging up behind her as the front was flattened against him. She really has a terrific body, at the same time rounder and more muscular than mine. She was not wearing very high-soled shoes, presumably because it was him she was coming to see, and so she was only half an inch taller than him, a few inches taller than me.

'I'm not dancing this evening so I thought I'd give you a treat,' she said, so expertly winding herself about him that she was kissing the back of his neck before I could see how she'd managed it. 'This odious army business, we have not met each other for so long.'

He caressed her so boldly that I was shocked.

But he had still not disillusioned her about her new status as his ex-official mistress. Perhaps he really meant not to forgo the pleasures she could bring now she was here, but in any case it was obvious it was not her but myself that he was in a hurry to get jealous.

'I'll go and get you both some refreshment before I go for my walk,' I promised with cordial grace, and made for the door.

'Ah, don't bother,' she sighed disdainfully, meaning "I want none of the fruits of this household's kitchen". As I went she turned to look at me and she saw my trousers. Her eyes widened.

'I like the gold tracery on your ankles,' she said expressionlessly.

'Do you?' I smiled my nicest delighted-smile and closed the door on them. I felt so happy for some reason as I went down the stairs.

Avoiding too many streets, I crossed the bridge and wandered in the countryside. The trees were mainly in blossom and the air loud with song and insects. I took off my sandals and felt the grasses between my toes. Everywhere were flowers dancing with their shadows. Breezes chased ripplings of light and shadow across the meadows. I heard the maa'aa'aaing of goats and the tinkle of bells. The goatherd greeted me from the distance and when I reached him we sat down together on the bank of a blue and white stream, gurgling with stones, and ate black bread and goats' cheese. As if it was very important we discussed the seasoning of cheeses, comparing our opinions. I felt like a girl in the mountains with the peasants again. It is so long since I have been a real girl, able to toss my hair on my shoulders and smile innocently as I watch a man's eyes come shyly to my breasts, then away, then again, exploring, wondering. Perhaps they would have married me to Turg if the law-men had not come, and I should not have minded. I am of godly blood, but events have pitchforked me far from my natural niche and meadow air is the sweetest and yet the tangiest. I felt a nostalgia for Lel, whom I remembered I have not visited for so long, but there is nothing left of the wild timid brat in the little town lady with the flow of refined chatter and the nest of sophisticated vicious patrons. The goatherd and I leaned back on the bank and chewed long grasses, making their feathery tips twist in the air far out from our teeth. He was a boy my age, heavily built, his arms and legs and torso shining bronze, his greenish eyes startling pale and live in his bronze face, his grin a flash of teeth which looked clean against his face, his feet chalky with stale dust and dirt; he wore peasant boy's clothes, a goatskin jacket, a sash full of pockets, tools and knives, a pair of full, faded, blue, ragged knee-pants.

As dusk closed in the crickets came out. They went kreeep-kreeep. Kreeep-kreeep. Kreeep-kreeep.

The boy took a pipe from his sash and blew into it. The maa'aa'aa'ing increased around us from all directions and what sounded all distances. The boy bounded to his feet, held down a hand for me. His was large, the horniest and most callused whose fingers have ever caged mine, yet if ever a hand could have a respectful expression this was it.

I nodded and smiled through the twilight, and walked towards the city. The breeze made the grass a silky sea-edge about my ankles. I felt young and supple and feminine through and through, the whole universe loved and was at one with my ankles. My dress, the breeze being against me, followed the movements of my legs. I looked down and realised my dress, simple and attractive as it was, was Smahil's shirt; I shrugged. Moths flowed on the air in and out among the pin-prick stars, the sky was still china blue. The gurgle and gush of the stream down beside me in its stony bed mingled with the bells and bleating as the goats gathered. There was a smell of onions and cheese superimposed on the heady scent of meadow twilight; the boy loomed up beside me, his eyes shining on me from the bronze.

I faced him in the breeze.

'What be your name?' he asked.

'Cija.'

'Keeya.' His voice was hoarse as it hushed to handle the name. 'I'll remember,' he said simply.

I ran on into the dusk which gathered like a swift sigh from a vast purple mouth half enfolding the world. All the scents in the meadow sharpened. My sandals swung against my side; from my trousers as much as from my slim, delicate mould the peasant boy must have thought me a fine city girl.

Suddenly a hill reared up above me. A stony track, deep on either side with drifts of wild flowers among the trees' roots, led up to its crown, dim in this light but I could see its wooded shape. Was it?—My shoulders bowed and my body ached.

The mountain conical guardian of the City rose hugely black beyond the conical shadow of the hill.

I climbed the stairs slowly and entered immediately

after knocking. I hadn't expected to find Terez still there.

The light in the room seemed exactly the same as when I'd left: the seven dusty sunbeams seemed hardly redder. I'd been away little more than an hour.

Terez was squatting mainly naked on the edge of the open cupboard bed. Her hair was dishevelled, her lips swollen and her eyes glinted topaz from under languid violet-stained lids. But in sharp contrast to her physical satisfaction was the bitchiness she forced out upon me.

She glared at me with the greedy topazes as I walked to the middle of the room and again kicked off my sandals. Her head swung to follow me without a stare-flicker.

It was now I saw Smahil. He was lying back behind her in the bed-gloom, sinewy-naked, munching an apple. His face was chiselled and remote, the face of the audience at some primitive, savage blood-sport. For the first time I could expect no help from him.

And it was true. I did feel a stir of jealousy. Do I look like that when Smahil has finished with me? How intricate and yet passionate their love must have been, here in my familiar lonely room, in the hour I was gone. Of course she is a practised mistress in the art, which to me is only a new willy-nilly experience, something which happens to me.

'Slut!'

She hissed.

Suddenly I wanted to laugh. I knew that I am this particular courtesan's superior in wit, in whatever else I might be her inferior. 'You look so much more yourself, madam, as you are.' And, just as I had smiled at her earlier, I gave my very nicest, most genuine, candid chuckle.

She leaped up, her claws shimmering. For a moment I didn't even mind inciting her to draw blood. God knows, I am used enough to fighting women, it has been consistently forced upon me. But, as she plunged on to me, I remembered again that she is my superior in size and strength and certainly in experience. I remembered again her hell-cat reputation. Oh, Cousin, *damn* Smahil and his looker's-on desire to see me at last forced into displaying some strong emotion-action for *him*. *Damn* his cruel, self-ridden, looker's-on, masturbating hate for me—the curse, swift as it had to be, was like a gush of venom in my brain.

I was under her and she unremittingly heavy as any lover, without hesitation, the first thing, her nails straight for my eyes, I shall be torn and blinded and the pain—

I spat in her face and twisted, burying my face in the rug. This strained my neck almost to breaking point. The nails dug themselves into my scalp and pain stung through my eyes and ears. She was wrenching at my hair. My hand groped convulsively for something to hang on to, my only chance was to keep my face away from her, and my fingers felt something long and smooth. For a moment they didn't think to inquire what it was; then—a thong! The ribbon thong of my sandal! I clutched on it, drew the sandal in towards me, got a frenzied grip on it, turned and bashed it into her eye as the nails tore down my cheek. '*Oh*youfilthylittlesoandso,' she screamed all in one gasp. It was so piercing that I was assailed by acute nausea. I tensed all my muscles ready for the next onslaught but she had got up and was clutching her eye. 'Oh, oh, you've driven it right through my head,' she moaned and staggered, calling me a string of the filthiest names I've ever heard, though filthy was the adjective she put for me in front of every one of them.

A few months ago I'd have been stricken with apprehension and compunction, but now I stood there, disregarding the hot blood streaming down my face and neck, a fierce alert triumph burning in the place of pity.

She had removed her cupped hand now and was blinking and grimacing. Suddenly she lurched to the chair her clothes lay on and flung them at me.

'Take them, take them all then, lice-spawn!'

As they sparkled to my feet she came at me with the last

garment in her hand, the jacket stiff with raised gold thread, and seizing me before I realised what she was about she was grinding it into my back. It was far worse than any fistful of gravel could be and I had to bite my lip to prevent myself screaming. I was strongly held, there was nothing I could do but endure this merciless vengeance.

I thought it would last for eternity and when she stopped my nerves were still writhing exactly as though the torture were still continuing.

'Remember that for the rest of your life as you sleep sore in your fair boy's arms,' she whispered.

I heard her dress and wrap rustle as she pulled them on and ran down the stairs and up the alley.

Weeping, I pulled back the hanging and looked down. An amber glowing beetle in the brick alley, scurrying along after the expression of a hate like a pus-filled sore always ready in her for this or that excuse, she seemed to me the most hideous thing in the world. I stooped and gathered up the shimmering skirt and blood-streaked jacket, holding them gingerly for I loathed their touch, and dropped them through the window. Behind her a group of gutter urchins without even looking up to see whence they had come fell on them dragging them from one another like animals and finally made off, some with the skirt, others with the jacket.

I turned slowly into the room again. I had not the strength to keep the hanging held up; I let it fall, shutting me in with the dreary, dank lack of light, and Smahil from whom I knew without testing it there would be no warmth, no compassion.

I felt like a very old woman. I was tired, I wanted to sleep, and sleep, and sleep. To sleep; nevermore to aspire to anything, to accept with my numbed mind my degradation, the humiliation of all my divinity and the rare high hopes I had been fashioned and born for; to accept with my numbed senses the pain which lapped me and which I was too utterly eternally exhausted to try to soothe alone.

'Your creamy back will hold those marks to your dying day,' Smahil's voice said. 'She rubbed till her arm fell with the fatigue of it.'

From a long way I dragged my voice, 'I have been whipped before.'

'But I have no unguents for you.' His voice was smooth and gloating . . . 'You see, I can't afford it—'

'Smahil, how could you?' I asked slowly. I only wanted to know this. 'You are not cruel for the sake of cruelty. Why did you let her . . .? She knows you let her.'

'I wanted to see you suffer.' His voice was quicker, nearer now, but I couldn't see him. Perhaps my eyes were closed, perhaps my weariness had blanked my sight after all. 'You never show emotion, you're always like an icicle, aloof, untouchable, untouched no matter what is done to you—You live, you breathe, you worry, but you don't reach out to other people, you keep your passion for the Reptile—'

His arms slid on my lacerated back, he was covering me with kisses. The sound of his panting roused me.

'Oh, my back,' I moaned.

He threw me into the bed where the stuffed bear's head still attached to the pelt glared at me in the murk.

I moaned and wept as he caressed me. Even the touch of the linen sheet beneath me was agony. I was too weak with pain and despair even to plead with him. But now my sight was no longer numb. I kept my eyes open.

Even . . .

He was not even gentle.

'You are good like this,' he mumbled. 'Terez is a clever fire—consuming me for itself—you are always mine, you cling to me as if I were a rock in Chaos, you cling to me—you'd cling to the marrow in my bones—I can feel even that moving towards the rhythm of your heart—poor little child—my Cija—poor little weeping child—'

I was nearly unconscious but I felt his tears on my mouth as I relaxed my always-pleading convulsive grip—

I lay for a long time in pain and darkness. Most of the time I could not keep even my vague instincts in a straight enough line for a thought, let alone enough thoughts in a line for an idea—it was all pain, degradation, despair, no one to turn to—that was it; no one to turn to, I have no friends, no one can help, no one can be kind to me—

It is not the pain that makes me ill, I thought; it is that I have no friend, no one who can help.

I was roused by Smahil, he was rubbing unguent with firm fingers into my wounds. I cried out, moaned and shuddered; he held me gently. I began to hear; he was whispering, frantically he whispered as he rubbed into my back the unguent which first was fire, and then was soothing. 'You'll be all right, Cija. I got this from the cavalry commander in exchange for my next three months' pay. It's all in arrears anyway. It's tremendously good, you won't be scarred, you will be healed and oh, so comfortable, you'll see. You'll be well, I'll make you happy, Cija. You mustn't cry, it's making you well again. If only I got to it in time . . .'

The hysteria is long over, it was not as bad as it seemed, there seems to be hope when the sun shines, there is hope—and preparations for the Atlan campaign go forward so slowly. There is something at work in the temple-palace beyond the mountain, something which wants in my opinion only to get from somebody high in the Northern army the secret of the scientific formula which is capable of filling with air the immense Vacuum; Smahil told me what Terez let him know, the reason for the infamous Southern attack on Northern headquarters.

The purpose, obvious enough to anyone who reflects for a moment if they already know as I do of the vital formula (very few even of the Northern side know of it, I'm not sure even Smahil does)—the purpose of that attack was that someone big wants to capture the General himself. Even if he doesn't know the exact formula, he's important enough for those who do to give up the secret in order to get him released. And according to Terez who has access to the highest table-talk, the Hammerfist instituted the attack, on the official grounds that immorality and impurity are too rife among the Northern controllers. He has not even kept out of it; the supreme insult to us, their allies, the Superlativity has presented Hammerfist with a medal of rock-crystal veined with gold for conspicuous gallantry and foresight in 'leading' an assault on impiety not to say treachery to the prevailing, pervading hospitable and holy religion of the Southern land of the most holy . . . etc. It is a weariness.

There is of course bloodshed everywhere in the streets. Our men are bitterly furious.

Everyone knows for which actual action the Hammerfist is being rewarded.

The officers no longer bother even to separate the forces, but instead join in when they come upon a mêlée, which is incessantly.

That too seems a weariness.

No more parades, or inspections, but broken heads, fury everywhere; no safety anywhere in stepping out of doors, and above all the bitter certainty that once we, the inferior force, are made to hand over our secret we shall be negligible, kicked aside, treated with contempt and worse, despised and also enslaved . . .

And as an accompaniment the mountain is rumbling to life, twice a week it is heard grumbling in the clouds and it belches out horrid little puffs of flame and smoke . . .

My back no longer hurts me, nevertheless I think I shall carry those scars to my death. They are very deep.

Smahil would not hold the mirrors to show me my back, but one day while I was alone I managed to arrange it for

myself. My back must have been in ribbons . . . The scars
are now clean and silver, raised weals which will presently
fade and fine down . . . And when I am old, if I ever do
live till then, they will shrink and draw my skin with them
in crumpling wrinkles.

The brand I love to feel on Smahil's back will be nothing
to that. 'How did you get it?' I asked him once. He was
quite surprised. 'I never knew it was a brand. Are you
sure you're not making a mistake?' 'Yes, it's very tiny but
it's a brand mark, a rusty black oval—' 'I don't know, no
one has ever branded me, I must have had it always . . .'

That is absurd, but I don't think it matters . . .

I don't think anything really matters . . .

The whispers have found my new dwelling-place.

That, too, is another of the things from which I feel
secure only in Smahil's arms. This place is so lonely all
day, so dank and dreary that sometimes I have to get up
and stride from corner to corner, back and forth, biting
my lip to prevent myself screaming; or I fall upon the bed
in a passion of weeping for which I can find no real reason.
I play endless games with myself; I redecorate the room as
I would if I had unlimited riches and resources, but how
futile it is, if I had them I should not keep this room. But
if I had to—But no. It is too pointless.

Smahil has forbidden me to go out, even to the river
bank in the country, and I confess I have no inclination to
go out either—not with the city in such a state of ferocious
turmoil. He has forbidden me even to visit Lel. He forbids a damn sight too much, but as I pointed out I intend
to obey him from my own sense.

Sometimes I go out of the room and down the stairs,
along the sleazy passage and back again. I even find myself
playing the game of walking on every third tile only; a
game much more interesting in the hot tower which pris-
oned my genuine, happier though even lonelier childhood,

for then there were great floors stretching far out ahead and to every side, squared with red and black marble. I would step only on the red, never on the black. Alas, I am sure it was the black that followed me with the red into the outside world. The horror I feel when my foot slips to the second instead of the third cracked tile is familiar. But the nervousness with which I scurry into the shadows or back to the staircase when anyone enters—that nervousness is so real, so far removed from make-believe, that it clutches at the pit of my throat and my hand leaves a moist print on the rail. But they are only other officers who live here. Sometimes I have to pass them on the stairs: they are always preoccupied and in a hurry. Northern officers are particularly harassed these days—not only by the danger of their position in the Capital at all, and by the growing insubordination of the troops who want only to harm as many of their allies as possible, but also by the fact that whereas the formula-greedy, power-confident Southerners are letting the campaign preparations go hang, our officers are desperately trying to get the whole business under way and the two armies mobilised; it perhaps would be disastrous, perhaps is our only chance.

It cannot be the normal life of cantoned military. For one tiny instance, we hardly ever get Smahil's or the other's friends in for supper or brief calls—and when they do come they are terribly for-tomorrow-we-die-jovial with sudden unexplained silences.

'Miss me?' Smahil says like the imitation of a conventional newly-wed, as he returns in the evening (later and later) flings his tunic at the table, his belt at the chair and looks gloatingly at me and at his hands before bringing us all together by a master's right.

'It is lonely all day. I am—I mean—Sometimes I feel a brooding presence—'

'Well, no presence with any gumption is going to brood in a dump like this—'

'My breasts are sore, don't crush them too hard—they've been getting sorer for days,' I said quickly.

He stepped back and gazed narrowly at me. 'Has it occurred to you that perhaps you're pregnant?'

'Yes . . .' I couldn't tell if he was pleased at the possibility. Of course, it would be an excuse for him to rejoice more than ever in his complete ownership, and of course it would be madness to bring a child into the world now. 'I have none of the other symptoms. I'm lucky to have had that time with the Beauty's household. The gossip taught me in a few weeks all the knowledge that another girl's upbringing would have given her by right, and which I might have missed so acutely—'

'You can sound appallingly *vulgar* at times,' he triumph-antly interrupted as he carried me to the bed.

'I'm glad I'm not having your child, Smahil,' I murmured, all languid and innocent, a simple remark.

'Why?'

His sudden defencelessness did amaze me.

'A child—I don't want a baby, not *now*,' I explained

His eyes questioned, 'Later?' My arms went round his neck. 'Oh, Smahil,' I murmured. He was pleased. I realised that I hardly ever vouchsafe any gesture, let alone any of affection. Of course, how often can I feel like it?

'Your breasts are growing,' he said. His tone in the darkness was strange—was it with a kind of wonder? I could not see his face. His hands were warm. 'They are high and firm and yet with such an unfathomable softness.' He whispered. 'I have made you a woman.'

I was thinking as I lay there with him that I am indeed physically richer now. Though even in the past they have been only women who called me plain. Now I have a rich rare appearance, a translucent skin, sparkling eyes which really reflect any sky of grey, azure or aquamarine, a full almost scarlet mouth, and hair, like stiff honey, springing, waving, heavy from my scalp. And my body too—always vivid with youth, and now with a kind of lusciousness, foreign to me and which I regard shyly, blooming over my slenderness—

Outside in the room there was the scrape of boots coming off, Anad or one of the others had entered, a yawn, the bang of a shutting bed-door.

From the other side, below in the street a scuffling on alley cobbles, cursing, the familiar almost nightly clash of steel on steel.

A lantern was lit in the alley as the sky became pitch black. Perhaps further away there was the flare and glow of the volcano.

Smahil's face hung poised above mine, a strained, pale, golden visitation, long pallid, eyelids and glinting eyes drained of colour by the light.

'Smahil . . .'

But afterwards a sort of fierceness pervaded him.

'You even breathe like a goddess. You tempt me at times to believe you a goddess, a small goddess. But you are really so ordinary. I must remind myself you are— this—remote, tender warmth—only because you have been reared from your conception to think of yourself as everything. That is what makes you care so little in the long run about what happens. In ordinary circumstances you would have had few hobbies and not been particularly clever.'

Abruptly he pulled up the bed-covers enough to show me, as in a warm, dark tunnel, our bodies still twisted together. They seemed to float contorted in a golden aureole of light, a lascivious unreality . . .

'That is the only reality. Remember it, my own Cija. I love you,' he whispered, 'I love you more than any other woman in the world.'

I could not make the mistake of believing he really loves me as I know the word.

He loves every pore of my body, every one of my

movements, the scent of me, the taste of me, my every eyelash: but it is not the love I want. When other people love, they love also the soul, the mind; but not Smahil, or not Smahil with me.

So he regarded me.

'I wonder why,' he said. 'You're by no means the most beautiful woman I've known.'

I fell asleep, clinging to this person Smahil, pressing my head to his chest, to his heart-beat, to hide my ears from the intangible.

I am still shaken by compulsive shudders as I write this. Tonight I had fallen asleep in the chair. I was awakened by a noise of loud talking around me. Smahil, Anad and Dani were in the room. Dani is another of the officers. The room was very cold, so that I shivered, and dark so I knew I had slept a long time. However, Smahil was now lighting the lamp.

'What is all this noise for?' I asked, sitting up.

'You were asleep and Anad came in and sat quietly opposite you, reading orders till the light failed, so as not to waken you, like the good little boy he is,' replied Smahil briskly. 'But he must have been dreaming too, for just as we came up the stairs we were brought rushing by his yell, and he says he saw the door open, he looked up thinking it was us, and a huge, gusty woman walked into the room and seized you by the arm—'

'I didn't say she was huge—I can't remember whether she was tall or short, she just seemed—*big*—' Anad was rubbing his eyes but was still too impressed by his dream to be shamefaced.

'And as he yelled out she disappeared. Then the door opened again and it really was us this time. Bursting in and finding nothing but a—'

I yawned and stretched my arms above my head. In a sudden silence I realised they were all staring at me, I myself finally looked up at my arm, from which the sleeve-folds had fallen. There on my flesh were the bruise-prints of four fingers and a thumb of more than usual size.

As I crawled with Smahil into our cupboard bed it seemed to smell more unpleasant than any shut place need when it has an open window.

'A *big* woman with gleaming eyes, but she did not look at me. If she had, I would have been unable to make a move, much less yell,' Anad mumbled, no longer inter-rupted. 'Gleaming silver eyes. I am glad for Cija's sake she was asleep . . .'

We received orders to be completely ready within a few days, to leave the Capital. Zerd was tenting the army outside. He officially claimed that the life in the City was being too much for the whole army, troops and officers, and that he was putting it outside under tentage in order to get it under control. 'More likely because you're scared we'll murder you all,' jeered the Southerners, stoning and pelting with filth the lines evacuating through the streets.

It was a savagely hot day, and the crowd's temper was savage.

Yapping dogs biting at calves of legs, gutter brats and even middle-class children with stones, women howling out their wrongs interrupted the order of the marching lines. The beggars rose up, forgot the weakening diseases they claim incurable, and belaboured the soldiers with their crutches; decent trades-people poured slop on them and reviled them from their windows. The men, grumbling, limping, pretending to ignore everything, were kept forc-ibly in line by officers chanelling their fury into discipline. Some of the Southerners also had split heads or were limping because of stones, but they didn't desist, though in the narrower streets it was hard for a missile always to get its intended mark.

It had taken me nearly half an hour to accompany this evacuation only for the length of three streets.

The sun broiled down, every temper was shocking, the streets seemed to burst with temper, and the thrumming of each regiment's small black drums instead of keeping upright our dignity only served to madden.

'This is impossible!' I cried furiously to the trooper beside me. I was not even with Smahil. 'I don't mind them stoning you, but any minute they're liable to get me too if they're not careful!' Sometimes, afraid of being swept to the back of the crowd, I clung to the uniformed arm; it was patchy with sweat.

Glancing at his officer in case he was noticing, my trooper thrust his scabbard point viciously into the stomach of a sturdy gutter-boy contesting his way. As the scabbard was worn very thin the steel came through, and the boy somersaulted aside with a shriek and then picked up a steaming fistful of manure, relic of the passage of our own baggage-train, and threw it. It caught my jacket at which I dabbed ineffectually and finally took off and threw away. A group of girls stopped stoning in order to pounce on it; then looked at me reproachfully. I clung again to the trooper's arm as we struck a bad patch. The marching could no longer follow even every second rhythm-beat of the drums. The trooper irritably shook my arm away.

'I need room,' he yelled, making it a kind of battle-cry, as this time he had to raise his scabbarded sword and use it like a club on the roaring townspeople.

I kicked the shins of a man who looked so angry that I darted into the ranks and sought a (somewhat jostled) protection among the most crowded troops, pushed in on each other's lines by the narrowness of the street—made even narrower by its walls of rabble.

'Here, you oughtn't be here,' stated a new neighbour, squinting at me.

'I know,' I said feelingly.

'I tell you what you ought to do,' he told me in snatches. 'You ought to find an empty house, there's plenty of billets suddenly empty right now, and stay there till we've all gone past.'

I found to my surprise that my presence had been noted by all the men around me, and another trooper now said to me, 'No, I tell you what you ought to do. You ought to stay here in the City the night, and go in to the camp tomorrow when we're all set up. They'll mistake you for one of themselves then, they'll all be flowing in, to bother the commission our Blue Scales has set up to deal with all their nasty little complaints: damage, rapes, begging your pardon, girlie, murders of providers, etc. My advice, miss.'

'Yes, thank you,' I gasped, knocked to one side by some sudden surge.

'Here,' he said kindly and I found he had rescued my bundle for me. 'OK now, miss?'

'Oh! Thanks,' and I struggled to the side once more.

Even at the back of the crowd I found movement against the main stream impossible.

I was about to give up (I was in the mood to call it despairing rather than resigning myself) when I lifted my head and recognised some buildings we were approaching. All this, four winding streets of it, had been unnecessary! Just like our Administrative Section, some incompetent staff-officer had mapped the path of our evacuation and we had taken a lovely wide detour, now passing again the barracks and inn. I could easily find my way to my own late billet from here. Forcing my way to the front through the cursing troops, into and through a corner of the baggage-train, skirting five Southern girls each with a presumably premature baby (for we haven't been here that long) be-sieging a soldier, past a group of civilians trying to pull a lowing ox out of place, I was presently once more in the familiar, small, cobbled courtyard, completely deserted, not even the horses and birds looked out from the stalls. They had all gone.

I went along the passage and up the stairs, quietly, though I knew the inn-woman had probably gone to join in the excitement.

The room was a furnace but when I heard steps on the stairs I thought I'd better hide as someone else had had my idea.

I slipped into the shut-bed which had been mine and Smahil's, taking care not to leave my bundle behind. This was just as well; for sure enough, it was the door of this very room which opened and there was quite a noise as about half a dozen people came in.

I recognised the voice of a man very high up on the Accoutrements Side, a man known to be a scientist.

'The birds seem to have flown.'

I was positively stifling in the shut-bed. Up through its window came the sound of the still passing army, and from the other side these voices.

'But this is the young leader's billet, sir.'

'We appear to be too late.'

'Well, now we're here it's as good a place as any to wait till that scum below have passed.'

I clutched my bundle and nodded at the stuffed head attached to the pelt. Yes. I know that voice.

What is our beloved General doing here?

'Look, here are some of his lady-friend's things still lying about. It's possible she'll return for them, then I can give her the message.'

How maddening, how unfair. I haven't left anything about, they're being encouraged to stay by a few beads and the discarded waist-ribbon left by Dani's last girl-friend. He didn't like her well enough to collect them for when he might see her next.

So here I am, I thought, imprisoned by the presence of—And who's that new voice?

'I'm glad you're at last considering me. The streets are torture.' (How can she have reached the stage of demanding his consideration for her welfare?) 'Oh, how is it, how is it we accept such real *monsters* as our allies?'

'Don't worry, I have my plans.' He sounded amused.

'All leading up to—' one of the scientists began smugly, and then I nearly jumped in my bed. What business had they mentioning *that* in front of her, the High General's wife though she is? For they went on to speak grimly, yet too casually, of the Formula which is their only hold over the Southerners. Once the secret of *that* is out—and I have it! I heard it! Not even here shall I write it down, I fear it might burn the paper, and I have told myself to forget it, but then at night I find myself repeating it in my head over and over. Then my tongue shrinks back and I am afraid I may have spoken it out loud.

'Do you suppose there's any food in this place?' One of them suggested after a pause.

'Yes, Gods' Fingerjoints, we could do with a little meat or wine or both, now that I come to think of it.'

'Perhaps in the kitchen . . .?'

'That'll be at the bottom of the stairs.'

They went out and I heard them making the staircase clatter; Zerd and the scientists—the action-commanders weren't here, I'd not heard their voices, they must be out presiding over the evacuation. I moved cautiously but then was warned by a sigh and a creak that one person had been left in the room and was leaning against my very door. I heard the rustle of a settling dress. It was a very fed-up sigh now in private. Why would a woman begin to scold Zerd? She was unsure of him, to say the least, and I could guess that her life must be a continuous ill-tasting search for ways to hold him.

Oh, this warring, this lust for dominance, even she has it. And he, it's his whole vile life, possession, penetration, air flooding with a hiss of sudden turbulence, moiling with

all its bacteria and currents the great nothingness, the wall
of passive protection to peace—swords, blood, torture,
grief brought for its own sake to the only shores one might
have considered safe, the last stronghold in the world of
the *purely* Divinely-descended race . . .

Abruptly as she leant on it the bed-door, which had not
been fastened, swung. She turned. We stared into each
other's faces.

Now a funny thing happened. It could so easily have
happened at any time in the last few months, but now was
just the time it was most unlikely. But it was as her late
stew-boy she recognised me. The little hostage-slave Cija
doesn't seem to have taken up much space in most people's
lives—except of course in that hostage's who is now an
officer and spent his time in greed for all of her. But now
in the shadows of the bed perhaps I did still resemble
Jaleril. I was wearing a low-class Southern teenager's
leggings, all we could afford, instead of a lady's full trousers,
and my plain, short, cotton dress was hanging outside my
belt, like a shirt, because of the heat. My hair, in one
thick braid, must have been behind my head and out of
sight in the shadows. Anyway, this delightful princess
gave one sharp stare and then as the door opened to admit
the General balancing two plates of meat and rather wrinkled fruits and a wine-jug, she disarranged her hair and
bodice and ran to him sobbing.

'Oh, Zerd, Zerd, my Zerd—avenge me—as soon as you
left me alone that door opened and the boy who'd been
there all the time came out and started to assault me—'

He didn't say anything but set down the plates and jug
on the table as she flung herself sobbing and crowing for
hysterical breath against him.

Her face was blotchy and she had worked herself so
ingeniously into real tears which revealed with their devastating damp just how much paint she laid on her skin. For

the first time I was shaken by pity. Not compassion—but pity for her *efforts*.

He strode to the cupboard and looked in at me. At another time I might have laughed.

'See—he was—'

'Our stew-boy, yes.' Suddenly this big, genial, half-human man in his black and scarlet highest-General's uniform turned and spat into the cleft between his wife's breasts in her self-disarranged *décollatage*.

She fell back, silent except for her panting, her eyes fixed with a look of horror on his face. He was still genial but he looked her once down and up with contempt.

As there was no alternative except to skulk like a fool, I gathered my bundle and walked into the room.

The General's hand heavy on my shoulder turned me and he smiled without pleasantness, at my braid, at my chest, at every line of me.

'Our stew-boy, yes, but I don't think there was an assault.'

This was an intensely personal incident now, for as I tipped back my head to stare into the eyes they were as intent as mine. He knew me. My hands, my body were clammy. It seemed an irrelevant interruption as the poor wife, believing the room filled with her humiliation and tragedy, bowed her head and crawled to his side.

'Forgive me, Zerd—I made a mistake . . .'

'The other gentlemen are in the kitchen,' he said coldly and she ran from the room.

The General sat on the floor and leaned against the door. He balanced a plate on his upraised knee.

She only wanted to make you jealous and protective, I wanted to say, but found that my mouth wouldn't speak. I also found that I had backed against the table and was facing him in a ridiculous position like a beast at bay. I lifted my head and willing my hands at least not to shake, I began to drink from the jug, a reason for having come to the table.

'So you've been here all the time?'

'It *is* my billet.'

'And that of several young leaders—I'm sorry I won't be able to send the leader Smahil any greeting via you.'

His eyes widened on my fingers trembling, gripping the table edge.

'But you did hear the Formula, didn't you?'

'I am afraid so.'

'But this is very unwonted humility. You've changed, flosshair.'

'Well, there are two compartments in my mind now,' I said wryly.

'What a pity this all is. Isn't it? But I'm afraid I can't let anyone loose on the world, as you might say, with such a secret on the tip of their—charming—tongue.'

He was drawling, slurring his words with an air of disregarding them, letting them come as they would, as he watched with the straight-browed, glowing, black gaze every movement I made, every expression. I tried to still all emotion. I didn't even notice the effect of cool courage which resulted.

'Everyone has to die, General. I'm sure you won't torture me unnecessarily.'

'Dear me, what a life of tenterhooks you must have been living to be able to put on so readily such resignation. You don't cling to life? I know camp-following can be rather dreary, but you seemed to enjoy yourself sometimes with the pots.'

'You watched me?'

He bowed courteously over his meat. 'But could you doubt it?'

'You guessed I was not a boy?'

'When you ran into my arms the first night, in the inn, it was deliciously obvious you were not a boy. Then of course there was very little difficulty in recognising my most interesting hostage, in fact now I come to think of it,

I can't remember ever having had any quite as interesting, though many more accommodating. It amused me to watch you after that.'

I inclined my head.

'How nice to have been able to lighten some of your hours of duty.'

'Hm . . . So you ask nothing more and will presently be put out like a light?'

I remained silent, analysing his mockery, and presently he ran two fingers across his chin while above his gaze never shifted. 'As a matter of fact I am really loth to waste this . . . Doesn't it seem, even to yourself, that you have outgrown your little fair playmate?'

My mind tuned in. It is true. I have sloughed the need for girlish, kittenish, desperate, adroit lying every different moment, and with it the genuine adolescent whose mother let her out of the tower. I have outgrown Smahil.

'You are asking me to sleep with you.'

'I am asking you to be my mistress, a securer position, involving regular sleeping-habits—'

'But then when you tired of me the danger would be as before.'

He raised the brows.

'The temporary reprieve doesn't seem to you worth it? Your death, as you remarked, is unlikely to be unnecessarily painful, you don't want merely to postpone it? You are perhaps over-modest as well as certainly uncomplimentary. Perhaps by the time I tire of you the conquest of the Continent will already have been accomplished and your danger-potential nullified.'

Nullified . . . Always that word following me, pseudo-urgent.

There was only one temptation, but I knew it wasn't in me to assassinate *anyone* in cold blood. I could make up my mind wonderfully, but I would put it off till tomorrow, till tomorrow, till an even better opportunity. He must know that too, and/or be determined never to let me near him with a dagger, otherwise he'd not be willing to take me on after the accusation Ooldra must have made before she left for home. So I'd never get the chance anyway.

'Yes, General, I do believe it isn't worth it. You had better execute me after lunch.'

'You mean it.' He peered at me. 'What calm determination. Am I, on mature reflection, so unattractive to you? Is it still because I am the enemy of your country?'

'Of every country, I think. Apart from that you are usually quite pleasant, except of course—'

'My skin? I am, naturally, quite inferior to the human army I lead. But women never previously seem to have taken exception to that.'

His naïvety thrilled me.

Is it possible he has always been a little sensitive about his difference, inherited from his father's predilection for the big, black women of the sub-human Northern tribes?

'Come, hostage.'

I shook my head. I felt nothing, I knew only that I could not let this power-poison touch me.

'You will be placed under close arrest.' He did not look at me again, but still leaning against the door transferred his complete attention to the meal.

It was ugly really, but when I saw again the hard, hot sky which is that blue because of its depth, and smelt the unattractive, real, big bird smell of the bird the General had mounted, I knew I wanted to *live*. The—potency—of this world we have been born into clamours more *in* our veins than our blood does, though sometimes I have thought *it is* our blood. But this has nothing to do with courage, though a lot to do with determination. Zerd dismissed the scientists on to the various places where they'd presently be needed. Lara went with one, not looking at us. 'Here, up,' Zerd said.

I mounted reasonably well and swiftly without touching his proffered hand.

When up behind him I had to hold on in order not to be dashed into the crowd because of the bird's gait. However, I crooked into his belt only one finger, though it soon ached.

'We're going to the camp where you'll be guarded for the short time till your execution,' he said conversationally.

He chuckled, really as if helluva amused, and with the reins in one hand he half-turned back to me and without urgency removed from round his neck the black kerchief worn in hot weather and in whose folds had been caught most of his sweat. This is now stuffed into my mouth before I realised what was intended. Then he took both my hands in his and turned to the front again so that my arms were round his waist.

'In case you decide to shout the dread secret out to these ladies and gentlemen, though it's doubtful that even the nearness of death could make you feel such kindness for the Southerners, and it's also doubtful that any of them'd hear over their own vociferation,' he explained. 'But then, it really is quite an important formula.'

I tried to spit the pungent cloth out of my mouth, but he had tucked it in with the dexterous hand probably of experience. I was exposed to full view and as I was again dressed as myself I felt remarkably embarrassed. I kept my eyes lowered, afraid of meeting some recognisable gaze.

The way he had pulled my arms meant that I was stretched close against him. Because of the heat, the scarlet cloak had been looped to one side and I felt through his black shirt the smoothly-scaled ripple of the muscles of the mighty bas-relief back. The sway of the bird was enough to ensure that my own breasts had just sufficient maddening freedom to quiver or be thrust against these muscles, so that I was as shamed as someone can be whose main consciousness is centred on approaching severance from life itself. The only reason I was glad he was wearing only a shirt, no jerkin even, was that it was poor protection if anybody happened to throw something very pointed at him. But we were among the Golds, and the streets were wider, and somehow it didn't happen.

I kept my hands lax in his. I hoped he might slacken his attention. Then maybe I'd be able to get at least one arm free. But even when he raised a hand to wave a brief greeting to another commander, he kept my fingers barred in his and my arm was raised to make the wave too.

It would probably be beheading. They were good with their swords, some of those guards, swift and sure. It was only the imminent, quickly nearer, unknown I had to fear, not the pain. Yet in the confusion and business of getting under tentage on a hot day after demonstrations from a hostile public—might they entrust me to an inferior executioner, someone badly practised? Or might even the best man's sword slip? Everyone makes a few mistakes in a lifetime, but what is a mistake for a craftsman who is annoyance and pride promises himself, 'Better next time', can mean agony for the particular victim who happens to catch the mistake. Yes, as I bared my neck ready I would be shaking with fear, panic of butchery as well as of the unknown. And if I shook I'd be a bad mark . . .

I am terrified. Oh, if only he gives me another chance, if only he asks me again before the moment . . .

But you know, with luck, your immediate reflex would be to say 'No'. Better to suffer a little physical pain . . .

Every minute, every jogging moment, every second, O God, Oh Cousin, every sharp second is bringing it nearer.

We are still riding through the Golds and the shouting crowd but the roar is only the roar in my ears. It's all broken up into sharp stabs of colour and each a second of the time—the only Time allotted to me. How hot the sun is. How hard these cruel hands round mine, the rippling of this against my breasts, which I am beginning in my panic to feel physically chafed, ceaselessly . . .

Suddenly I had a thought which seemed to me so dazzlingly, brilliantly simple that I knew why neither he nor I had foreseen it. With a fatuous joy I kicked hard with both feet simultaneously at the bird's sides. I heard its bark and it started sidling. I had time to kick it once more, so that it reared nervously because it couldn't dash forward owing to the thickness of the crowd before it. The General with a shout gave both hands, still holding mine, to the reins. I wrenched mine free and jumped.

My hands caught the stone of the bridge I had seen above us.

It seemed unbearably rough and gritty.

I heaved myself up but I'm not acrobatic and my thudding heart and my panting almost split me in two. Sweat had started out on my forehead and my fingers were sliding before they'd groped the few inches up to the balustrade-edge.

Would the desperation of my need give me unusual strength?

That thought did it. I slipped and, with a gurgle behind my stuffed mouth, clutching frantically at nothing—I fell—

I landed on something harsh and prickly but soft enough to break my fall. This was a big, jolting straw-cart on to whose immense high-piled load I had fallen.

As I looked up in amazement at the fatal grey-stone bridge-thoroughfare spanning the road, I saw Zerd on foot race on to it. How quickly he must have seen my jump, leaped from his bird and up the steps on to the bridge as he saw me clambering on to it. But he was in quite the wrong place, wasn't he? I saw him shoulder his way through the townspeople crammed on the bridge to watch the army's passing, and his dark face turning swiftly and concentratedly here and there. Even in this while I was busily removing the black linen sweat-rag from my mouth.

The pungent taste it left seemed bitterer when struck by air than when the thing itself had been there. I shook my head with my mouth hanging open, to dry out the taste, and looked down about me at the carts and the Golds marching, ahead. At this moment I heard a shout. Zerd was leaning over the parapet. He had seen me. The great General turned and disappeared into the crowd up there. The cart lurched on.

Well, what to do now?

Breathlessly safe, but for how long?

He knew this cart now, and wouldn't I be abler on my feet dodging through this multitude?

I scrambled across the hay to its edge. The load was very high. The closely-packed heads beneath seemed very far away, the invisible ground therefore even farther.

Nevertheless, I half-scrambled, half-slid down the precarious swaying load and vehicle. I now discovered my hands had been hurt by the bridge, there was a lot of skin off them and a lot of blood on them. I hurt them even more now, but it was one of those times when you don't feel pain except as just another urgent sensation.

At the bottom of my journey I found myself grasped by numbers of the Golds who had laughingly watched. They should not have so much as *glanced* out of line, particularly they who are so jealous of their reputation against the other regiments', but there was so much need for action during the marching today that those who hadn't been stoned were treating the whole thing as a holiday. Almost complete anarchy reigned everywhere.

I hardly heard the laughing, lewd shouts of welcome I received, I hardly felt the many rough grasps and breaths.

The glare of heat on my uncovered head was making me feel, as I dashed between the marchers, that I was getting ringing head-blows. My eyes and ears were confused, my panting was drying my tongue till it swelled, and to run was a real bodily effort. I was not thinking at all now. This is proved by the fact that only at the end of the chase did I put my had up to my throat and think, 'Oh, so this sore ache is my tight collar and not the beheading blade!'

The threat pursued me. What a threat—big, scarlet, black, muscular, tall, important! My heart thudded.

Well. I ran through the soldiery, the soldiery marching through thrown stones and verbal and physical filth.

I sensed the pursuit.

Except as I turned corners I never saw the General. I was too busy looking ahead, but I heard behind me the pounding of his swift, steady running-strides, the respectful murmurs of the men as they crowded together to let him pass, and as I passed soldiers who took no notice of me I saw them turn to stare at his approach. Before they could realise that there was not merely a pursuer but a pursued, I was ahead again.

A soldier presumably intent on approbation or even promotion started to chase me, but was soon behind the General.

I blundered into another part of the baggage-train.

'Cija!'

The word was repeated twice before it became a name, and again before it made sense to me. I stumbled aside, one step, and saw a little boy grinning anxiously at me.

Ow, the goat-boy, Narra's brother.

'You be in hurry, Lady Cija.'

As if I'd never been away. Had he, in his little goat-herd world, even noticed my long absence—and his sister's?

'Ow, I'm running away from someone who's *furious* to punish me—' His urchin's eyes glittered. '—Ow, for Gods' sakes drive your goats across the street, behind me—'

I lurched on, my whole being a prayer.

The goats surged across the street, I could hear their numberless, disharmonious separate bleatings, their acrid stink burdened the air.

As I turned the next corner I glanced back.

Away at the entrance to the street the baggage-train was blocked by the goats. Drovers were cursing. The curses became frantic and still the animals milled aimlessly, effectively. Among them, not in the least dignified, flailing his arms and lashing out with his boots, was the big black and scarlet threat.

So now I had a head-start.

I doubled through a long tavern room. It was crammed with good Southern gentlemen who had come in to refresh themselves during their hard day's work, and who'd stayed till now incapable, poor dears, of throwing a single stone. I knocked against several who hit their neighbours, either because they blamed the knock on them or because they aimed for me and missed. As I nipped out of the back window I saw the General caught in the fighting, moiling room. At first exasperated, temper still in his face from the goat-incident, he tried to shoulder his way through the drunken turmoil but soon had to defend himself from fists eager for any mark. He shoved men aside and struck down others, impatiently, but was caught and had to fight in earnest. That would keep him going for some time. I clambered over the sill and for an instant between the fighters in the length of the room he looked up and saw me.

I felt the same stab in the diaphragm that I have had several times from him.

I found myself in the tavern's back yard, a tiny square almost all taken up with a vast, peak-topped dung-hill.

I skirted this but found the paling-fence behind it impossible to climb. I tried again and again, but it was just too tall, the palings had pointed tops, and my foot slipped even when I could get it between them. I hurt my feet, wrenching them desperately out when they got jammed, I had no time to ease them out properly, and my hands were full of long nasty splinters. It was one of those ventures when every movement slips and ends wrong, my chin descended heavily on the points of the palings as my feet and hands slipped, and I bit my tongue, and my chin hurt so sore and was covered in blood, and I think I wailed. I turned frantically to find another means of getting out of the yard.

There was a door into the kitchen, full of fires and movement but perhaps no one would stop me, but meanwhile a figure had appeared at the window. Landing a last blow on someone behind him, he swung out. I hid behind the dungheap. I had wasted my precious hard-won breathing space on that wretched paling fence.

I was sobbing, silently I think, and my gullet where I felt the blade was cold.

He didn't speak, but strode round towards me, his boots and sleeves catching dung. We circled once and then by changing his direction unexpectedly he had me. The black eyes glittered grimly down on me. The mouth smiled. I bit his hand, my teeth grated so that I thought I had struck bone, so savage was my determination, but I could not even puncture those scales.

'I carry my own armour-plating with me, you see.'

His voice hurt me.

'Reptile!'

His expression, beneath its surface of grim triumph, was unfathomable.

He was so inescapable in that tiny squalid space, I nearly despaired.

As his other hand came to me, fingers flexing to frighten me and impress me with my helplessness which Gods knew weighed on me already as heavy as the pattern going through marqueterie, I seized the pitchfork sticking in the hill behind me and lunged it at his face. I longed to see blood gush from his face by an action of mine, that thick, dark blood. He let go my wrist, seized the fork. This was like a game of chess, he knew I would be away again but I had checked him, he had to admit to the efficacy of that sharp threat.

He cursed me, angry now, and I fled.

I made for the kitchen door, but he was between me and that and there was no room to pass him even if I were adroit enough. The window to the long room was behind him too.

I sprang up on the yielding soggy hill, and before I could sink in it I leaped for the nearby shed-roof. It wasn't high.

I ran along the top of this, hoisted myself on to the inn-roof. He threw the clattering pitchfork, missed, and was up after me. He had the speed of some horrible, nimble, big animal, a panther or, yes, a crocodile. I had to flee so fast that there was no time to choose a route and soon I was splashing in the roof-gutters. These were at a sloping angle and my panic heightened. I held out my arms to balance myself as though tightrope-walking. He came on. He was laughing now, stalking me slowly, steadily—certainly. I leaped for the next roof, landed sprawled on my knees in its gutter. Tried to climb up the roof-slope, but a tile fell and me nearly with it.

There were just I and the General, more an animal, more a brilliant kind of brute able to lead the higher species because of his instinct for savagery and his form of love for prey, now up in a little roof-top world of grey and blue tiles, dormer windows, clouds, the roofs of narrow, easily-leapt, back streets where not even a dog yapped below, streets deserted for the procession—a scrambling, slanting grey world with this one live black and scarlet focal point, a laughing animal, striding over the street-spaces I leapt wildly, and I the prey.

The air itself struck sparks from the hot tiles till the grey and gold neutralised each other, swimming in tension.

The blast from a chimney under which some big kitchen-fire had suddenly been lit nearly sent me flying.

A panic scream wailed till far away on the heat's tension, it was mine. I was crying. He laughed and came on. Our speeds were about equal, he was gaining but imperceptibly, but whereas mine was maintained by wild leaps and clutches and sprawls, leaps up-again, accompanied by a frantic sobbing, torn clothes, bitten lips and bloodied hands, his was easy and competent. He was stalking me surely. His big head was thrown back, and his gaze on me, noting every humiliating effort, his mouth open, his laughing coming out never-ending, real mirth, harsh, ferocious, ringing.

Big clouds gathered above the heat haze.

The desolation grumbled.

The dusty tiles were pitted with moist roundels.

A great crocodile went thundering round the sky and back again. The heat haze trembled, split. Water came pouring down. I clung with both arms round a chimney-stack as my only defence against being washed away down the roof-slope. For a moment even he was hidden by the mass of rain. The gutters gurgled.

Still he approached, he was very near. It was as if there had been no change.

I screamed because he is a demon.

I flung wide a half-open window and somehow got through it—a tiny attic window. The attic was evidently that of an upper middle-class home, judging by the lumber of outdated glitter-sewn ball-dresses and trousers, curl-toed slippers, curtains, a pile of tarnished silver plate two generations old, a big chair with ripped upholstery. I dodged over all this musty richness, through a door there, and locked it behind me.

I blessed its key which I had so miraculously found in the lock, and tiptoed down the carpeted stairs.

This was some near-noble's town home, as I guessed from the furnishings and rooms I glimpsed, but deserted as far as I could make out. In the upper storeys there had been the brief pounding of the General's boots on the door he'd found locked after he followed me through the window, but though I had waited appalled, quieting even my breathing, no one had come.

Now I did hear a sound, down below. The General had entered below.

The tradesmen's entrance must have been open. And there was no mistaking the sound of that stride—so sure, so untroubled, so inescapable, so aware of its inescapability.

I dashed aside through another door banging it behind me, there was no key in this one. But thank Gods the room was empty. Yes, the house was quite deserted, everyone must have gone off like loyal patriots to the allies-baiting.

I ran across this room to the farther door which opened on another staircase.

'Cija!'

The empty rooms reverberated.

I ran as silently as possible but soon had to sacrifice quietness to speed. He was on my trail.

'Come, little hostage, don't you find the game is tedious when it has no more point?'

I searched the lock of every door I passed, but there were no more keys. My clothes dried a little. I could hear the rainflurry on the dark-silvered windows. Up the top of a narrow, dark staircase, the first without a carpeting, on which I'd found myself suddenly as I ran from a light airy room littered with a child's toys, I heard a moaning.

Startled, I was still for a moment, listening fearfully, till I was reminded of the pursuit by the click of a door just below me.

No help for it, so up the stairs and into that moaning room.

As I entered that dark, ill-smelling, shut-up room an old woman sitting by the bed rose up.

'What are you?' she said.

I strode to the window and opened it.

She shrieked.

'What will Zerd think?' I thought.

'And this will benefit your patient,' I said. The fresh air swirled into the room, forced into eddies against the sick-room atmosphere. I leaned out, into the pouring rain. The ground was very far below. Before I could make sure of the means I saw of climbing down, the General entered.

He came over and his hand turned me.

'Shouldn't jump if I were you,' he said. It was a wolfish tone, resonant with complete victory. And that death awaited me behind it.

The heap on the bed stirred.

She sat up.

I shuddered as I saw the eyes fixed on him, staring out from that discoloured face. It took me back to the heat, the terror, the smells of that time when I nursed Smahil all discoloured with blue poison—and in the weeks since I had last seen this woman, the poison must have spread across her whole body.

The fever-bright eyes glared on him, a wasted blotchy blue arm was raised.

She got out of bed, drew closer to him. Her white shift was dark with bitter sweat. I turned my eyes from the blue blotching of her breasts, whose swell had once been so proud and white.

She gripped him, pressing against him.

'Do you want me now, Zerd? Great General? Does my skin at last match yours which tired of mine? Let me lay it against yours. If only the poison would spread back to whence it came and prove deadly now augmented with mine, for Gods know I hate you deadly enough. You, who have allowed me a few days more to live, hidden away like a cancer in my father's house, till swollen blue with your derision—'

The harsh whisper which she had left of her voice continued and continued.

I didn't wait for it, I didn't wait to look at his fascinated, amused, proud, inhuman *man*-formed face—I was out of the window and my hands soon on the wall-creeper out there. The rain tried to tear it and me apart, but when it eventually won and ripped my hand from the stem I was near enough to the ground for it not to matter.

Now I knew another secret of the General's—the secret even Smahil had not dared do more than hint at.

And she was the woman whom I had last seen hanging, panting, near-nude, like a drowning woman on Zerd on the Night of the Dinosaur.

I was on the brick river-wharf.
The river boiled under the rain.

Crouched in a little boat among rows of empty others, jamming myself under its plank-bench, soon myself impregnated with the smell of sodden wood, I saw him through the rainsheets, emerged from the house, scanning the street, the windows, the roofs, the river.

He turned away, walking across the brick bridge, a silhouette in the drumming, leaden air. He did not even shrug, his rather leonine profile containing every possible expression and each negating the others, but there was a definite expression to his shoulders as he disappeared in the maze of rainy brick alleys the other side of the bridge.

The abandoned rainfall slashed at the river.

I climbed from my little boat on to a bigger one, hid among the baled goods unseen by the rain-weary watch before the crew boarded her, and was miles up-river and at their destination before, a night and day later, they discovered me.

— II —

THE PALACE

As I write this I lean my book on a thick, quashy, purple cushion. As I wriggle with the satisfaction of what I write, my bed on the end of its chain from the ceiling sways and springs, responding to my every emotion, the most aimless of my kicks at this superfluity of coloured cushions. It is a very different bed from that cupboard I've been incarcerated in for the last weeks.

The morning sunlight was pale and fluttered on the waves. It struck sharp directly through my thin clothes which had seemed so much too heavy a day ago. With the sharpness of a knife it divided the deck, pale strips between the clear-cut shadows of moving men, shadows diagonal across the vertical lines of the deck-planks. Because of the ship's gentle heave and roll on the waves, the slanting of these actually-vertical lines gave the illusion that they were sliding apart from one another in independent motion, and presently the ship would disintegrate and we would all, captain, crew, cargo and stowaway, be ourselves rolling in the blue water, but it did not seem to matter at all.

I leaned back at my ease among the crates. I watched the crew swabbing the deck, and later preparations for landing.

White birds made dozens of tiny arches over the ship.

They alighted in rows on the bulwarks; and the crew, big bronzed men in red sashes and very little else except for metal jewellery and knives, threw to them meat-scraps I wouldn't have disdained.

One bird alighted on a crate up-ended beside me. It peered down at me with a pearly pink eye. It was so far the only being on this ship which had discovered me.

In spite of my emptiness, stiffness and chilliness I was more contented than I could ever remember and, as I looked around at water, sky, wind and sunlight, I kept realising that there was a fond, perhaps faintly foolish smile on my face.

I knew I should be discovered when we landed and unloaded: if I were a boy I should have been kicked, bullied, perhaps made to work for the passage I'd taken; but when I behaved like a charming little lady I should be off in a few minutes.

Then, what should I do in a unknown port? It might be difficult, I was quite alone and a stranger, and my bundle of humble but useful belongings had been the only thing I'd lost in my flight from the General.

But I had a feeling I should begin a new life in this new place. Helped by this core of balance I had this morning discovered born in me—acceptance, confidence, ableness to deal with whatever life would send and which I should accept—a balance somehow fostered by the sunlight, the wind, the creak of boards, the crack of a sail against the mast, the slap of spray on the gunwales and of water swilling in the bilge. This was complete freedom. A continuance of life in a *new* world miles even from memories of everything before.

I have never felt as though inexperience were a part of me which would soon be overlaid with 'the wonder of Experience': I felt as if inexperience were a thing, a thing like a pall, hanging over me and clouding my intrinsic

Experience and its truth; and soon that pall would be twisted away and there I would stand, at last myself.

This was the first time I'd been on a ship—well, this didn't deserve the name; this was a river-trader. I was enjoying myself and very proud that I was evidently one of those things 'a good sailor'. Actually I had felt a little queasy when she moved off last night, so it was a good thing I'd nothing in my stomach. But this morning I was hungry and had remained in the same position for hours under a chill wind, and I'd never felt so healthy. Every smell was a delight: I had smelt this river for the last half-dozen months or so, but never had it smelt like this, so wide, so salt, so *free*. There was the smell of tar and galley-smells which made me vividly hungry.

It was hard, among the piled crates, to catch many glimpses of the shore, but I don't think I'd have seen much more from any position on deck. The river was tremendously wide here. The shores were far, hazy lines, here suggesting plains by their flat grey-yellow haze, here forests or a hilly town by their undulating grey-green haze. There were other boats though, yammering before the wind, down-river over the whorls and swelling, swaying, green currents and the blue, sunlit, wind-whipped waves.

There was almost always a sail, near or far, faded orange or striped, patched and bellying, rakish-slanted or stolidly rectangular, even on my limited horizon.

The hoarse shouts of the crews, cross-wind from each other, and the froth and leap of the waters all spoke with one virile voice: it was summer, the river was bounding away from the brick City and bearing me heart-bounding on it.

When the sun was high there was much tacking of sails by men scrambling in what rigging there was, and some of the crates farthest from where I lay began to be shifted, with grunting.

I braced myself for the rapidly approaching climax of my lovely illicit passage; pushed the salt-stiff hair back from my eyes and tried moving what parts of me I could.

Presently I heard bustle of a different sort, far more voices than the crew possessed, a different sound to the splash, and though we still lurched and rocked I could tell we had nearly stopped because of the slackening of the wind on my eyeballs—the rest of my face and body was by now too numb with continuous wind to feel it at all. There was the creaking of ropes and the men began singing, all together, some song in a foreign language with few words and those few much-repeated in a slow beat-beating rhythm. I peeped out.

Yes, we had berthed and were unloading.

All I could see of shore was that it was a high-sided stone wharf, equipped with great metal rings for the ships' ropes, and that it rose in stone steps which were covered with the most active crowd I'd ever seen. I could see no buildings behind them, but perhaps if I strained my neck—

Long before I was in the right frame of mind, the crates hiding me were yanked aside.

There was a split instant while I was still not-seen, and then—

'We-e-ell,' said a gravelly voice and I was looking straight ahead at a pair of wide salt-rimed boots.

This was an abrupt change from the endless crates which had been my companions, and there was yet another moment suspended before I raised my head and met the eyes of the captain himself who had been assisting in unloading. You could tell he was the captain, Gods know not by the quality of his clothes but because he was wearing several.

He stood looking down at me with one fist on his hip, thumb hooked in weapon-belt, the other hand pulling at his lip.

'Found something, Shaj?'

'My oath, yes,' said the captain.

The other speaker came forward. He was not the mate as I had expected, but a visitor just fresh from shore, a tall, lean man in a black robe, caught in folds to one side by a plain gold belt. As the newcomer's eyes rested on me I was sure I had met that gaze somewhere before (always memories, after all, catching up with you, but it was not an unpleasant memory).

'Just wanting, sir, to show you the prize of our cargo,' said the captain, 'and . . .'

'If you stand back I'll have room to stand up,' I said.

'And I'm not sure that you haven't found the prize,' said the newcomer.

The captain automatically stepped back and I got shakily to my feet. My ankles were for a moment too stiff to hold me up, and I put a hand to the crates behind me to support me. Before I touched them the newcomer had placed an arm round me and held me the moment I needed.

'She's not part of my cargo, you know,' the captain apologised. 'She's a stowaway.'

'Evidently.'

'Yeah.'

I was the apex of the triangle. They considered me while I considered them, the circulation returning to my legs and my mind like a frog's tongue leaping for a fly a quarter-inch out of reach—where had I met this man before, and if we had met before did he recognise me? It was impossible to tell from his eyes, candid though their consideration seemed.

The captain wore in his right ear a red jewel which glinted in the sunlight and hypnotised me a little. He couldn't wear anything in his other ear, you could see under his coarse hair the half-healed scar where it had been. That must have been quite a recent fight. It was much warmer in the sun when we were not on the move.

'Excuse me, sir,' I said to the tall man. 'I've a feeling we've met before, but I can't put a name to your face.'

'More or less what I was about to ask you,' said the captain. 'Usual question with stowaways. Who are you?'

'I can't pay you for the journey I've had,' I said. 'I'd better make that clear at the outset. But I've had only a night and three-quarters of a day, and they were cramped and cold—and no food.'

'Ho. And have you reached your destination, or aren't you satisfied with the time of your discovery?'

'I'm quite happy here, thank you.'

'*Good.*'

He continued to pull at his lip, red-brown in his beard, then turned to the other and burst out, 'Damnedest things, stowaways. Rare and you never can tell with them. It is true you've met her someplace, sir?'

'It's possible she's seen me.'

'Of course. You don't remember noticing her? Probably seen you in one of your processions. Do you want her?' said the captain on a kind of open-handed appeal. 'There's nothing I can do with a young lady, what with people unwilling to take her on the market because they'd be afraid she's been stolen, and she's obviously one, for all her lack of *means* . . .' I was longing for him to bow and apologise for my uncomfortable journey but going that far did not occur to him.

'What would *I* do with her?' said the tall man, amused, but with a strange inflexion in his voice.

The captain looked as though he'd committed a social solecism but didn't think it would be taken too badly. 'Ah, you should know that better'n me,' he said. 'There's always the vaults for secrets . . .'

'Why did you leave the Capital?' the man asked me.

I was startled. At first I thought he must have recognised me after all and remembered seeing me in the City, then I realised it was obvious where I'd come from by the number of days I'd said my voyage had lasted.

'I was fed up there,' I said.

'And what about your poor parents?' cried the captain virtuously. 'They might pay to get you back?' he suggested.

'I've none.'

'No guardian?'

I thought briefly of the General, my legal guardian, in whose care my mother placed me. 'No guardian.'

I looked round me. 'What is this place?' I asked.

The captain began with hoarse pride to recite the full name of his ship, foreign and full of ceremoniously guttural words, but I said, 'No, I mean the name of this town.'

'Thought you said you meant to come here?' stared the captain.

'No, I didn't.'

'This is the Superlativity's Temple-town,' said the tall man.

At that I recognised him as the Priest Kaselm. Now I was not so sure that he could possibly recognise me, he'd hardly noticed me and I'd been a boy then. Why had his face suggested a pleasant memory? Gods know, it had been a terrible occasion, neither had I thought at the time that his keen shrewd gaze had struck me as at all likeable.

'I need lodging and food and I've no money,' I said. 'Can you tell me an inn that needs a girl?'

'Several, but not your sort,' interpolated the captain chuckling.

'No,' said the Priest.

I was taken aback by such a flat denial. 'I've no right to ask, but can't you advise me?'

'Come with me.'

Without giving myself time to catch my breath at his abrupt decision, I followed him—I had to, he was already on the gang-plank. He was my only hope at the moment, and this morning I had made myself a motto I meant to keep like a rule—'All or nothing; you can expect to obtain nothing without demand or risk.'

I have already lived long enough in the Outside to know that I have led a far more adventurous life since I left the tower of my childhood than most people ever do. And when I was little I thought that everyone in the World lived lives of incredible interest! So they do, compared to my early life—but fate is making up to me for that now. I felt very confident as behind the Priest Kaselm I threaded my way through the crowd up the wharf-steps. I will go on making my way through adventures.

So far I have come out of most of them reasonably well, though I am neither strong, athletic, very knowledgeable nor devastatingly beautiful. Even when the worst comes to the worst, somehow one eventually does find some reserve of power, of *acceptance* therefore resurgence, which enables one to emerge after all worthwhile. So I thought now—for though I knew that there are in the World kinds of *the worst* from which no one can ever recover, I sensed through all my youth and health and resilience, in my toes to the tips of my fingers to my breast-tips to the ends of my hair, and all young and real and *mine*, that I should always withstand diseases and maiming.

The Priest did not turn to see whether I still followed—now I came to think of it, he had not even turned after he first said, 'Come with me' to see whether I followed at all. Indeed it was rather difficult through a crowd of this turbulence.

Presently doubts began to creep through me, but so exalted was I this morning that they did not bother me at all.

'Escape'—that was actually the story of my life.

Only once had I met tragedy face to stark face, and it had not marked me. In deeper moments I wondered if it should have marked me, and knew myself lacking, but for the fact that it had not I blamed the big terrible bird, and from it too I had now separated myself. I! I was learning, really learning at last, the intoxication of the reality of self.

Suppose the Priest is taking me to the lair of the Superlativity, suppose he remembers having seen me as a Northern army-server, and wishes to sacrifice me on the altar of his masters' hate for their allies? No matter what he means, it is what my fate means that will be.

A white wall leaned before us without warning—the Priest took a bold black key from his belt and unlocked a rotting wooden gate in the wall. This gate he locked again after I'd followed him through it.

We were in a green garden, and so thick was the wall that the garden was also quiet.

Still without a word the Priest led me across the springy sward, past a bed of pink plants, under another arched gate, along a cold, blue-white, stone passage unlit, through a nail-studded black door and into a small rather bare room where he signalled me to seat myself—I asked first for a fountain-room, he directed me farther up the passage, I came back to the room and seated myself on a stool opposite him.

'Well?' I said composedly. It seemed I had lost even that persistent habit of feeling my heart beat hard and irregular every so often in the nerve-racking life I lead.

The Priest leaned forward, elbows on knees, hands in opposite sleeves, conversational mouth pushed a little forward.

'Are you here as a spy for the Northern General Zerd?'

'No.'

'Then . . .?'

'I should like sanctuary from him.' I paused. 'You remember having seen me—in his—household?'

'On the occasion of a very interesting entertainment he provided.'

'I am a hostage whose—privileges he abused. I fled

from the army during the confusion of its being placed
under tentage—you've heard of that?—and beg sanctuary.'

'How do I know you are not a spy?'

'Send me anywhere if you will not keep me here. I did
not mean to come here.' I thought of the liquidation by
these people of the priests of the older sect. 'I wanted
merely to leave the Capital. And if you decide to let me
stay I will work at anything; you can place me under any
surveillace.'

'You say you were a hostage. From what land?'

'The lad north of the forests, north of the plains, north
of your mountains—the land south of the Northern
Kingdom—'

'The land of a female dictator?'

'I am her daughter.'

He leaned forward, rocking the stool, black eyes intent
and mouth pushed into a silent whistle.

'You would have to prove that.'

'I can see no need to prove it. I can only insist that I am
a hostage and not a spy. Besides, I can't see how I could
prove it.'

'The Dictatress has had reputed liaison with only one
man—The High Priest there.'

My spine became just a little colder and this time I did
not answer.

'What is your name?' Kaselm asked.

'Do you know what it should be if I am telling the
truth?'

'Yes.'

'And what will happen to me if I give the right answer?'

He smiled for the first time since I'd met him that
morning, but it wasn't a reassuring smile, the amusement
was to cold, too self-shared. 'Now you say *if* instead of
when—and your hesitation is most eloquent. Well, Cija,
come with me to the Superlativity.'

That gentleman admitted me almost at once. There was

hardly any time to wait with the dry-smiling Kaselm outside the August Apartments. The messenger returned almost immediately to admit us, and I could not tell from
Kaselm's behaviour whether I were to prove myself to an
order of death. After all, a High Priest's daughter in a
town where a priest's chastity and austerity was his point
of honour—

The Superlativity lives in four rooms farther up the
same blue-white stone passage. They are larger rooms
than Kaselm's, but as austere.

He himself came forward to greet us. A gaunt man, with
sunken cheeks and large-pupiled obviously short-sighted
eyes, he was surprisingly not much taller than myself. He
wore a scrupulously neat, belted, black robe, skirts fluttering round him like a brisk dowager's, and his gaze was all
for me. We all three seated ourselves. The whole conversation took place in the presence of a black-robed young
man who was writing over at a desk before a window. The
window overlooked the pleasant sward-stretch.

'You—forgive me, we must be sure—*call yourself* the
daughter of the High Priest of the land south of the
Northern Kingdom?' eagerly asked the Superlativity.

'Yes,' I said, not too vehemently.

'And your name—?'

'Cija.'

'Your father sent you—a goddess, descended from parents each descended from parents descended on both
sides from the gods—as a hostage with the Northern
hordes?'

'There were reasons . . . You know a lot about the tiny
country divided from you by so many dangerous lands.'

I had risked that. To my surprise he was almost
apologetic.

'Please do not think this catechism presumptuous. You
understand we cannot indulge ourselves in mistakes. However, we shall soon learn if you are indeed the goddess

Cija; I know much of that land from my own High Priest Kaselm's personal experience of it during his years of travel—ah, yes, there can be little communication between us but your father is in his country working for the same ends as we in ours—the Pious Rape of the Introvert Soil of Atlan—

'Why did your father send you with the Northerner?' Kaselm asked.

So they revered my father—I must risk the possibility that they were pretending esteem for him in order to lead me on. The Superlativity, in the manner of great little men, seemed intense but transparent enough.

'There was a prophecy at my birth—' I said.

I had to tell them even of my assassination-task, but it only aroused the Superlativity's sympathy. He patted me on the shoulder with his solid, papery-covered hand—a hand rather like my mother's, but severely innocent of rings.

'That is all over, Goddess. In your sincere *efforts* to dispose of the monster, you have in effect nullified the prophecy. You are too far from your beloved country ever to bring it to harm. A noble sacrifice, self-imposed banishment. Noble efforts against odds too great for a young girl alone even if fired with divine blood.'

But he was immediately brisk again; you had the impression that his emotions were in rigidly separated cupboards, just like his papers in the care of that industrious young black-robe over there, cupboards which he could open and shut with an automatic, perfect sense of what was appropriate to each moment of each occasion. It is an unattractive, chilling fact, of which adjectives applied to himself he constitutionally can have no inkling, that he is utterly sincere in these Emotions as far as they go. It is not that by discipline he keeps them in their place and forbids them to affect his work of administration: he is simply what his own type call a model human being. He lacks some kind of a core—but I can't call such a lack a drawback, seeing that it has left him free to build up his own clear-cut empire.

He would shed tears with a man apprehensive of execution, then with quivering distaste order the execution. I should guess he never does anything with cold disinterest—he *feels* the emotion appropriate to each action.

Anyway, I convinced him of my identity.

Apparently, my birth-prophecy was a hush-hush bit of knowledge which even Kaselm (who seems to be a man of resource) had difficulty getting hold of. My own knowledge of it, combined with several other matters I mentioned, was conclusive.

My mother was not mentioned at all.

I took care not to mention her. If they hold my father in such esteem, they must hate her, his rival for rulership.

I longed to ask what my father is like, but dared not betray such ignorance.

As I was led away to the apartments and slaves which were to be mine, I wondered how much Kaselm knew that he'd not told the Superlativity, and if he'd even tell him now. He had been the colleague of my father, who wants me dead—had apparently discussed me with my father, since he knew my name and the prophecy—and yet seemingly did not know my father's hate for me? He has not even asked me why I was in boy's clothes when he first saw me.

No, the Priest Kaselm is playing a game of his own. It is almost certainly a very deep one. I must watch myself when I am with him—it will do me no good to watch *him* when I am with him, his bland, lean, black-a-vised face will tell me nothing.

I received my biggest surprise of the day when I came to my own apartments.

They are tremendously luxurious.

They are in the Court attached to the Temple—a Court at the moment chock-full of the Southern nobility most of whom seem to have deserted the Capital as soon as the Northern army marched in. This was because they didn't want to be in the midst of the trouble—and trouble they knew there'd be. The exacerbation of the allies was planned well ahead on the part of the South.

This court has also been the home of Southern nobility for longer than it has been the home of the Southern religion-emperor.

The result is that the Court, while paying *very elaborate* lip-service to the religion, continues in its own sweet way. It seems to me most corrupt. The Superlativity keeps to his own bare suite in the Temple and can't know much of his subjects' *life*, only of their elaborate attention to ceremony, ritual and his theories. But the Court is full of black-robes, scurrying here and there on religious and/or administrative business. I think some of them are too unworldly, or too sure of their way, to see beyond the Court's surface; others are power-seekers, toadies to Court as much as to Temple.

And one great lady has already said outright to me, 'A fastidious noblewoman must always prefer her lover to be a priest. Ordinary men are all very well for common women; but a priest's manhood is superior because it is never stunted by the wearing of breeches.'

It is so nice to be priggish in my Diary about the corruptness of this Court; then to go down and enjoy being made a fuss of by all the corrupt noblemen and some of the corrupt noblewomen.

It is so nice to be Goddess again; but I am not quite certain about this. Their words have the correct reverence, but the tones and behaviour and glances and actions of all the men seem to show that they think of me only as a very young (and very desirable) girl. It is not that they don't believe I've divine blood: just that they don't know how much that ought to mean.

Another nice thing is that though I am the fashion because I am new here, I think the way they treat me as desirable is sincere. This is the kind of civilised society to which I am afraid I am just suited. Not stupid children, nor envious peasants, nor uncouth young officers on their worst, most informal behaviour before what they called a strumpet—this is a Court of polished sex-addicts, the majority young, some jaded, all with time on their hands, genuinely thrilled by anything new, unresentful of the chase which they find all-absorbing. They all know how to make themselves pleasant, they have wonderful manners and know almost exactly when to use them, though the fashion at the moment is for mock-boorish standing-off-ceremony.

The pretty women are divided in their behaviour towards me. A percentage, those who were till now the accepted 'goddesses' or were chasing noblemen now devoted to me—these ladies are very jealous and do anything to throw a spoke in my wheel. Of this the noblemen are all aware. It all makes for more fun for everyone.

Other women, equally pretty, have found that they genuinely like me. We make good companions for each other and have already had lots of very happy times. They know that in a few months, more or less, my brilliant meteor will have settled and I shall be ranged with them when another extra-fabulous newcomer arrives. But when a meteor has settled, the other stars rise once more.

I am having such a really lovely time mainly because I gather I have a new sort of appeal. I found it out almost by accident but it is now obvious.

I am not very witty, I can't indulge in hours of brilliant back-chat and I sometimes take seriously things which turn out to be sophisticated and long-established witticisms. This amuses people who have lots of mounting hysteria at my expense. I never resent it, I am not even embarrassed by it, because it is done openly and with fondness.

I am sincere, usually tell the truth because I have an ineradicable idea that people want to hear the truth in answer to their questions, also I am shy. None of the other ladies have these qualities, but are richly endowed with their opposites: it is the way they have been brought up.

I am also obviously virtuous; bets are being laid on to whom I shall give in first. I am not supposed to know about them.

I am virtuous, not because no one attracts me: almost everyone does. That's the trouble; they have almost all the same appeal. It would seem so wasteful to take one kind, gay, tender, handsome, irresponsible, protective young lover when I could have had any one of nearly a hundred others.

At times, yes, I wake and find my body lonely for the love Smahil taught it to be so used to; in the night I wake blindly and reach out to absence. I find no shoulder for my head, no throat for my brief sleepy mouth, no hands for my breasts as though they were sleepy doves which might fly away, no Smahil to mutter his dreams. The bed becomes a vast abyss, acres wide, and I am tiny and lost in it.

At times, yes, I yearn till occasionally I smile with surprise to find tears in my eyes from the very intensity of my yearning, for a lover who would look after me, never demand too much of me, and not spend his time finding jealous fault with me; but no, really, it is too much to ask me to do, take a whole new lover, another human being. I have never needed people and don't have to start now. Of course I am not lonely.

There is also a large minority, a leavening of respectable nobles and their women, old or elderly or even young, who look on my set and therefore myself as nothing more than—well, I won't use the word. They certainly never would.

These people whisk their skirts away from me when I pass.

It is all rather unjust, I am neither really in one camp nor in the other, but the camp that provides most fun likes it just so.

Everybody wears fabulous clothes, including myself.

Almost all the clothes at Court have been at least partially designed by their owners. Original ideas, no matter how bizarre, count at the moment far more than elegance.

Every morning everybody takes a long walk in The Cloisters (they are vastly long-pillared arcades surrounding gardens open to the sky) in order to exchange gossip and compare their clothes with everyone else's. A ridiculous custom has grown up of waving your arms in the strangest gesticulations at whoever you're speaking to. You place your arms in any one of the hundreds of possible variations: you hold them there for about twenty seconds, then change to another position. You can hold your arms out at different angles, place one on your hip and the other on your head—anything at all strange, in fact. All this while you talk and laugh quite naturally. After fifteen or twenty minutes with one companion, you leave each other by some mutual timing-instinct and move on to the next friend, acquaintance or enemy. You can do the rounds of The Cloisters singly, in pairs, or in threes. Any larger group is infra dig till you get to about ten, which is again permissible. All these rules, crazy gestures, etc. are only for The Cloisters. Anywhere else in the Court you behave normally (more or less).

Clothes take almost any pattern but there are male and female motifs.

Women's dress revolves almost all round the *veil*: this floats from the head, the shoulders, the top of a peaked headdress, or even from one wrist. If it is a long veil, its end is held by the little attendant page almost everyone has. I have a conventionally delicious, rather insolent nobleman, very chubby and with marvellous, red curls, five years old. I wish I could have had Ow. A secondary motif in the ladies' clothing is the elaborate matching of the trousers to the dress. This has always been the basis of peasants' clothes, which of course are made, trousers and dress, from the same piece of woven cloth—now at this Court the nobility have adopted and embellished it.

The central motif of the men's dress is the codpiece. There are some adorable ones, on which much thought and fond care have obviously been lavished: some stick out inches, most are in ingenious shapes, such as a big shell or a huge fruit drenched in appropriate scent.

It is a lovely Court—most of its life revolving about the bedrooms, the gardens, the staircases, banqueting halls and of course The Cloisters.

There are flowers everywhere, trained up the walls if they can't be present any other way, or blossoming creep ers encircling the pillars. These incredibly tall, incredibly slender, silvery blue pillars rise everywhere, ostensibly holding the rafters, or flanking the staircases which recede into watery blue distance in stately convolutions, up and down. Fountains spring over balustrades of peculiarly high, slender, narrow marble staircases rearing like steep hills in and out of the lines of pillars and the complicated rafters of the Court, sometimes in the open air for no reason.

(I am told these fountains are turned off in winter so only their statues remain, decorative jewelled, metal figures and abstract shapes without the yards-high jets springing from their orifices.)

Every here and there in the Court, from a base of flowers and fountains rises a vastly tall, glass screen. The water spreads itself upon this, fanwise against it, or jets from its very top and drops swiftly, a tempestuous, artificial waterfall.

The rafters of the Court halls are very mazy. White and turquoise birds perch on them or fly cooing amongst them. There are droppings everywhere, one has to get used to them, even on one's favourite dress, even on the banqueting table.

There are lots of organised games, and almost everyone can play a musical instrument or sing. There are songs of which everyone knows the words and which are sung all the time till they are loved to death and the next song becomes the fashion. Every song harps on love and presents it in a lyrically physical way which promises all joy but ignores the existence of any spirit. They are a form of art, for the words if heard or read without their music are puerile in content and punk as writing, and the music if heard without the words is empty rhythm; together they lend an emotional depth to each other, their meaning and their quality, and also to love, life . . .

I persuade myself, almost, that life here is not an unreal dream, that it can last and last without cloying me, without wakening any ambition in me, without dissolving into war.

I am very happy.

Occasionally the Court receives news of the Northern army's manoeuvres.

I have pieced together what has evidently been happening.

Zerd drilled his troops unmercifully for nearly a week outside the Capital, to harden them for marching, but the Southerners said it was because he wanted to regain harsh discipline. One dark night he marched them on about ten miles—towards the Southern coast but also towards this temple-town of the Superlativity. He is now immobile again, a focus of conjecture to everyone—does he intend to visit the Superlativity? Does he (horrors!) intend to make the Atlan campaign himself, dispensing after all with the troublesome allies, and to overcome the Southern fleet on the coast and sail complete with secret of formula intact?

Meanwhile he just sits tight there, under tentage again, drilling all day (now, according to reports, with a more practised air as if merely to keep boredom at bay) on the plain beside the river I sailed down at the beginning of summer, a maddening mystery to everyone.

I bet he's enjoying himself in his grim, competent, contemptuous, vivid way.

I escaped today from a picnic. There were so many rustly billowy skirts, so much back-chat, so much fuss about where to sit—perfectly delightful mossy hollows were impossible because everyone's skirts were too wide to fit in—and I do like compliments, but not when they are couched in difficult metaphors that you have to be awfully quick at answering. It's not fair, it's easy enough to make a compliment but horrible to have to answer right away and in the same metaphor, and it gives you absolutely no time to gloat over actually getting the compliment, and if you just blush and look away you are laying yourself open to being sniggered at.

I found that the grounds stretch right down to the river—and beyond too, only I couldn't find a bridge.

They get quite wild, untended, and bordering the river there is a part of the orchard where, as I ventured into it, I thought 'I shouldn't think anyone has been here for ages'.

The trees, five different kinds of fruit-trees, had been planted wide apart but now are tangled together. The undergrowth is thick, but not alarming—that gentle country kind of undergrowth, furry seed-balls, tickling-headed grasses, docks near any nettles, pleasant with bees. I

wandered amongst it, my head bent, watching the tiny
insects scurrying and passing each other on perpendicular
stems. The foliages were tangled together by loops of
flowering creeper, and in spring the mass of blossom in
this old-orchard must be tremendous, but now the trees
were dotted rather sparsely with little wrinkled fruits, the
kind that come from trees whose inspiration is just about
over, so I was breathing in all the scents but watching the
undergrowth and picking occasional spiders off my frills—
when I banged into a foot.

At first I thought it was a bough or creeper my head had
struck, and tried to brush it away without raising my
eyes—but it swung rather nastily.

I stood there, among the pretty flowers, looking up at
the row of men. Six men, and a small boy, in peasants' and
artisans' clothes, and all in varying stages of decomposition,
one of the men nearly quite rotted away. But the latest
could only have been strung up yesterday or this morning
at the earliest—the cheeks and lips still pink and fresh-
smooth, the skin almost pulsing with life, a beard, I'd've
sworn it, pushing itself through. I stood there watching
them, one of a society which had been in this part of the
orchard for some time—the men and boy dancing a little
on every breeze, the bees communicating with them, a
couple of spiders friendly in a web depending from one
foot to another, the web lissome and elastic when necessary,
a few buzzing bluebottles crawling in and out of clothing
folds—of course the nearly decomposed gentleman was
nearly alive again with flies, whirring, scintillating; gregari-
ous chips of fur-legged lapislazuli. There was a sweetish
stale smell—of course each must have had his own separate smell according to his age but all together—oh, no,
really, it's not a thing to stay calm about. I stood there far
too long, several seconds, so every detail was stamped
indelibly into my brain as I turned to dash away, blunder-
ing through grasses and tangles, splashing through a stream

hidden under fronds, insects spattering from what I touched like specks of spray—

The nightmares have caught me by the throat again. They have found me in my new happy existence—I think the sight in the orchard laid me open to them.

I hear vague knockings at night as I start awake in bed, which is soon clammy with my own sweat—they seem to advance, retreat, advance as if anxious to break through—not the wall, they're not against the wall, they're always just above my head and the tempo quickens, I'm sure they'll break through one night, *one* night soon, and then—? And yet as soon as I'm not hearing them I doubt if I have, memories of the nightmare, I tell myself, and everyone has nightmares.

I think the time has come for me to face it—at least the question: Is something trying to get at me? Oh, Gods, at least let me keep the questionmark, not—not Something is . . .

Gods, Cija, face it, write it down, put it on your page, can a nightmare break through into waking life and *that* into—into vivid supra-life, something reaching to destroy, something out there intent on me, drawing even nearer, reaching its concentration out to *me* all the time from the other side—nearer and nearer, no longer whispers as in the City, here in the kind laughing Court that leaves me quite alone at night while I lie sweating and rigid, small and unknowledgeable and terrified and utterly alone, while it draws steadily nearer night by night, knocking, not stealthily but calmly, little groups of knocks on the wall separating it from reality—quite ready to flow through—reaching all ready and eager to reach for *me*—its long goal—and it may *be* tonight.

The talk at the evening feast was all of the Northern army's approach.

'Pouf, what can the Dragon-General do even if he does come here? With his straggling little army of fretful novices—'

'Rest assured, he'll not even reach here.'

'Well, I couldn't be sorrier. I'd like at least to see him before it's all over. He's said to be devastating.'

'Couldn't we all arrange an excursion and go and watch while our Temple Guard do their slaughtering? You might see him quite close to.'

Forialk peeled some nuts for me and teased me to open my mouth so he could feed me. He is the one with a conceited line of blond beard emphasising his jaw-line—which, I must admit, is a good one, young and strong and clear-cut and arrogant. Would he keep me safe tonight, when eventually even this late feast reached its finale and I had to go up and—fear—? In his arms, would anything intangible be able to grip me?

I explored his dark-blue gaze. Deep down there was more potential kindness than I'd expected. The pupils widened and I could not look away—I realised that, with a stab of triumph, the boy had misinterpreted my intentness.

(Why I think of him as a boy I don't know, he's several years older than I am.)

Suddenly in our own private quietness at that noisy table, he turned my hand over and ran his finger down the back of it.

I smiled indulgently even while the tingle went through me.

How many young men have used my hand so? A favourite trick among the officers who frequented the Beauty's tent—

Couldn't I really find someone better?

And yet—tonight—I would want to run sobbing pleading after him, as soon as I clicked my door shut on myself alone tonight—

I took my hand from his, careful not to snatch it.

'I'm not hungry tonight, Forialk. Are you?'

His eyes widened on mine, he shook his head.

'Let's walk, outside.'

I rose and walked away from the table. I didn't bother to turn to see him following me. As we went between the tables to the courtyard, questions and those eternal conundrums were laughed at us, but no one was seriously interested. They are all so used to my unassailable virtue— they are quite sure it will crack one day but it never seems likely at the moment. However, as we got nearer the courtyard entrance something in Forialk's eager, taut, smug-cornered smile must have awakened suspicion—the young noble Ecir caught the velvet swing of Forialk's sleeve and said quietly, 'Where are you taking the Goddess?'

Forialk disengaged his sleeve, smiling his provocative smile.

Ecir started to his feet.

'Goddess—' he offered his arm, his eyes pleading.

He had realised the imminence of urgency.

I glanced from one to the other, while we were watched with covert interest by those near, openly by those farther up the table.

While there was still time to choose, which did I prefer of these two who had presented themselves out of a hundred tonight for my need?

As I glanced from Forialk's impatient arrogance (he was tapping his feet and his eyes on me were hot) to Ecir's speaking glance, I realised that Ecir is in love with me. His lips were trembling, he was pouring a message to me through his eyes. At a word from me Forialk would be dealt with—but they both knew it was for me to choose. I hesitated no longer after I pictured the involvement of giving myself to someone who would tell me he adores me and would later tell me that gave him rights where I am concerned, who would most probably become wild at times and the other times glower at me from corners—I placed my fingers again on Forialk's sleeve and we went out together without looking again at Ecir.

In the courtyard the tall fountains were striped with starlight. There was cooing from innumerable hidden sleepy birds.

I knew Forialk was looking at me but I kept my profile clear.

This courtyard was not deserted, there were figures in the colonnades, lovers mostly, but there a group of pages talking with spasmodic horseplay in torchlight, and now and then a sedate or scurrying black-robe, and there the priest Kaselm, for his stride at its most casual is easily recognised from anyone else's.

The next courtyard was nearly empty, and silent but for fountains and birds, and a breeze in the creepers.

Forialk turned me to face him when I was about to walk on.

'Whoa, what's the hurry?'

'I thought we came out for a walk.'

I was being not only discouraging but rather obvious. My usual idea is not to show that I know what they want of me in starlit courtyards—it saves embarrassment at times. This evening I couldn't care less. It was enough to make his eyes flicker uncertainly before mine and he walked on mechanically a few steps before recollecting himself and again turning me to him.

His hands were firm on my shoulders, as I stared straight ahead at his shapely lips they parted and his large teeth caught the starlight.

He looked down at me for a moment, then gave a strange tender little laugh in his throat and pressed me to him, his hands strong against my shoulder-blades. I had to hang on to the points of his big starched collar in order not to lose my balance.

I didn't return his kiss but I was complaisant till I realised the character of the kiss. It was a passionate kiss, greedy but not hungry, not respectful enough considering that I am the little goddess Cija, most sought-after noblewoman of the Court and just about the one with the best blood, and he knew this is the first time I've been kissed since arriving at Court. He's tried once or twice before, himself.

I stood there under his kiss, my mind now working separately, while he worried at my mouth like a young bear at feeding-time.

This man would make a rotten lover. Well, for my purpose anyway. He'd be generous and gay and ardent. But he'd pooh-pooh any ideas that he had to stay with me all of every night. He'd be bound to be off dicing and drinking in places where a lady couldn't follow and wouldn't be wanted if she did. And it would be even harder to change from him than from someone like Ecir who's in love with me—once he had me he'd take care to keep me because I'm the prize of the Court. There'd be annoying ugly scenes, maybe duels.

At least it wasn't a phoney-maudlin kiss, he wasn't insulting me by pretending to be in love with me. But it was time it was ended—I was finding it difficult to breathe, anyway.

I stepped back and twisted from his grasp when he wasn't expecting me to.

Now that he'd kissed me his gaze burned into me so that I shivered.

'Please, Forialk,' I said, 'let's walk on.'

It was as if he hadn't bothered to hear my words, he reached for me again.

'Or even go back,' I added.

'I thought this was what you wanted.'

My gaze dropped. I had indeed led him on. If I denied it, he'd believe me because of my reputation, he'd think he'd made the mistake. Still . . . It was better not to be

frank, and he was no good, I must discard him even at the
risk of a night of horror on my own.

'I'm sorry, Forialk. It's not what I wanted. Will you take
me on to look at the gardens—or back, if you're not
interested in the gardens—?'

I looked at him almost humbly.

He took a deep breath of the darkness. Suddenly he
gripped my hands in his and led me over to a bench
half-covered in a seclusion of tangled creepers. We sat
facing the whites of each other's eyes, which was just
about all we could see there, our knees nearly touching.

'Now that I've got you here I'm certainly not taking you
back in. Look—You're acting strangely this night, Cija
. . .' He tried the name on his palate. Of course it's not
the first time he'd used it, but now he was giving it an
intimate flavour. 'You're like a disconnected doll—you
don't seem to care about anything much, yet something's
worrying you. Give. What's up?'

His voice became unbelievably gentle.

'Tell me . . .?'

I felt the wry twist of my mouth. I thought of telling
Forialk that I have nightmares, that I am neurotic enough
to think them so bad I was prepared to take a lover to
keep me company during them, that his kiss had convinced me he was no good . . .

'Cija?'

Pause.

'You are worried about something, aren't you?'

I had hesitated too long now for a denial.

'Yes, I am, but it's nothing—only I'm a little depressed.'

'Let me fix it?' There was a pause of a couple of heart-
beats before he added hurriedly, 'Let me try?' Then his
mouth was down on mine again, his tongue was ruthless,
the closed firmness of his embrace invincible. It was a
very—not exactly ungentle, but an exacting way of com-

forting. But curiously enough, I did find it comforting. It was so real.

Swimmingly I raised my eyelids and his eyes glinted down at me, probably slightly crossed because of the close range, but so unnerving as to be endearing.

When he comes up for air, I promised myself vaguely, I'll entrust myself to him, I'll tell my loneliness and fears and he'll say I'm sweet and be kind and carry me up that big, chilly, creeper-grown staircase until it winds under the rafters and comes to his living-quarters.

Forialk's head was yanked back by a tense-knuckled hand. I immediately recognised the big topaz ring.

Forialk turned with a curse, saw his assailant, released me and stood up. He wasn't allowed more than a second before Ecir knocked him down again with a crack that shivered the creepers even before Forialk crashed into them. Forialk started up, immediately furious, and there were some fierce blows with both boys swaying on the balls of their feet. I watched for a minute but neither even looked at me. I couldn't be sure which would win, they were evenly matched. I couldn't even be sure which I wanted to win. I backed away, found myself in the shadows of the colonnade, someone steadying with my shoulders.

'Take it easy, they probably won't kill each other.'

'Holy Kaselm! I'm quite calm, I assure you. But aren't you going to stop them?'

'I'm not going to inconvenience myself so, Goddess—unless, of course, your wish is to be my command?' He bowed in the gloom.

I pushed my hair out of my eyes. 'Oh, no, by all means don't bother—' I seated myself on the plinth of a pillar. The sound of blows continued out in the starlight but I wasn't watching. What is going to become of me tonight? I was busy wondering, and it wasn't pleasant for me.

'You were having trouble?' In spite of his tone, I felt the question too familiar to be courteous. 'I'm sorry I didn't

know as I was passing. I assure you it would then have
been myself who would have interfered.' He set a foot on
the plinth beside me, rested a hand on his upraised knee,
his chin in the palm of the hand. In the starlight shiftingly
magnified by the fountains, I saw the wide absent-minded
meditation of the black eyes. The worldly black robe,
caught in folds to one side of the belt, fell away from the
priest's long lean thigh, long, hard, flat muscles and sinews tautening the black tights.

'You are trembling, Goddess?' But he wasn't looking at
me, nor at the fight.

'I am cold, Holy Kaselm.'

'That's too bad. You are wearing a velvet wrap and it's a
summer evening.'

'I—I am afraid, Holy Kaselm.' He waited, and I turned
to him and let it come in a rush before I could be sorry
and control myself. 'Lately I have been having terrible
nightmares, really terrible ones, I am afraid of being alone
at night, I have no one to turn to, I cannot sleep with my
friends among the noblewomen—'

'They are usually accompanied by harsher comrades?'

I bowed my head.

'They—sleep lightly for companions, Holy Kaselm.'

'You do well to blush for them, Goddess. So you wish
for a safe place of sleep, with an unfrightened companion
close by? Your personal maid is unobtainable?'

'At night, I would not like to claim her away from—for
the sake of night-fears—'

'And yet they are really bad?'

I whispered bleakly, 'Yes.'

I added, 'I couldn't be calling her all the time. I need
another presence—something to keep them away—'

'Them?'

'I hear knockings . . .' I began to cry. I gulped myself to
a stop, shuddered, stared quietly ahead again.

'If you agree, Goddess, I shall offer you the sanctity of

the priestly Corridors until you feel yourself safe again from these night-terrors. This means that you would sleep in my cell. I would be a few feet away, readily within call. I would know as soon as you were in distress.'

I turned my head to stare at him.

'I can only say Thank you, Holy Kaselm. I—I would be tremendously grateful, it sounds a solution, a security. I have been—May I ask you one thing? Do you believe in ghosts?'

'I don't, Goddess.'

'My maid does. It's one of the reasons she'd be no good—'

'I know how terrible dreams can be. I have seen sane men crazy from them—'

A splash recalled us to the fight. Ecir sprawled in the basin of a heavy fountain.

Forialk lurched towards me, bowed when he saw the priest Kaselm. 'Your slave, Holy . . . Cija . . .' He presented an arm. There was a bloody contusion on his forehead, his dishevelled hair falling stickily across it, one velvet sleeve hanging in tatters. His mouth was open, he blinked at me from between swollen lids.

'How many teeth have you lost?'

Forialk glanced at the priest, unsure how to take this.

'None, Holy Kaselm—I think.'

'I'm going with the priest, Forialk. He has offered me—sanctuary—'

'What are you talking about?'

'I have been having uncomfortable nights. I shall feel better, I am sure, in the holy quiet of the Corridors.'

I half-put out my hand, for an instant touched the split lip which so recently had been whole hard on mine. The priest was already walking away. 'Have someone see to you, my lord . . .'

He woke into life again as I began to follow the priest.

'Cija—Goddess—You can't go, not with him, that priest is known—'

A fragmentary protest meant nothing to me. I followed Holy Kaselm over the pillars' shadows. My mind and body were already vague, longing for rest with the confidence which, if strong enough, was all that was needed to defeat the fear.

A single candle hazed the small bare room. I was already in the priest's black shirt, too large for me, between the rough linen sheets, when he returned with a flask of wine and two exquisitely wrought goblets, obviously Temple property and so not to be looked upon as luxury. His shadow wavered over wall and ceiling, surged into the impenetrable, stagnant shadow curving the room's corners.

'Of course, tomorrow the most important parts of your wardrobe will be transferred here. I have enough space.'

'Your priests' shirts are very like the officers' shirts of the Northern army, in which they also sleep.'

'You have experience of that, naturally.' He held out one full goblet to me.

'Yes, I was with the Northern army more than a year. Also the men sleep in their boots—even in billets, at least according to the ladies of your Capital who sued for various damages . . .' I didn't realise till later that I was avoiding an awkwardness.

'Something to eat, bread and cheese?'

'Please. I hear he's coming here?'

'Who?'

'Zerd—'

'Don't worry. He'll not get far with that army. Their regulars were a tiny nucleus before this giant campaign was recruited for—the scum of the Northern drinking-shops. Anyone with any money bought himself off—At a pinch even a war-office can be warred against, but not the little individual officials in it—' Kaselm munched placidly, his shadow jerking a parody of each mastication.

'He's held them so far,' I said dubiously. 'It wasn't a pretty journey, actually, Holy Kaselm.'

'He's a good general, that's acknowledged through the known world. But he's not yet had one battle to try those raw recruits—and men can ford streams hand-in-hand even in the most exotic scenery, it doesn't stop them being raw till they've seen a bit of action—more than half his youthful raggle-taggle will break in battle, and unfortunately for him their first is going to be pretty important.'

'I shouldn't think he'd be risking so much if that were so.'

'No? He's little to lose, hasn't he? The whole idea was a suicide-jaunt from the first. The Dragon-General has seemed a threat under the Northern King's nose for some years—'

'Isn't it possible Zerd accepted the job with enough faith in his own ability to pull it off, Atlan and all?'

'Anything's possible,' the priest agreed, 'but I should think he's found out his mistake in the last few months bogged down by the ominous on every side, trapped, cut off behind our mountains.'

'He's dangerous enough. I know he gathers in the tail-ends of every plan-structure before making his next move, he takes account of every aspect of living for his army from movement to movement, week to week—month by month they've survived far more than his King presumably expected. He's brilliant enough to be taking account of the greater plan, too. He's the calmest person in the world. *I* should be very surprised,' I said, embarking on a cheese sandwich, 'to find that he has ever considered the word failure.'

'No matter how brilliant in himself, I don't think we need fear his advent. How could one man hold together such a deplorable force, very aware that they're ludi-

crously outnumbered in enemy territory—unless he's
superhuman.'

'He's ab-human. The Superlativity will surely declare
open war on an ally whose great-grandmother was a crocodile—who—who can turn any enemies blue like himself,
filling them with the poison which is his element but alien
to his victims who die within a few days. He must be
exterminated!'

The priest turned a stare on me.

'How do you know this?'

I whispered, 'I must be one of the only three people in
the world who know this and still live.'

'How does he inflict the poison?'

'A bite, a scratch, maybe at times without purpose,
through carelessness—I couldn't be sure of the exact way.'

'The Superlativity may be interested by this information,'
Kaselm said thoughtfully, snuffing the candle. I nodded
sleepily. 'Kill the Demon.' I snuggled into my pillow.

What seemed the next instant the room was flooded
with light. Bird song liquefied space. The priest Kaselm
was nowhere to be seen.

My sleep must have been immediate and profound—
and long. The priest had gone to the Temple morning-
meal, leaving me to rouse myself in time for the later
breakfast of the Court. I yawned and stretched. I was
already feeling better for my sanctuary. I wriggled out of
bed and the priest's spare shirt, dressed in my own clothes,
went to the doorway, started down the long, bare, fresh,
clean corridor. I felt well and alive. It occurred to me for
the first time that the priest might have drugged my wine
to ensure a profound sleep. The friendly sound of my
footsteps kept up with me.

Out in the Temple grounds, where I'd never been before,
I realised just how early it was though. I'd emerged from
the wrong end of the corridor and had a mile, perhaps a

little less, to traverse before I got back to Court. I didn't mind a bit. The grass was silver-gold with dew. Flower petals could just about be seen unfurling. The morning was swift with that kind of movement, but there was not another human being to be seen.

The resilient turf stretched up. I followed the incline beside a long white wall, formed of blocks decayed in places. There were not even any windows. I felt so healthy and happy, it was the last place in the world I expected to hear groans.

Muffled groans, as if subterranean, but with no attempt at concealment. They were reckless wild groans, the expression of despair, but the angry expression.

Such bad-tempered hopelessness from below ground—I knelt beside the wall. There was a crash as if something unwieldy but substantial had been thrown. My hand came to a rusty grating—the top segment of a barred window, just enough to admit air to an underground chamber—the rest of the window must face earth. I scrabbled a bit and pulled away enough weed to be able to peer through the grating. There was nothing, no darkness, nothing, a suffused colourless yet murky gloom.

I put my lips to the grating and called clearly but softly. 'Is anybody there?'

There was hardly an instant of breathless silence, then a rush and suddenly strong, pale fingers were round the bars before me, then fast groping savagely out between them. My face was touched before I backed with a gasp; the fingers followed but the hand-knuckles were unable to pass through.

I was afraid I had meddled with a shut-up madman, so I didn't say anything and was getting ready to up and run when a hoarse voice came from the invisible. 'Who are you?'

'Who are you?' I countered.

'Who do you think?' The hoarseness stumbled on a laugh. The tone struck me as contemptuous.

'Listen,' I said. 'I'm no one. I don't belong here. I was passing and I heard you, that's all.'

'What do you mean you don't belong here? Are you trespassing?'

'I've a right at least to be here, I've been with a priest. What were you throwing?'

'How—?' 'When I heard you—'

'Dead rat. At least it was dead when it hit the wall, after I threw it.' The fingers were gripping the bars again. 'Listen, you sound very young—Why are you talking to me?'

'I don't know. Curiosity, at first, and now I just haven't left yet. Are you shut up down there or can you get out if you like?'

There was a burst of fierce laughter. He was laughing his head off. The fingers shook on the bars.

'You're a criminal? That's a Temple dungeon?'

'Sure, sure, very pretty, all correct.'

'Is there anyone else with you?'

'No.' He was relaxed again. He sounded uninterested. His fingers were long and the nails jet-black rimmed, the skin a pale tan under a lot of dirt. 'Hey kid—boy or girl? Girl isn't it—that's nice. Can you get me something to eat? Something little, something fresh and nice—Y'know? just shove it through—'

'Why not skin and eat your rat?'

'*No fooling*—' I was glad he couldn't get at me.

'I'm glad you can't get at me, with a violent temper like that.'

I heard swearing behind me as I went to the nearest fruit tree. I returned with three ripes, which I pushed through to him. 'Gods bless your dear little heart—'

'I only brought three because you can't have too many to hide, your gaoler would notice—Have you anything at all to hide things in, down there?'

'Filthy straw—'

'I'll bring more to eat tomorrow morning—How well do they feed you here?'

'Bowl of weevily gruel a day, big bowl, I wolf it down, maybe a hunk of meat with something wrong with it; there's a pitcher of water, always in the corner, always gets a green scum before they change it. I let the rats pee in it, leave it alone, unless I'm particularly thirsty.'

He was eating the fruit now, the hands had left the bars, I could hear him, also the spitting out of pips.

'I may be able to bring a flask of wine. Could you hide that amongst your straw?'

'Sure. Sure.' There was a short pause while he gnawed thoughtfully at the fruit. 'Why you doing this?'

'Just tell me why you were put in here.'

'I'm Kond,' he said, but hearing that didn't ring a bell, 'second-in-command of Ael.'

'Where's Ael?'

'*Where's Ael?* Look, lovey, you a moron or what? Ael, you know, Ael.'

'Doesn't matter how clearly you hiss it, I don't know it.'

'*Him*. Most dreaded bandit chief in the Empire, especially in these hills.'

'I didn't even know there were hills near here.' I was disillusioned; I had fondly believed I was doing good for a rebel of the old Religion, since he was stuck in the Temple dungeons. 'Listen, whoever you are, I will be back tomorrow unless discovered—is there anything else you want?'

'A knife.'

The Court have taken it in good part that I am sleeping in the Corridors because of nightmares. Some of the ladies seem to envy me for being under Kaselm's protection, but when I seemed bewildered everyone believed at once in my innocence and there have even passed conniving glances—nobody means to enlighten me in case I am worried.

There was sympathy and well-wishing about my night-mares. My night-things and some of my clothes have been transferred to Kaselm's cell.

I saw Forialk at two of the meals. He was rather band-aged and has two black eyes and a split lip and looks very dashing. He would have spoken to me but there was too much of a crowd. I can't remember whether I saw Ecir.

At night there was a big send-off, I was escorted with streamers to the Temple, but managed to hide some things under my cloak.

In the candlelit cell I drained my goblet.

'You drug my wine, don't you, Kaselm?'

'I won't if you don't wish it.'

'I've tried sleeping-daughts myself but they were never strong enough.'

'I hope this will prove so tonight. You were far more tired last night.'

'Kaselm—Tell me, who is Ael?'

'The bandit leader? Who told you about him?'

'I heard of him today in the Court.'

'Oh, he's nothing but one of the thorns in the flesh of the law. His gang are impregnable in the hills, they roost in a network of caves and swoop on travellers. Not even the best armed escorts can be certain of being much use—apart from the fact that many of them are secretly in Ael's pay. He doesn't scruple to rob or kill the most important personages—'

'What is he like?'

'A big, ugly tyrant, nearing forty in appearance but he's said to be in his late twenties, half his nose gone and his whole skin a patchwork of scars—'

'And his second-in-command? Haven't you got him here?' I held my breath, wondering whether the Court are sup-posed to know that.

'Yes, I believe we did catch him, several months ago. Of

course Ael will have found someone else now, so he's no longer a valuable prisoner.'

'Haven't the gang tried a rescue-swoop?'

'Why should they bother? They could never get far, whereas in their eyrie . . . Ael's surrounded by too many competent toughs to repine over their individual loss in fight or capture. No, our young man is safe with us, and when we need the dungeon for someone else we'll have him executed without trouble.'

Once in the night I awoke and found myself shuddering in every limb. A sound of knocking seemed to converge upon my ears from every side. I pressed my hands to my eyes and moaned. In a swift movement the priest Kaselm had rolled over on his pallet, risen, and was crouched at my side. 'All right, all right, little one.' He lit a candle and held my hands till I stopped shuddering. He did not blow out the flame when at last I lay weakly back again.

In the morning the priest was gone and I was alone in the light- and song-flooded room. I dressed, hid the objects under my cloak, and went out into the sunlight.

I found the grating after a little difficulty, I hadn't properly memorised where it is, knelt to it and called softly.

'Kond.'

There was a sound of movement.

'Here I am.'

'Here is a flask of wine and some cold meat, as I promised . . .'

He groped and took them, breathing heavily. 'I'm sure you'll get to heaven . . .'

'You can manage OK? You're standing with your arms raised?'

'I don't mind the strain, for this . . .' There was a pause. 'Did you bring it?'

'You want to kill the jailer, don't you?'

'What else.'

'Then you'd be out, killing anyone else who got in the way, and up to the hills again.'

'Well?'

'I'm not eager to help you . . .'

'Can't you get it? Can't you try for tomorrow?'

'I may bring you food again, but I don't want to help a brigand to be at large again—'

He grasped the bars fiercely, if the bars had been a little less hard they would have winced, and I knew they were meant to be my throat. 'Listen, what do you mean, what are you talking about? Of course you want to help me—'

'I don't no.'

'Damn your soul,' he whispered after a while.

'I see how you want it.'

'No, you don't. You're not going, are you? Look, there's no reason we can't work something out, I can give in a bit, don't leave me after we got friendly—' He was saying with frantic persuasiveness at trip-tongue speed when I whispered fiercely, '*Shut up.*'

'Good morning, holy priest,' I added.

'Good morning, my child. What are you doing here?'

I held up a ragged bunch I'd been pulling up absently while talking to the prisoner. 'Picking flowers, holy priest.'

'But they're weeds, child!'

'Oh, I think they're pretty, holy priest!' I looked at them with affection, holding back from their rank smell. I walked away with the old priest, chattering as disarmingly as possible.

This morning I did not go to the grating. I've had enough of helping people, it's time I learnt that lesson.

I stood in the front row of the spectators on the biggest ground floor balcony. I had a basket of roses to throw, but my hands were too listless. They all cheered so my head ached, the crowd along the route were so many (*so many*) stupid specks, beginning to churn into a vortex attacking my eyes. In other words I had a splitting headache, it was mainly the sense of injustice. All those people had been hanging round for hours in the sun-glare to ensure that nobody pinched their chance of a good view, yet they were awfully energetic. I'd only been out a few minutes because everyone knew I must be in front—already I wanted coolness and dark.

The procession was already approaching. The cheering was spreading towards us, a sure forerunner. Damn enthusiastic fools, they were not only treating him as the ally the Superlativity had declared he still definitely is, they were already taking him to their hearts because he is to be a novel treat, a handsome, famous, scale-skinned—

'Mainly your work, mine and yours,' Kaselm had said last night. 'I told my master the Superlativity of the Dragon-General's personal—er—well, powers. He seems to be convinced that the ally can only be a demon, perhaps equal to his godhead, and must be treated with discretion until it becomes clearer what plan of action should be employed.'

My ear-drums throbbed angrily as the crowd below and the aristocrats with me cheered. They began to toss flowers. The sun whirled round and round in an unnecessary perhaps-would-be decorative maelstrom of curly fire, the only part one's eyes could bear.

Small black drums flanked the Northern army's horns, hideous as mastodons' squeals.

The crowd were delighted by the birds. They advanced eight abreast, claws sixteen abreast, on the petal-deep roadway. Their crests were up and they shied at the ceaseless fragrant shower. The crowd's cheering extinguished the riders' muttering but not the tightness of their mouths and the white knuckles of their rein-hands. I had a handful of roses but had thrown nothing. My pulses spun as I saw the red cloak, bright and immaculate, recently dry-cleaned, spread regally over the crupper of the high, black, thoroughbred bird. My pulses steadied to a staccato as I saw the black mane, held in a silver band studded with agate.

It was a thousand to one chance that he would look up then, this being the last and most important balcony above his route, but a fair-haired girl in the crowd had thrown a big pink-edged magnolia and he was busy catching it and bowing.

My mouth relaxed. The flowers slid between my fingers.

I'd never been in the main hall of the Temple before, but I wasn't getting much idea of it now either because it was all pitch dark. There were a lot of people standing round to every side of one, but they were not rustling or whispering much. I think a lot of it was awe. The only lit thing there was the throne, an ancient boulder of jade, roughly shaped ages ago into a chair-shape and with a stiff net of wrought gold over it. Where the loops of gold crossed each other jewels had been set, some big, some tiny, and apparently scattered quite haphazardly, no pattern. It was cunningly lit by some hidden lamp or something, and it was what we were all looking at but it seemed a long way away even to me. I was again in the front row of the crowd owing to my divinity, which was the only clue we had in the dark of the hall's hugeness. The throne stayed empty a long time.

Then there was a spreading rustle of heads turning and one saw little lights advancing from a distance. Or rather, it looked like one little light jerking in a stately way towards us. This also lasted a long time. Then suddenly the little light had reached the throne and was no more, and there instead was the Superlativity sitting in it, all bathed in the throne's glory and wearing a loose black robe which was supposed to symbolise simplicity but actually made him look pregnant. I was very impressed, even though Kaselm had already explained the lights to me the night before. Three attendants were with the Superlativity as he approached in darkness, one casting down little balls, the second lighting them by touching them with a stick which ignites at a touch, the third extinguishing them: so his progress through darkness was marked by spasmodic balls of fire.

We all laid our faces to the ground when we saw the Superlativity suddenly on the throne; and a lot of heavenly voices from some unseen gallery above us burst into a song of praise that the nation's god had deigned to appear in the flesh amongst us. He blessed us, and then benignly made us all get up because he said that though worship is necessary for us it means nothing to him. Then, over the heavenly choir which was badly organised and got too loud at times—making it difficult to hear him—he gave a long speech welcoming among us the leader of the men who will help us at last in the near future to break down the selfish barrier with which the continent Atlan has for so long cut off herself and her resources from her sister continents, from her loving ready-with-forgiveness mother the World.

This went on for ages. Then all the lights came on with a blaze. Everyone blinked and rubbed their eyes for a moment and then saw the Northern General going up to the Superlativity. He made a speech, thanking the Superlativity and his people for their kindness and cordiality and saying how we were all together in this undertaking of (in effect) rescuing Atlan from herself, and he called forth beauteous slaves, mainly golden-skinned ones—they're always good for effect but becoming almost conventional—who laid their foreheads to the step of the throne and presented the Superlativity with presents. There were one or two awfully good presents—had Zerd had them all the time or how had he got hold of them?—mastodons' tusks hooped with gold, that sort of thing. The hooping was rather clumsy, perhaps home-made by the army, but it gave a barbaric sort of look, as if they were old and therefore just as valuable. But the balance of the presents were just fill-ups, rather poor stuff, hastily gathered together, hand-embroidered cloaks (probably done by Lara and her ladies) and uncut gems: just bulk, nothing exquisite. There were feathers, and a quartz drinking-trough which I'd seen hundreds of times before and never thought anything special, and as the *piece de résistance* a young white bird was brought in. The Superlativity accepted these gifts graciously and with every sign of proper pleasure. I'm sure it wasn't tact, he always believes in what he's doing at the moment, he's a wonderful god really, intrinsically proper and respectable. It's what nations need. And then he blessed Zerd and with a wave of his hand included us in the blessing before the lights went out again and away went the little fire-balls. I was sure he must be awfully stiff, probably etched all over after sitting in that tracery-covered throne.

When the lights went on again we were all free to crowd round the presents and Zerd and his commanders and household, and touch and make cooing noises. The only presents I wanted to look at closely were some pterodactyls' eggs. I wasn't sure whether they were fake or not, but in any case . . . Everyone was thrilled by the white bird, the men asking his grooms questions and the ladies recoiling with screams every time he moved. He was quite good-tempered considering all the confusion, but stood on the eggs before I had a chance to get at them.

Lara was being made an awful fuss of by about a dozen nobles. I was contemptuous at first and then suddenly realised that there are a lot of factors in favour of her being the next Court meteor. The Northern General's pretty little wife, and of course she is quite pretty, was wearing a pink dress over pink trousers banded in sequins; Forialk was one of those making most fuss of her which brought me comfort. The way he ignores me, never even looks at me let alone speaks even when we're put together, it's most flattering. Then someone led me over to Zerd before I realised—

'General, one of our most adorable ladies, the Goddess Cija. You should have a lot in common with each other, I believe she was born somewhere north of our mountains, you were, weren't you, darling?'

The General did not bow for a perceptible while.

He stood looking at my face, seeming to search it. I was close enough to see the smoothly overlapping texture of his skin, simply the colour of a thunder-cloud against his red cloak and over his polished leather breastplate. I could smell his sweat, faint this afternoon, pungent. I believe he saw my nostrils widen.

'Goddess—'

He bowed.

I nodded coolly, then smiled as a gracious afterthought. 'We really are glad to have you among us, General.' The right brand of aristocratic-female mock-cordial cordiality. I was not in just any grand pretty dress—it was white lace, slim, long-sleeved. I was elegant and immaculate. I moved away amongst the crowd, no need to glide, no need to try for effect, I was in effect in myself, the best kind. Safe. But watch out for lonely walks, watch out for villainous-looking Northern sergeants, you know the formula, the most important factor there is, the key to the war, he must be pretty certain you haven't told it yet but you're dynamite, alas.

'You are pale.'

'Yes, it was—it was—seeing him again today—' I shall not tell him Zerd wants to kill me, I might get protection, on the other hand they might find out I know the formula and I want to hold that as a trump-card.

'You are safe here.'

'I know, Holy Kaselm.'

'Just never let him bite you—' He smiled as he handed me the wine. 'Do you know if anyone has ever survived that?'

'A friend of mine, owing to prompt and exhaustive care, but it may have been an accident that he was harmed, I can think of no reason—'

'The Superlativity is grateful to you for this knowledge concerning the General—he is now satisfied that the General is a demon as he himself is a god, and if he hadn't known that he would be at battle with him now, maybe unfortunately, instead of welcoming him as an ally while he feels his way. So he thanks you—'

'I am very surprised I have not been condemned to execution because my father is a priest vowed to sacred celibacy—'

'Your father is not an ordinary priest.' Kaselm trimmed the candle. 'He and your mother both have divine blood on both sides—it is permissible, even high-minded—for a priest to bring into the world a *divine* child.' He lay down, turned his head sideways on the pillow to smile at me. 'That's a new rule: it hadn't been invented before, it hadn't been needed; you are unique.'

Two smiles from the black-a-vised Kaselm in one evening.

Zerd's main army is cantoned outside the town, but with his household and commanders he is occupying a very large grand building on the road to the Court.

Lara is the new meteor.

The ladies are *very* sympathetic to me.

Life has become rather flatter.

Zerd is not often at Court.

*   *   *

It poured with rain today. Of course, autumn is drawing nearer. In the open courtyards one couldn't tell which was fountains and which rain. In the distance there were red flashes.

'What are those red flashes—there, miles off through the rain?'

'The mountain must be erupting again.'

It rained for hours. There was no boundary between day and evening; when evening came the sky was as grim as it had been all day. None of the servants had thought to turn off the fountains. A strong wind had been blowing for a couple of hours and there were pools everywhere. Coming down a staircase, Lara slipped in water and immediately there was a crowd of nobles about her. They began to carry her to the bottom. She ignores me, whether because she has recognised me and doesn't know what line to take or because of simple arrogance, I don't know. One's foot splashed at nearly every step on the marble. The songs played in the cushioned hall were nearly all about Lara. The others are about me, but I don't like out-of-date modern-culture anyway. It is the first time the Court has seemed dreary to me. At an impulse I wrapped my cloak about me and scurried out into the wet gloaming.

'Kond, it's me, are you awake?'

'Yes, nearly half drowned.'

'I was afraid that's how you'd be in this weather. I thought the earth wall before your window might have turned into slime and deluged your cell a bit—'

'Very kind of you to come and bother to see—' His dignified hostility was precarious, under it there was a terrific surprise that I'd come, and maybe twice as much gladness. He now proceeded with cunning tact to doff the defiance and gradually smarm me back into the right state of mind.

'Brought the knife this time, gorgeous?'

He added, 'Why you laughing?'

'I'm sorry. I just realise why my attitude to you last time was wrong.'

'Yeah, that's it,' he said eagerly. 'But I wouldn't hold it against you, you're a nice kid. How old are you?'

'Eighteen, I think, so I'm not so young. I know I sound it. I've brought you some meat and wine and fruit. I wish I could give you a blanket too but your jailer would notice.'

'Look, darling. Why not the knife?'

I spoke in the same voice of reason. 'You're a notorious brigand. You'll kill with the knife. You'll get out and back to your tribe and you'll kill and pillage. I'm not to know that the very first man you'd kill, the jailer, isn't a very nice good man and just the sort I'd like.'

'He's a bastard.'

'I'm not to know.'

'I can tell you're a kind little girl, full of sweetness and all. You want to be kind to everyone. All right. You don't want me to be executed soon? I know it is soon. I don't know when, but I know it's soon. They're doing us systematic, bunch by bunch, and it's our turn soon, me and a couple of sneak-thiefs and the old priest across the passage—'

'Old priest? What's he like?'

'I been loosening the earth with me fingers, well the rain done that for good and all only it bakes up again, I been at the bars but a *knife*, for the love of—'

'What is the priest like?'

'Old, I dunno, wears priest-clothes—'

'Is he—is he—' How could I put it? 'Anyway, does he belong to the old religion?'

'Wouldn't be in here unless.'

'If I gave you the knife could you get him out too?'

'What is this?'

'I'm against executing priests—'

'Oh.' He didn't let himself take offence. 'All right, darling, you give me a knife and I'll do whatever you want.'

'I want a guarantee.'

'Ah, now you're being difficult.' He sounded annoyed. 'How can you expect all this nonsense, I'm in a difficult position enough. Don't you trust me?'

'No. And keep a civil tongue in your head, I needn't stay here any more kneeling in the dark on the drenched grass—'

'Of course you needn't. You've a lovely heart and I don't deserve the use of it. But then, did I ever say I did? Now you want to help the priest and I'll get him out sure if I kill the jailer, I've only to take his keys.'

'I can only trust you. I know you'll do no better with the life I'm giving you, but I hope you'll let him out too before you go. Please risk the extra minutes, Kond. I'll bring a knife tomorrow morning.'

He muttered, 'Thank you.' He said quietly, 'I hope you don't get a chill from being here.'

'I'm sure I won't. Well —'

'If the jailer's here when you come tomorrow I'll put up my arm like I was stretching and flex my fingers. You whistle when you come. This mustn't go wrong.'

'I can't whistle.'

'What a kid. Well—well—I dunno. Can you sing?'

'I'll sing this marching song.' I hummed the tune.

'Pretty, pretty. Tomorrow then.'

I walked away humming it through the rain.

It was raining heavily the next morning. It is the first time I have ever wakened in the priest's cell and thought it not yet morning, so dark was the silver of the light. But I found the priest gone and I huddled myself into my cloak.

Out in the long cold corridor.

Out in the deafening, dreary tintinnabulation of the downpour.

My thin summer sandals were soon totally water-logged, there were squelchings between my toes and at each step the grass would let my soles go only with a sucking sound after an effort on my part. Up visible through the rain and seeming a separated phenomenon, clouds like juice-swelled plums. Foliage showered my shoulders. The marching-song caught like croup in my throat.

I knelt on the queasy ground by the grating.

'Kond! . . . Kond?'

Louder.

'Kond!'

I peered through the grating, but there was no hand to be seen no matter how pale in the gloom. There was no sound.

Is he asleep? Or perhaps it is a trap, perhaps they've found out and are waiting for me to declare myself?

I looked behind me, to either side. I started up and began to run, in bad slow-motion, for the grass wanted my feet and even the hems of my trousers and cloak were heavy with a rim of slow globules.

The thunder blockaded the clouds. The trees were obscene cataracts.

In spite of the rain, I saw them some way ahead of me. The slow procession, black-robes, no chanting, not even a little mumbling, silent, under the black canopy held over their holy heads making a sound like a big black drum as the raindrops bounced on it like so many humourless imps on a trampoline.

I darted up the incline, keeping among the trees. Now I was alongside the procession. The black-robes were mainly short, grizzled nonentities. I couldn't see Kaselm among them. The prisoners were flanked to either side, and were hard to get glimpses of. As far as I could see there were indeed four, walking separately with only their hands tied behind them, and most important, one *was* in the grey leather robe of the priests who refuse to accept the Superlativity as the national god. Slipping between the trees, I kept beside them, one freezing hand clutching the cloak in its cowled folds round my shoulders and head, the other hand now curling as if for dreamlike reassurance round the knife in the cloak's swinging inside-pocket.

The procession turned in to the trees and I was only just in time behind a great, fragrant, moss-slimed trunk.

Here there were drifts of bluebell flowers between the roots. The black-robes were wet-ankle-deep. They all seemed to be hopping a little now.

A wind skirled and fleered out from behind the thunder as I followed, not a heavy wind but thin and keen, and the bluebells lashed at my legs in a purple frenzy.

Yes, here we are, a tree with a big out-sticking bough and they're stopping in front of it. The priests break formation and shuffle to each other to discuss proceedings, and the prisoners stand hands-tied and eye the bough and the bough faces back at them, ready with a cordial welcome. I can see the prisoners unobscured now, mainly their backs; I might be able to see their profiles if I sneak round among the trees, but on the other hand the priests might then spy me.

A priest in grey leather, his white hair plastered to his skull by the weight of rain he's been respectfully escorted through (only driblets reach us here, slipping and sliding and oddly spurting precariously through layers and levels of leaves); a thin, rat-bearded, middle-aged man with slumped shoulders under his rags; a young brown-haired man likewise huddled morosely in rags; another young tough with a blood-stained headband and a striped mantle, full of holes, its edging of tassels fluttering above the fluttering bluebells.

Through these now come a little coven of priests, hopping to keep their hems at least half as dry as possible, bearing a length of rope. It is a long coil and they are going to quarter it. One produces a pair of ivory-handled

gold Temple scissors. The prisoners have turned a little to
watch, I can see their faces as, silently and without
expression, they watch what is to be their last scene.'

It is, it is my priest! Anywhere I'd know that lined
urchin's face!

This must be stopped, I can't see them hang him.

I dodged closer. He is separated from me by Tassel-
fringe and the morose one, Tassel-fringe is the nearest to
me and Rat-beard farthest away. Which is Kond? I begin
to hum the marching-song, at first it is only a thread
amongst the rain-noises, then it swells a little and I think
the prisoners have heard it. The only black-robe who
might hear is the one by them cutting the rope, I pray
he's too busy. The prisoners are glancing round, anything
is interesting to them when it is to be their last experience.
Which is Kond? A burst of thunder drowns the song. The
rain must have doubled its force, it teems white upon the
priests who look up in alarm at the foliage and tut-tut.
They move away and try to pull their tight necklines up
about their ears, but there is nowhere for them to go.
Only a few can pack under the canopy. They are miserable.
What a day for the execution to have been scheduled for.
They look impatiently at their brother measuring the long
rope for its next place of snipping. The prisoners cannot
be more drenched than they are, they stand in their
sodden rags, each hole a waterfall, flowers springing between their hairy toes, some of the least stale dirt sluicing
off. The blood on Tassel-fringe's bandage is fresh, he must
have fought them when they came for him this morning.
The priest makes a sign with his scissors over each half-
yard of rope before he measures it off, and before he
makes any cut. This must be a kind of ceremony, necessary to be done just before the execution. Our whole little
world under the trees seems to be sternly crackling and
beating: it is only the rain. I squelch even closer and begin
to hum again as loudly as I can, which makes it nasal.

All the prisoners are listening.

I am thinking I'll bet on Tassel-fringe, his bandage makes him seem the most belligerent though his unshaven upper lip is slack, when the morose young man behind him turns round slowly, as though aimlessly to keep movement in his legs, facing in each direction for several moments. As his back comes to view, I notice his hands: wrists caught together in the brace behind him, his fingers flexing. He begins to whistle my tune.

I fumble in my pocket, bring out the knife, get a mobile-wristed grip on it and there it is quivering in the wet grass by his foot, rain already trickling down the hilt.

This is real slow-motion now. I watch every detail of every second so that it seems four minutes where it is half a minute. The prisoners are silent and still, none has yet even drawn a breath. Kond stoops by the knife; the others' eyes are on the snipping priest. But his head comes up; he has heard the little swish of the thrown knife. Tassel-fringe makes a pace towards him, his back now to me, the ball of his calf gleaming. The priest sees Kond: Kond draws his bound wrists across the blade stuck upright by its point in the grass, the priest gurgles and gestures. Tassel-fringe reaches him, glaring meaningly, but the priest will not look at him, he embarks on a better gurgle. There is a line of blood bright on Kond's arm, the blade wobbles and collapses but a strand of cord hangs loose. Kond strains his wrists apart, the cord taken by surprise gives a little and before it can tighten again one hand is through and in one movement is grasping the knife while the other hand shakes off the wide, now useless, bracelet of cord. Tassel-fringe leaps upon the priest who trembles and raises the scissors. He is thrown to the ground, under Tassel-fringe's full length, but has the ill-sense to screech. Kond bounds forward, at a slash severs Tassel-fringe's cords, and they both begin to throttle the poor old priest who drops the scissors and gasps. The other priests turn towards the screech. They see the heap on the ground and with expressions of horror hurry across. I curse Kond: my priest is still bound. I risk everything.

'Kond!' I cry. 'Free the priest!'

Tassel-fringe has throttled the black-robe who lies still. Kond, knife in hand, turns crouching a little to face the others. One of them has snatched up the scissors and without compunction is closing in ready to stab Kond in the stomach. Rat-beard begins to stamp and moan with shivering impatience. He tries to tug his wrists apart and chafes the flesh. My priest stands by as though watching a carnival-tournament, his head a little bowed, his eyes very bright over their large debauched-looking bags, no smile and no grimness on his compassionate mouth.

The black-robe with the scissors stabs. Kond catches his wrist with one hand, twists the knife forward and up, rips into the belly. First there is only the sound of tearing cloth, then a gushing of blood. The blackrobe falls untidily to the grass, where the blood is soon diluted with rainwater. Kond stoops for the scissors, has to tug because they're caught in a loop of entrail, shoves them at Tassel-fringe who grabs them and shows his teeth. The black-robes stand at bay. Tassel-fringe and Kond go forward stooping. Tassel-fringe beats a black-robe over the head with the scissors, Kond thrusts down another who jabbers for mercy even while he's dying. They're cutting down potential pursuit before making their getaway, though I'm not sure it's necessary, and that's taking a tolerant view of it; it looks like plain viciousness, and it's sheer slaughter for there isn't a single weapon among all the black-robes. I've unleashed this pointless brutishness and my priest is still bound. Rat-beard is whimpering, not because of the slaughter around him but because he's afraid they're going to make off soon without their bound companions. So am I.

'Kond!—'

Kond leaps towards the priest, slashes apart his wrists.
My priest, non-bewildered gravity, bows.

Tassel-fringe runs bent double among the trees, towards
the open, back the way I usually take to the Temple wall.
The priest picks up his skirts and follows, his old competent feet slapping down the grasping grass. Kond comes to
the side, his hand is on me before I understand. 'Let me
look at you, my little sweetheart—' He pulls me round.

'Let me go, you fool, you must get away and I must
too.'

'Pretty,' says Kond's familiar voice, his familiar hand
under my chin, his unfamiliar face appraising mine. 'Sure,
and together, you're just the girl I always wanted in the
hills. I'll thank you there.'

'I'm not coming with you—'

I chop his hand away with the edge of mine and am
away, farther on among the trees. He had grasped my
cloak, but torn only part of the edge. I know he daren't
detour from his direction to get me.

The rat-bearded man screams a curse and falls weeping
to the grass, his bound hands thrashing.

I got back to Court and was greeted with amazement and
alarm.

'I fell on my way back in the rain, the thunder frightened me and I ran too fast—'

'But part of your cloak is torn right off—'

I brushed them aside and ran up to my room.

I washed off the blood, Kond's hand had grasped me
after reaching for the scissors in the pool of the murdered
blackrobe's blood.

Those ornate and valuable, not to mention sanctified
Temple scissors must now be somewhere in the rocky hills
of Ael's brigandry.

The news did not reach Court till the evening meal.

'This morning several prisoners about to be executed

broke free and murdered nearly half the priests escorting them. All the prisoners except one escaped, including a priest of the old religion who is believed to have been a spy for Atlan. Every effort has been made to recapture him but he seems to have disappeared.'

I received curious looks.

'Did you see any of this, Cija? You arrived so upset and dishevelled this morning—'

'I saw nothing. I heard screams, I was frightened but thought them part of the storm—'

'You are odd—'

Lara began to whisper behind her hand. A pretty scandal, the goddess Cija connected with some of the things she can tell them, and her word that of an honourable accepted ally.

To make worse matters which could hardly have been nastier in the first place, I have a perfectly horrid cold and am sneezing and sniffling all over the place. I wanted to stay in bed but that would have looked cowardly, so I have gone round inflicting germs on everyone who gives me sidelong glances—and they all do, for one reason or another.

Last night Kaselm asked me if I had seen any part of the escape. I said 'No.'

Tomorrow night I have to face an evening feast in honour of Zerd and his wife.

I am glad to be able to report that trouble is, however, starting up again between the allies in the town, though they are so sweet to each other in higher places. You just can't keep it down for long. Down by the wharfs the Northern army have been unloading a lot of stores they've taken the opportunity to order. They got them all right, but their loading line was prevented from getting much done by a Southern horseman of high rank riding ceaselessly back and forth along the ramp and therefore through the line. The Northern sentry came up to the officer in charge.

'This bastard's stopping all work, sir; shall I do him?' The officer rubbed a finger down the side of his nose. 'Of course you mustn't do him. What are you talking of, corporal? By the way, I shall be looking in that direction over there for the next ten minutes.' When the rider next passed a spear went through his cloak, half-hooking, half-pushing him right off his saddle into the mud. The officer said it was an unavoidable incident, the sentry was turning and his spear accidentally swung too far. No action was taken.

This story was told to the Court by the Northern officer in question. Everybody laughed pleasantly.

The only part of day I now look forward to is night when I take my drugged wine and sleep in Kaselm's cell, in which he leaves the candle burning all night for my sake. I don't even like the early morning walks, the half-hidden grating seems to shriek its emptiness. There is still no news as to whether the priest has been recaptured. Thank my Cousin. I had no idea my priest was working for Atlan.

I am quite sure I am the object of a Court scandal, especially the way Lara and her especial friends look at me and titter.

I still have my own friends, but they also would and do slander their own mothers for the sake of a little gossip, and I suppose I laid myself open to anything like this exciting them because of my impregnable virtue during my months here. It won't be long, in my opinion, before Lara takes to publicly calling me 'Winegirl'. Being a hostage to the Northern army had indescribably more cachet, though even that I tried to mention to as few people as possible. As I have still given no cause for scandal since coming here, I may in time live this down but at the moment it hasn't even reached its height.

* * *

The feast was quite interesting I suppose.

It was held on the Central Lawn because it was a fine night lit by stars and the distant misbehavings of the volcano, and everyone arrived in litters, and wearing shoes with such long tasselled points that it was difficult to walk even a few steps in them—it's a new fashion, signing that one belongs without doubt to the idle nobility.

I wore a dramatic velvet scabbard of a dress, black, making my skin glow white, with a cloud of white gossamer trailing from each wrist, and a haughty gold-encrusted headdress adding several inches to my height, also gold-encrusted trousers. The effect of all this may have been vaguely spoilt by the fact that I kept sniffing and snuffling all the time and had to keep hunting down my neckline for the hanky which I'd put between my breasts for want of anywhere else, as my sleeves were too wide and I had no pocket.

In my opinion Lara's hat was a pointless idea, but lots of people cooed over it. It was a little gilded cage in which a turquoise and pink humming bird had barely room to stretch its wings. A rim all round the bottom of the cage protected the wearer from any droppings.

However, my cold seemed to have aroused sympathy or something, because undoubtedly I was the success of the evening, though not the unqualified success I have been at other times. However, the crowd round me was larger than hers. Even Forialk has got fed up with hanging round her, and brought me some wine.

'You may have noticed that I haven't spoken to you lately,' he said in a low voice, which struck me as rather naïve so I didn't have the heart to retort that I hadn't been noticing him at all.

'I am glad to see your eyes better, my lord.'

He was looking very eloquent, the arrows embroidered on his clothes all pointing to the centre of his anatomy, those on his jerkin pointing downwards, those on his tights upwards, those on his right side to the left, vice versa. All this embroidered clamour drew attention to a cod-piece shaped and coiled like a beautiful huge rose.

'The points of your shoulders are stars to light us, Goddess,' said someone beside me, it embarrassed me that it was Ecir with a frighteningly sincere poetic look, he hadn't noticed Forialk. In order to avoid a clash which might worsen my reputation I allowed myself to be drawn away to the buffet by an uninteresting elderly intellectual and later I was awfully sorry because neither of them got near me again all evening, not even separately.

To say I was the success of the evening, of course, is only counting the females. The real success of the evening was His Mightiness the Dragon-General, for while the young nobles were divided between Lara and myself with me winning slightly, all the other women, young and old, flocked round him. He got a little drunk, whirled a delighted young lady of high degree round in his arms till her underskirts knocked down a small table, kissed various shoulders and necks (he prefers fleshy springy ones) and gave an exhibition of sword-twirling and thrusting; and it all only made him more swooned over than ever. His eyes glittered black all over the place. He was dressed mainly in uniform, probably because he hasn't much else, but the sides of his jerkin fell in tasselled points to either side of his codpiece to accentuate its size. I had the distinction of being the only woman he came up to, the whole evening he was submerged in females but they all swarmed up to him.

He came up, bowed, flashed a courteous grin meant to be a smile, offered his arm.

'Would you do me the honour of a few words, Goddess?'

I was able not only to refuse for the sake of my safety, but to do it with style, because of course a goddess is more important than a foreign general.

'Wait a moment, please; I just have to go and give

someone something to take somewhere . . .' I drifted vaguely away, found my page playing with others under the buffet, and told him to run a message to Kaselm that I should be late. After that I sat in an arbour and listened to songs about myself. Having been undernourished for a while, I have rediscovered a taste for them.

I'm still not sure what happened, nor indeed how, but here I am locked in my own room. I was talking in The Cloisters, and a number of priests came by, nobody ever takes much notice of them, and then Rat-beard was pushed forward by one of them. He said, 'That's her,' and the priests seized me by the shoulders and led me away and everybody stared like anything and called out questions and I just smiled in a bewildered way and opened my hands and shrugged my shoulders, and the priests brought me up to my room and wouldn't answer when I said things to them and they locked me in and went away—

I never before realised what an inconvenient room this would be to be locked in, there is indeed a balcony outside the long windows but it is terribly high up and there is no way of reaching any roof or any other balcony from it. I have been here several hours now, getting hungry, have rung repeatedly for my maid but she must have been ordered not to answer.

I have only just thought of writing in my Diary, but there is nothing to write except these few salient, deeply ominous facts.

I have been trying the chimney, it is far too narrow for me to get even my shoulders up.

I have been out on the balcony several times, but there is no way of getting away from it. Far below the grounds begin to haze as sunset approaches, they are empty, there is no one down there to whom I can signal, they are all in the banqueting hall now. Earlier there were people about, I waved my arms frantically and called but the distance is just too wide to carry sound, no one looked up except one large lady, too far away for me to recognise her, she waved back to me and went on leisurely walking, obviously think-ing I was just being friendly.

It is evening—the hangings are not drawn across the big windows through which pours golden light dimmed, as it were, and made dusty by the age of the evening. Indeed I have never known such a long evening. The raised designs on the rich ceiling throw straight blue shadows upon it and each other.

I count the geometrically placed knobs on the ceiling and join them with imaginary lines, which raises me to such a pitch of the sense of futility as I wait literally in a trap that my nerves are raw and my stomach seems to be whirling in extreme anger.

I feel very alone in the huge, desolate, empty room. The rafters above the grand ceiling clatter at the force of the wind upon the roof. I shudder at the lengthy eerie moaning of it, I wonder what I would do if at any moment the huge disc-shaped grey face of the wind appeared to me at a window. Terror uses me at the thought, which I cannot keep from my mind. I get up again from my chair and hysterically pace the room, flinching at the always rising heights of noise attained by the wind, every minute or two forcing myself to turn round to the windows to see if the face is there. My fingers clench so tightly into my hands that when I open them I find the palms swollen and disfigured with the deep indentations of my nails.

I heard Them coming long before they actually entered. The building was empty, this part of it, at this time, except for me and now them. Up the staircase, along the gallery in a bevy, their robes whispering friendlily and a little ashamed of it. They unlocked the door in an ordinary, everyday way as if nothing were farther from their collec-tive mind than matters of life and death—the ancient peevish lock snarled at the rapist key, unattractive ancients together, the hand of the procurer priest faltered with casual incompetence and had to try again, the handle turned, metal heavy with the opulent way it was wrought, had to be turned twice. It really seemed all like that to me and when they came in I was weak with the obscene suspense of a couple of seconds.

'Sit down, holy gentlemen,' I said and flopped into a chair.

They did not sit. Clustered in a group facing me, accusing jawlines jutting so righteously at me they were nearly free of their saggy neckcords.

'Goddess. The Superlativity is tremendously grieved that you have been keeping from him something you knew important to him.'

I inclined my head. 'And that something . . .?'

'Why, Goddess, that you are a spy for Atlan.'

The spokesman priest was a tall greyhead with an actor's hands. He must be enjoying himself. He was presenting to me this deadly grimness with an incongruous, cruel absurdity.

'I am in my turn grieved,' I said, 'that the Superlativity could think this of me. Perhaps he has been faithlessly counselled?' The priest ignored my last remark.

'Even goddesses can blaspheme, against higher gods. And blasphemy it was, triple blasphemy, Goddess. You offended the Superlativity as a host, as a god, and as the head of all Temple affairs—'

At this quibbling mention of the Temple I realised what this was likely to be all about.

'Rat-beard managed to gabble a betrayal before his own execution, revenging himself on me because he was the only prisoner unable to slaughter and escape—'

'The thief we would have hanged today, yes, he betrayed you if you call it that. But you underestimate the importance of his information to us. We were so pleased to get it we even let him go free—'

'To keep the gallows free for bigger game?'

'Crude, Goddess.' He was pained. And the gazes around him were all on me, all avid. No sympathy among all those holy, elderly gentlemen for the girl with her hands clammy and her feet trembling and her throat knotted at the effort of verbal defiance. 'Have you any warrant for believing me an Atlantean spy simply because I rescued one of your prisoners who adheres to the old faith? He was my friend.'

'Exactly. He is also a spy for the cause of Atlan.'

'I swear to you, I am not.'

'Come, come, Goddess, don't sound so heated. It is all one, spy or blasphemy, the penalty is the same. But that priest is dangerous loose. He seems to be one of those spies' top people. Where is he?'

'I don't know.' I sneezed.

'And yet it was you who went to all the trouble of arranging his escape?—thus *betraying*, since that is your own word, the debt of gratitude you owed the Superlativity, and blaspheming his divine will—'

'I do not know the present whereabouts of the priest,' I said slowly and reasonably, 'nor where he went after he had been—rescued. I didn't even see which way he went. For a moment or two I was—detained by one of the other prisoners. I apologise that they got away. It was unavoidable.'

'I must warn you, Goddess, this ignorance is foolish. I said the penalties for spying and blasphemy are both the rope.' And truly the dignified straining of his throat reminded me of cord. . . . 'But unless you give the whereabouts of the spy-priest, you will be tortured.'

'Listen,' I said, each breath shallow and scorching, I was so afraid I wouldn't get the right number of words out in time, 'I have not tried to deny my hand in his escape. I don't know where he went. I didn't know he was an Atlan-partisan. In earnest of my good faith I will tell you something which will convince you torture would be useless, and you will hang me without this fuss. I will give you the formula which unlocks the Atlan vacuum.'

In hope, my lungs sore, I watched their faces. It did not matter at all to me that I was losing this war for the Northerners. Now the Southerners would be their masters, place their ray-spurred boots upon the neck of the little Northern army which had for so long staved off this hour, in another few weeks the Southern army would embark and the veil be torn, the ancient Peace destroyed . . .

'You cannot possibly mean this, Goddess.'

'I do, I do. I overheard the General—He knows, he wanted me killed but I escaped. Escape, it was a thing I used always to be lucky about, only I always went to something worse—Please believe me. That's why I came here. And he knows I know and he's been trying to get me alone but he didn't try frantically enough, did he? He knew I hadn't told your Superlativity yet and he thought there was some time, he knew I'd hold such a secret till I could use it to save myself from something or push some great bargain. He didn't know I'd rescue an old priest who was my friend and be in the greatest danger right away—'

Their faces were all glowing with a triumph so strong they didn't fear for it, even at this early stage. They didn't hold it in, their eyes gleamed, still no room for any thought of me as human and in need. It is the first time I have loathed the divinity in my blood. They know I am different from them and they don't care that the difference is only slight.

'You tell us this to save yourself torture?' said the spokesman. 'And yet you withheld this—this *vital*—from the Superlativity when you first arrived here—and have known for so long how greatly we desire this one piece of all-important knowledge. Really, Goddess, the extent of your loyalty to the South which has welcomed you is hardly—'

'And nor is my loyalty to the North,' I gabbled. 'I tell

you, I heard the formula. And my loyalty is my own to place. I am *here* because of my loyalty to one of the only friends I've ever had, I helped to kill the other, and of course maybe I *would* have let this one die too if I'd known quite how I'd end up by helping him, and now my real loyalty is to myself and I want to be hanged not tortured—'

They waited courteously for me to finish all that, as if I were an eminent drunk at the maudlin stage.

And I told them the formula I overheard on that hot, stinking, noisy day in the shut-bed Smahil and I used to share.

They went away.

My trembling grew until I was relieved of my tension, and I thought of the little moment of pain. I felt my throat and it is so delicate, easy to break. I think of the green orchard where I shall hang, one of the brotherhood of the bees and the fragrances, until I am a sweet odour myself and I will fall and all my friends of the orchard will grow richer and riper because of me . . .

Quietly I wait for them to come back.

They were back in less than an hour, I'd laid down my pen and was waiting quietly like I last wrote, and they said, 'We've checked that formula with our scientists. It was an impossible formula. You've tried to trick us.' 'You're bluffing.' 'We must remind you that insolence may be dearly paid for—Tell us the true formula or the priest's whereabouts.' 'I don't know either.' 'You have three hours. At the end of that time if you have told us what we want to know you will be hanged. If not, you will receive the traditional torture of a spy—' 'But I don't *know* any other formula! I thought that was the right one! He wanted to kill me because I knew it—I don't understand!' 'In any case, you're a spy. Tell us where the priest is—we shall come at the end of the three hours. If you do not tell us then you will immediately be flayed . . . slowly . . . upwards from the feet . . . you'll be able to watch, right till the last, the slow curling back of the peeling skin, the veins all laid bare, the curling . . . curling . . .' 'You must be a frustrated poet.'

They have left me alone.

Help me, God. God. God. God. God. God. God.

(There follow four pages of God, scrawled each time very large with great intensity and with slow, slow, elaborate curlicues added afterwards. J. G.)

When the door was next unlocked I was behind the wimpled-glass screen separating the fountain from the rest of the room. I had one tiny chance. And at least I had nothing to lose. No matter how I infuriated them, they couldn't take worse action than was already to be inflicted on me. I had filled my priceless big coral vase with water and threw it all over the black-robe who entered. I made a dash for the door but the black-robe caught me. 'You're in a hurry,' he said, and proceeded to brush the water off himself.

'May I borrow this?' He scrubbed his head briefly with my embroidered towel.

I had nothing to say after 'Kaselm—' I was wondering whether it would be worse or better to be tortured by someone I knew well, at least whose face I knew well though I'd never be able to fathom his thoughts or feelings. I decided it didn't make any difference.

'I had no idea you'd get yourself into this,' he said in a low but untroubled voice. 'Why didn't you tell me? It's lucky I found out in time. Put on your cloak.'

'You mean—You're going to—'

'If I can. Don't hush yourself. Keep talking as much as you like, though not loudly.' We were now out of that gorgeous room which in one evening had become the most hateful of places, and we were walking down the stairs, he casually, myself trying but with melting knees, a lady and a priest in conversation. Oh, no one look closely. 'Unluckily I found out only a quarter of an hour ago that you were in such danger. If only I could have come during the feasting hours when the rest of the place is deserted—on the other hand we'll be less conspicuous.'

'And there are few lights now because they embarrass the courting courtiers—'

'When I came in and found you in your fountain-room I thought you were emulating the last woman we tortured, who took care to bathe beforehand—'

'I'm awfully sorry I soused you like that,' I said with trembling contrition. This was no time to boast that I actually do bathe generally once a week.

This heavy Diary which I'd surreptitiously put in my cloak-pocket banged against my knee.

A bull-necked priest was about to pass us on the staircase. He peered at me. 'Hey, hey!' He grasped my arm and started to pull me. I whimpered. Kaselm's hands encircled his bullneck from behind. 'Keep walking up the stairs,' he said in a grim whisper. 'Don't turn round. As soon as you show signs of turning, you'll get a thrown knife between your shoulder-blades. Keep on up the stairs and turn along the passage at the top.'

Kaselm released the bull-neck, who started resentfully quivering up the stairs. Kaselm pulled me into a dark corner and we watched for a few seconds, then he dragged me out and shoved me down the next flight. We were hidden from above.

'He'll raise the alarm,' Kaselm said. 'Run as though your Dragon-General were after you.'

Down more flights, his hand hard on the small of my back. I had no thoughts, but trust in his competence and strength. In the very back of my head was a doubt that he might not be trustworthy, but I had no option. The vague doubt sprang from the facts that I have rarely been able to

trust anyone at all for more than a short while, and I've
long suspected Kaselm of a deep game.

Down more flights, completely unlit. Now below courtyard level. I'd never been this low before, and expected
that we'd soon strike the servers' quarters. But we continued down, his strong fingers now over mine in the
blackness, and somehow I did not stumble.

'Do you really have a knife?' I dared to whisper hopefully when we reached a deserted, low-roofed, dim-lit
corridor, and could hurry on the flat for a while.

'You think a High Priest would carry a knife?' he whispered reprovingly and pulled from under the side-loop of
his robe a curved gold sheath which must usually hang
hidden against his thigh.

'Will you suffer greatly for helping me?'

He laughed quietly, the sound resonant in the pit of his
throat.

'I am the Superlativity's right ear, right eye, right arm.
I have my finger in a thousand plots of my own and if any
dare to accuse me weightily I have all the clever vermin of
the wharfs at my back.'

I remembered how I'd met him talking like an old
friend to the captain of the boat I'd stowed away on. I'd
wondered then about such things as smuggling, no more . . .

At the end of this corridor, down again. Damp blackness.
And now we could hear some kind of commotion above
us, but descending.

'Kaselm— They're coming!'

He pulled me right against a blank wall. His hand, still
with mine in it, went over the wall surface which was very
old and musty and scarred with cracks and split seams. A
little trickle of mouldy mortar drifted down. I sneezed and
began to snuffle. The priest's finger found one crack, which
seemed to me indistinguishable from the rest of the network,
and there was a grating noise right before us. I started and
clung to him.

'In, child. Part of the wall has swung open. Get in.'

I groped. Suddenly my hand went right through the wall. A damp, musty breeze breathed straight in my face. I tried to scramble through but my knee struck wall. My hands were already through and I was in a panic. Strong arms hoisted me up from behind. I dropped into a cold, stony dark, landed on one knee and scraped my hand on rough stone paving. I heard him come through after me and then the harsh grating as the wall swung to shut out the growing noise of pursuit as righteous priests flurried down the wooden flights, clattering in their hurry against the treads and each other. We heard them go past on the other side of the wall.

Kaselm and I, hand in hand, started walking. I was sure the echoes from the stone enclosing us must be heard for hundreds of yards. The steady sounds of our steps hit the walls and roof more than the pavings. From the sounds I thought the roof must be vaulted.

Speaking of vermin, scuttlings now began across our path. I knew they must be rats and kept calm. But a whirr above my face, flapping a wind through my hair, made my hand twist in Kaselm's.

'Bats,' he said. 'It's not the last you'll meet now. They don't like to be disturbed but probably they won't attack. However, the only sure thing to keep them off would be a fierce torch held high.'

I murmured an acknowledgment of the information. Speaking frightened me. Kaselm's voice still reverberated.

Soon the whirring flapping above us became intense, multitudinous. The tip of a hooked leather wing lashed across my face. I heard the priest draw his knife from its sheath. He continuously whirled and flashed the knife above his head. There were occasional little grunts or moans from above us and the flapping diminished as far as we were concerned, though I could hear the rest of the vaulting thick with it. The flashing knife also gave a sort of intermittent gleam which was not much good to see by but was comforting down here. It reminded one that light did exist. Once, however, his arm tired and he stopped. Immediately the bats were at us again.

I offered to take a turn, but he pointed out that I was too short and would only succeed in cutting his eye open.

Presently there assailed our eyes what I thought was a blaze of light. It was only the saffron of torches in iron wall-sockets, turning the stone walls umber. The presence of torches did not even mean someone had lit them recently, down here there was little to stop them slow-burning for days. There are no bats in the lit sections of these vaults.

But I decided with wonder that there were inhabitants. Other passages divided off the main one. Kaselm always seemed to know which to take. His stride never faltered. We were no longer even in a hurry. It was as though now, down in these vaults, Kaselm was in his kingdom—more primitively, in his element. I took my hand from his. I no longer needed help for haste in dark, and I rarely like being touched by people. It worries me.

There were almost definite signs of present habitation. Ragged but not mouldering curtains hung across rather smelly orifices in the walls, here and there a spear lay or leaned, not at all rusty, there were sometimes fountain-basins in the middle of a cross-space where several passages branched. The fountains were not springing but there were unrusty metal cups chained to them and puddles by them. Insects, centipedes and horned beetles, bustled in the upside-down forests of fungi on the ceilings.

'Do these fountains still work, Holy Kas—?'

He stepped to one, pressed the knob of a metal figure's navel and there were glug-glug sounds and then water gushed from one of her nipples and jetted from the other, and began plop-plopping and gurgling down the vortex of the basin-drain. There was a chugging of subterranean water-pipes, but no doubt about it, they were working.

Kaselm filled the chained cup and offered it to me. I drank though it was quite dirty. It was extremely cold and had almost a dry taste.

At this moment I actually saw one of the inhabitants. He emerged from a side-passage and padded past us and disappeared into another. He gave a palm-up salute to Kaselm as he passed, which Kaselm answered. He was dressed in a filthy leather tunic with a hood hanging at the back. He also wore wide, slit-sided, striped breeches with fringed bottoms, a floppy leather boot and one foot bare. His belt was stuck full of variously and murderously shaped weapons—knives, a chain with a spiked ball on one end, a saw-edged dagger. He was pale and had a lot of greasy hair of an indeterminate colour.

Kaselm and I moved on.

'Who lives in these labyrinths?' I said.

'Oh—various people who prefer it to any other life,' he said.

Those I saw were all ruffianly and pale. Most ignored us, but some saluted Kaselm and he replied in kind. What were they? Gangs of smugglers? Wanted criminals who at some time or other had escaped justice? Families who had been here since ancient centuries?

'Do the Court and Temple know of them?'

'They don't know the labyrinth exists. We're a long way underground here, you know.'

At this moment my breath caught in my throat. A blackrobe was coming towards us. Kaselm advanced without surprise. Could he mean to betray me after all? Were the torture-chambers at least down here? As the figure passed I saw it was a girl, walking demurely, painted lids lowered, pink-nailed fingers catching up a trailing fold of black vestment.

There were several layers of labyrinth, for we passed stairs leading down and up. There were occasional gratings and ventilation-chutes. The temperature in the lit sections was tepid, even warm at times.

I saw none of the ruffians' women, unless they look exactly like the men, but in a hewed alcove we passed three children. They all had a lot of unkempt hair falling over their pale faces, and stopped their work to stare at us from violet-rimmed eyes hard with unafraid appraising suspicion. A boy about eleven was sharpening a blade, a fierce blonde girl of eight or nine was feeding spoonfuls of chunky meat-gravy to a thin baby playing with a jewel-studded bracelet. An iron pot hung on a chain from the alcove roof, over a fire full of blue flames.

Later our feet splashed in pools of water but there were no fountains about. I kept quiet for a while, till I noticed a bunch of real sea-weed in one of these large puddles.

'Where does this water appear from, Kaselm?' Somehow I no longer thought to call him Holy.

He didn't bother to answer. He turned a corner and a sudden blast of air got me clutching my cloak to myself. At the same time I found myself up to my calves in water, fresh moving brine-water, a virile salt wind scudding it in long ripples hard against me—Kaselm's hand plucked me back. I stood behind him and sneezed as I looked up a slope and through a tunnel-arch of black green-slimed stone. All I could see was a pale sky, all movement, clouds scudding in it pursued by the wind as it pursued water. Because it was late evening the paleness of the sky had a violet tone richening its wild dreariness, but there must have been squally weather while we were traveling in the labyrinth—there was no gleam of setting sun nor rising star.

The tunnel slope before us was sliding with brine, collecting in the anciently worn hollow at the bottom, but there was no other sign of life except that a gull could be seen wheeling mewing for an instant in the patch of sky. But I didn't miss the rails on the slope for crates.

'Has no visitor to the wharfs ever noticed this hole?'

'Maybe. But none can come down here to find out what goes on. Even a punitive force wouldn't dare it. It wouldn't matter if they did. The people here don't bother with passwords which can be betrayed even from day to day— they kill or capture and use anyone they don't know they can trust.'

'Can I get away from this point—? A boat?'

'Where is your goal?'

'I've no idea,' I said after a pause of amazement that I'd not considered this. 'For one year after leaving my own country I had no goal but the Southern Capital. My months at the Court here I never thought of my future if I could help it—it was deliberately a state of being, an existence to relax, to slough off all the stresses of that former life which rose to screaming-point—I would never have gone except that now existence is again a threatened thing—'

'You've no wish to stay here?'

'In the Labyrinth? My personal God tells me No.'

'Have you any ambition?'

'No.'

'Consider. You are a displaced person, wanted by the Temple as a spy'—and by the law as a murderess, I added silently—'and you have no friend, no family, no chosen home, no purpose. To go out, alone and small and as far as I can tell impetuously incompetent, and with a bad cold, into a dangerous alien land thirsty for your pain and blood, just in order to find a roof and food, it isn't worth it.'

'I want more than food and shelter from weather. I want freedom—and the knowledge that not only tomorrow, but the next day and the next will find me secure in the same place.'

'You shudder at the thought of existence in these vaults. They would provide shelter, food, drink, warmth—and complete safety under my guardianship.'

'Among wild men and animals, crime and dirt?'

'Do you hope even to cross the harbour up there safely—to find at once the clean friendly home you seek in a land racked with war and a dozen internal strifes?'

'Frankly, Holy Kaselm, I don't want to be so near the Temple and the Court, to feel them pressing down upon me from above. I am eternally grateful for what you have done this evening. But you tell me your finger is in a thousand plots—and I know you are far too intelligent to worry about using me as a pawn in any of them.'

Seeing that I realise him to be ruthless, he didn't try to press or reassure me, thus merely worrying me further. I am beginning to prize him properly only now.

'I'll find you a boatman who'll take you to some little secluded place of safety, far from here,' he said. 'Wrap your cloak closer. At least you'll be fed soon.'

I followed him away, down another passage.

Presently a man emerged from a side-turning. He looked at me but saw Kaselm and saluted. 'Wait, Guts,' said Kaselm. 'Your boat is leaving tonight? How soon?'

'The wind is blowing from the convenient fourth of the world, and the tide will be right in less'n an hour.'

'Have you room for a passenger?'

Guts looked at me. 'Her—? She'll fit in.'

'We'll discuss terms and wherefores over a meal,' said Kaselm, but it was quite settled. Guts now grunted and led us along farther till we came to a leather curtain which he lifted. Kaselm's arm round me guided me into a big, smoky, pungent, dark cavern, crimson and gold fires roaring gustily; and, sitting round eating and drinking with crude concentration which left little time for speech but wasn't exactly noiseless, a whole crowd of ruffians, their giant shadows dovetailing with the flames. Guts, Kaselm and I sat down in a group which made room for us. Someone handed Guts three sizzling chops which he evened between us. Various people saluted Kaselm. Almost at once I felt a great warmth soothe the long anxiety of my very bones. I sneezed, yawned, found in my eyes tears of weariness so intense it was voluptuous.

Kaselm supported my shoulders with one arm, set a goblet to my lips. The wine was very harsh, my head swam and my inside burned beautifully.

While I sleepily busied myself digging kidney out of my chop (and getting rather muzzy with wine as well as sleepiness) Kaselm and Guts had a long quiet conversation.

What seemed at the same time much later and far too soon, Kaselm was standing me up and laughing. 'Ready, child?' I don't think he has ever called me Goddess. Anyway, I can't remember him ever calling me Goddess.

'Going now?' I said.

'The tide won't wait. Listen, Guts is taking you to his mother's village, three weeks down-river. You can trust him implicitly—he won't let a priest or lawman set an eye near you. Don't bother about giving him money. I've seen to it.'

'I couldn't anyway, I have none now. Oh, thank you, Holy Kaselm.'

We went with Guts to the tunnel-slope. The patch of sky was now murky black. 'A good, starless night,' Guts grunted. He whistled and we waited. Presently a rope slid down the chute and jerked. Guts tied one end to his belt, jerked, and was drawn climbing up.

'Your turn in a moment,' Kaselm said. 'Ready?' I nodded sickly.

The rope came down. He tied it round me, then folded me in his arms. I remembered all the warnings at Court. Rocking me a little, he kissed me on the cheek. He jerked on the rope before I could say anything. I went up, dizzy, scraping an arm on the side. Guts and two other men seized me, steadied me on the wharf and untied the rope. Kaselm did not come. They hustled me up the gangplank.

— III —

ESCAPE

THE small ship swayed on the black currents. There were no stars, only wind and clouds in the sliding sky. The clouds were ghostly-looking, a slightly-luminous-middled black in blackness. I huddled in my cloak against the poop. The small crew took no notice of me. There were various stacks of crates about, some haphazardly 'hidden', with more faith than anything else, behind sailcloth. It was none of my business. In my mother's country I would have hated and despised smugglers, but I don't care how the economic balance of this nation is mucked about with.

I was enclosed in my own thoughts and did not notice the commotion till its cause was far too near.

'As the wind is, we can bash right through their line.' 'And as the wind is, they'll be after us in no time.' 'Ah, we're a racier craft.' 'I'm not having her identified as a rogue ship, we'll stop and get through the usual. Like as not they'll take our word and not insist on opening 'em up. But keep your knives handy.' The sailors' voices impinged. 'Hey—wait—the girl!'

I started up and was just about blown for'ard, skimmed along the deck. 'Guts, Captain I mean—are those lawships out front?'

'Sure, we're all right with them. Routine check. But there's already a reward out for you. There's only a cubbyhole below. Can't even stow you lumpy and suspicious-looking under a bunk pallet, we kip on deck.'

'How near are they?' I quavered, peering ahead. 'Is that them?'

'Mp-hm.'

I tugged off my sandals. 'Goin' to swim for it?' they said, catching on fast. 'And not a moment too soon. You a good swimmer, missy? Make for that bank over there. Work forward. We may be able to pick you up at the ruined warehouse, though there's no saying.'

The muffled oars of the law, smugly and rather pathetic-ally certain it was sneaking up on these experienced river-farers, were now sending wash against our bows and making occasional plop noises which I suppose it fondly imagined would be mistaken for fish rising.

Guts helped me off with my dress, helped drag off my trousers. In my little shift I put my hands together and dived off the bulwark. I made the water with as little sound, just about, as the oars of the law. This now cried 'Halt!' in a loud voice. My heart froze so I didn't even notice the coldness of the new element. Guts' voice bawled back, 'Waddaya mean, Halt?' There was a clash of grap-pling hooks, canvas hauled down and my friends allowed themselves to be boarded. Something hit the water beside me. My sandals, straight down, knack-thrown. My dress, trousers and cloak in a bundle. They didn't want any trace of me left on board. A sudden sense of loss sent me for that bundle, entangling myself in the wash of the now floating vessels. I hit an oar and hoped like hell that no one was at the top of it. I got that bundle just as the cloth was beginning to spread out under the surface of the water. This heavy Diary in the swinging purse-like pocket of the cloak, it acted like a plummet-stone.

Swimming with the Diary bundled in the cloak clasped to my breast was difficult. The water was cold and sent little electric shivers against my limbs. I struck out for the bank they'd indicated. This was very different from swimming in the tower-top pool where I learnt. This was the farthest bank, the nearest one was a mass of wharfs and movements and lights, this was a row of gardens and big private mansions and little quiet, dark, private, landing-stages. Not too soon, I began to smell the wafted fragrance over the pervasion of salt and river-weed which in the small rounded enclosure of my nostrils seemed to suggest a wideness of miles.

Two lights ribboned past—long flutter-gilled eels, lambent in their own phosphorescence.

For a moment my swimming hand was lit underwater—a strange, thin, pearl object, a confident clawing on the element, on life . . .

I began to recognise some of the fragrances. Magnolias—sweet magnolia, heady magnolia, scent tangible as the flower itself, reclining languorous on the black air.

I pulled myself on to the little wooden landing-stage, which immediately creaked. The water was heavy now that I was half out of it, and I was very chilly. I got off the landing-stage. I was now on a narrow white path, disappearing as a thin thread into fogs of shrubbery. Over the patter of my feet was the silly pitter-pitter of sea-drops from my sodden self, shift and bundled cloak containing the Diary. I wanted to stop and see whether water had got into the bundle and harmed the Diary, though it would have been too dark to discover much; I wanted to stop and take off my horrible clammy shift, but I had now noticed lights advancing from the right and I hurried on through the gardens.

The shrubberies rustled, metal and marble statues gleamed out at me, the lights came nearer. Now more lights in front of me: but they are stationary. They are torches held by sentries in front of a great house. I pause, amazed, on the outskirts of the shrubbery. The sentries are indeed sentries, not sentinel servants, and are wearing Southern army uniform!

Of all the places to come to! I turn to dive back into the doubtful sanctuary of the shrubbery. But the other lights have come up on my right. They pass me at a distance of four or five yards. They are Northern soldiers, they are escorting the General himself home from a day at Court. He is not riding, but walking as though he were marching, as though he were one with his escort. His instincts are all soldier-instincts. Lara must have stayed later at Court, there are not even any girls with him. Eng walks beside him; they are both silent. Clor and Isad follow, talking.

They come to the marble staircase, each step a momentous scimitar-shaped sweep, on which Southern sentries stand. As the Northern soldiers approach, the sentries stiffen: they are longing at least to scowl, but they each raise their torches with a ceremonial-cry as the General passes them. He ignores them, except to salute their captain at whom he glances absemt-mindedly.

Of course I understand now. I have come to the very mansion lent by the Temple-Court to the Northern General for his stay here—and as an additional mark of honour they provided him with a sentry-corps of their own soldiers. Is he exasperated, for they must spy on him and would probably try to keep him prisoner if the circumstances arose?—He and his commanders disappeared into the great doorway.

Now comes the part which fills me with irrational shame, it's almost comic. Of all the ways to be discovered—I mean, there were about three hundred other likely ways for me to be discovered, if Fate insisted on it, but no, it has to be the classic way, the way heroines (and usually child-heroines, at that) were always discovered in the books I was actually *allowed* to read in my own childhood.

I sneezed.

The nearest sentry heard at once. He came straight towards me leisurely, holding up his torch.

I tried to creep back among the rustling swaying shrubs,

but I'd've done better to run madly and not bother about concealment. He saw my face anyway. That was that. He recognised me. He didn't yell out to his comrades; he wanted the reward all to himself.

He talked to me like a hunter to an animal trapped but edging away from him, like a soldier in a sacked town bothering to seduce a frightened girl he could rape.

'Come here, little coney, there's no safety behind you, only the sea's there, now, now, don't dash like that, it won't do you no good, you're only entangling yourself in the foliages, you're getting yourself in a panic, you need to keep your pecker up for what's coming, you'll have a bit to face but remember while they skin you that you've won an honest sentry a fat purse of *lovely* metal—ah, now, you're really getting excited. Here, just hold out your hand and I'll have you. No need to struggle any more for it ain't no use—'

His voice had belied the harshness of his grip when eventually he got me. He twisted the bundle from me, puckered his lips as we regarded each other.

'This your cloak? Best put it on, them legs are a bit bare, aren't they? Good thing your shift ain't a coupla inches shorter.' He flipped at its hem with heavy fingers and laughed as I recoiled. He laughed again as he looked at my face; I hadn't taken my eyes off his, I suppose I looked mesmerised already as a skinned rabbit. 'You don't want to interest my mates too much, do you now? Nor do I—they'll ask too many questions. Pull your hood over your sweet face, now.' The rhythm of his conversation reminded me of Kond's which used to come up from the blank impersonal grating: I felt almost homesick, for those had been safer moments.

His comrades were calling. 'Found what the noise was, Number 58?'

'Yeah, yeah, a trespasser, that's all.' He pulled the Diary from me. 'What's this?' He looked at it and said in wonder, 'A Book.' He opened it but could make little of my mixture of shorthand and abbreviations. He probably found reading difficult at the best of times. 'Well, I'm sure the Temple will find that interesting, too. A record of spying, I shouldn't wonder.' He put it in my pocket, pulled the hood over my eyes and propelled me forward again.

The Northern soldiers who'd been escorting the General were down the steps again by now, and just marching off to their barracks. Their leader saluted my captor, who saluted with his free arm. The Northern leader frowned; it was the wrong arm. 'Meant no disrespect, sir,' said my captor hurriedly hustling me to the other arm.

'What have you there?' said the Northern leader.

'A trespasser, sir, who I'm about to take to the Temple.'

He had the right arm free now, saluted, and was about to hurry on but the leader stopped him by speaking.

'Has another sentry been detailed to take your place?'

'Well, sir, I was about to go off duty anyway and this is an emergency—'

'You all go off duty a few minutes too early and without bothering to report. Just because most of the day there's nobody to watch you all but the statues . . . I find this a very slack outpost of your army. Go back to your post for the necessary five minutes.'

'Sergeant don't mind, sir—' said my captor almost bully-ingly, very aware of his superior nationality and army.

'Are you slandering your officer?' said the Northern leader smoothly. 'I am quite sure your sergeant minds. Leave the trespasser with me. I shall see he is taken, not to the Temple but to the General, whose grounds after all these are.'

The sentry saw his reward slipping through his fingers. The look he gave the leader was murderous but brief, he hurried back to his place on the steps as the leader, without one single glance at me, ordered a soldier to take me to the General.

I was marched away again, not up the steps, but to a small doorway round the corner of the building. We were passed in. This soldier had used his sense: by hurrying up the servers' stairs, we were in time to meet the General as he emerged leisurely on the second landing of the winding grand staircase inside the house.

We approached, the soldier saluted.

The General stopped. He was alone, the commanders no longer with him; he looked as if he were going to his chamber, continued taking off his jacket as he stood before us; his cloak was already over his arm.

'Caught a trespasser in the grounds sir,' said the soldier.

'A spy, hm?' said the General absent-mindedly.

I darted forward. The soldier was startled and reproachful, I'd been a good prisoner till then; he pinioned my arms again but I had got the General's attention. 'General,' I said, 'may I speak to you alone, only for a few minutes?'

'Ho, I don't advise that, sir,' said the soldier. 'Not but what it sounds like it's only a girl. But you never know with these assassins.'

'Yes, very likely, but you may go,' said the General. The soldier saluted and departed.

I fell forward into the arms. I was trembling horribly. 'They want to flay me.' My voice was small but hoarse: I thought, 'I sound hideous' but could not control it. 'There's a reward—they're all after me.' There was bile in my mouth. The checkered marble was spinning and rising.

'And you came to me?'

At the strange sound of his voice I looked up, my nausea arrested.

His eyes were on mine but somehow did not meet mine. He looked surprised, odd. 'Why to me?' he said. His gaze shifted away.

I was so anxious to show that I wasn't an idiot, that he *could* help, to beg from him, that I forgot to say that in any case it was an accident that the house I'd come to was his.

'Zerd, I know there is complete hatred between us, but you are the only one who can save me. Kill me, but don't let them torture me. I am yours, I surrender completely, I am your prisoner but don't let me be theirs.'

He had lifted me suddenly, one arm round my shoulders, the other under my knees. 'Why are you wet through?'

He carried me up the farther stairs, kicked open a decorated door, laid me on something soft. I was warm. I was in a big room, a fire gigantic in the hearth and torches round the walls. I was on a great circular bed which was covered by a musky musty fur.

He took off my cloak, and held up my arms, clasped together at the wrists in one of his hands. My teeth were chattering. He pulled my shift up over my head. 'Did he fish you out of the harbour?' I had closed my eyes. My eyelids were almost unbearably irritated, as though it was grit and not tears sliding from beneath them and streaming down my face. I felt him lifting the fur in handfuls and rubbing my body with it. 'Salt water, it'll be bad for the fur—' I think I jabbered. He lifted me again. I was aware of the sinews under the scales. He was tucking me into his bed, folding my arms like a baby's, smoothing the sheet. Was I asleep now? No, I couldn't be, because there was a thumping on the door. My heart? No, definitely on the door.

I opened my eyes. The General was flinging off his shirt, boots, belt. On his way to the door he dishevelled, with a thrust, the bed he'd just finished smoothing. He opened the door, scowling, doing up his belt again.

There was a force of Southern soldiers outside, green-jackets, not the sentries attached to this house. They fidgeted: the General didn't even say, 'Well?'

'It's been reported to us, sir, by one of our—your—sentries, that the wanted girl is in hiding here. We have orders to search.'

'Even in my bedchamber?'

They cleared their throats uncomfortably.

He stood aside, with an ironic gesture invited them blushing in. 'The only girl here, gentlemen, is this one.' They all looked at me in the dishevelled bed, at the General's scowling state of undress. 'But by all means search. I mustn't keep you from carrying out your duty. Look under the carpet, the floorboards, even the mattress. No spy must be allowed to escape.'

They searched very perfunctorily, their ears bright with embarrassment, keeping well away from me, poking tentative spears at hangings they took care not to tear. 'Thank you, sir. That'll be all. Obviously no one in here. Sorry to have interrupted—disturbed you—Sir.'

They all saluted while jostling each other out.

I was sitting in bed weeping.

He came and sat beside me, an arm round my shoulders. 'I needn't have saved you, but I did.'

'I *know* you needn't have.' A ridiculous, almost delicious suspicion struck me, as it did once before at another terrible moment when he was taking me to execution and I had refused to sleep with him and it had turned out that he is sensitive about his skin. I think he is actually rather naïve: a soldier, a lecher, a powerful leader, each aspect simple, brilliant but unadulterated. All that complicates him is his unaffected cynicism, his knowledge of human nature, the way *nothing* in any way unreal can sway him.

'General, I apologise for this, it can throw suspicion on you.'

'It has. But I'm glad you came.'

Then I remembered that he's wanted to get me for ages because I know the secret of the formula.

I said, 'If I were in my right mind I wouldn't tell you this, but death will seem kind when it is not—*that* way of dying—and you may be vengeful, you may torture me, but I don't think it will be that way either.' He was waiting, watching me with a sort of smile. I took a deep silent breath. 'I told the Temple black-robes the formula.'

His face went completely blank, the last thing I'd expected it to do. I went on, tripping a little over my own
tongue, 'They said they'd—flay me—if I didn't, so I did.
They must have been determined to finish me off anyway
because they came back and pretended it was the wrong
one. Then Kaselm helped me escape but he gave the
captain of the boat all that money to go to waste, because I
had to get off and I swam here—Kaselm is too clever and
powerful to suffer for helping me, he rules a whole kingdom underground—but I have brought trouble with me—
and I have told the formula—you must know—I am sorry
that I am a coward, and have made it impossible for you to
destroy Atlan.' I really was sorry, too. I felt utterly and
completely maudlin, as though it wasn't enough to offer
myself for execution in return for rescue from alien torture,
I had to be enormously, remorsefully overcome by my
ruining all the plans I had always hated.

'You have thought, all these months, that you knew the
formula?' I can understand your believing it in the first
shock, which I took advantage of, but that you never
realised afterwards—you are really incredibly naïve.' As I
had just finished thinking that of him I was rather nettled.

He was drawing two fingers across his chin when I
looked up at him again. 'Wait a moment,' he said. He got
up and went out, bare-chested and barefoot. He was away
about half an hour, as it turned out. I was still awake but
very drowsy when he came back. I was lying huddled in
the bed, curled as though in a dark, wonderful, safe womb,
luxuriating in safety as though I could quench thirst, feed
hunger and ease pain with it.

He sat down almost on my feet and I twisted to regard
him. I could feel the clearness of my own eyes. He gazed
into them with all the darkness of his.

'Can you sleep?'

'I think I no longer need to. I would sooner you talked,

General, if you don't actually despise the idea. I take it
I'm no longer facing imminent death?'

'You never faced it from me. Well—not since we reached
Southernland.' He said, 'Floss-hair.' Then he laughed. To
a certain extent, his eyes were glittering and his voice
vibrant. He was near excitement—he was waiting for something I didn't know about and I was connected with a kind
of expectation too. At the same time he was lazily amused
about everything—whatever everything was.

He leaned back, stretched, the now dimming flames
delirious on his calm, vibrant muscles. He has crazy elbows which go into sort of veined, mild whirlpools when
he straightens his arms. His crocodile-strength is apparent
in every part of his fabulous, almost mythical body.

'So,' he remarked, 'all summer you've been the Court's
rave under the impression that I was waiting to *get* you.
Charming. You're such an extraordinary child that you're
never pathetic. You were tremendously interesting to watch
in your kitchen days—and your legs were always fascinat-
ingly unselfconscious—but though it was obvious that at
times you had decided you were suffering, one never felt
it was time to step in. And I always put it off for another
day, like a wine which is all the better for the leaving, but
rarely for more than a day at a time, because you were so
invariably amusing in your certainty about your anonymity.
And then suddenly you were no longer there. And on that
very hot day at the beginning of summer, you overheard
that formula—did you seriously think about it and still
think we would have gone round mentioning the all-
important formula so casually? The formula you cherished
was that month's nickname for the real formula—a kind of
doggerel for it, not even a key-word, nothing to do with
the real signs of it. But I'm sorry it got you into trouble
with your hosts the black-robes.'

He paused, smiled, busy with his lazy amusement and
something else again.

'Have you ever had the sudden lift when you realise you can actually respect someone? Even though you were hoping for the sake of your plans that they'd succumb?'

I couldn't understand him, he meant he'd respected me at least once (I wasn't being too optimistic), but considering I'd been matter-of-factly selfish ever since he'd first noticed me . . .

'No, I could never have cared less if you told the Southerners that formula. The chase was solely for your benefit, to get you.'

I lay, not moving, but the clearness of my eyes was beginning to sear me and was no longer serenity, and safety became heavier. Those amused powerful lies to stampede me into sleeping with him. Did he care quite a bit about actually possessing this personality of mine he's been studying, or not at all?

There was no more to be said.

He had just saved me from what was literally far worse than death. I could not, by any stretch of the imagination, hear myself saying to him, 'It wasn't fair to get someone to sleep with you by pretending that the only alternative was immediate execution—and the only prospect execution anyway.'

He is cruel, lazily amused by analysis.

He sat watching me as I felt myself let go, drift back into drowsiness, still without moving.

'I hoped you would say something, anything, Floss-hair. In fact, I never thought that you would say nothing. But then, you are a very sleepy little thing, aren't you, and have been through a lot today, and you don't really understand being wanted. I am sure you have decided, there is no more to be said. Yes, sleep if you can. We'll be away before the first cock shocks the town.'

Away!

I woke as I was being lifted into the chariot. The air was outdoors air again, that was the first thing I noticed, chilly with that wind which skirls and fleers before the dawn, smelling of sea and magnolias—and birds. There was the busy sound of a large body of men and birds being as silent as possible without getting fussy over it.

I was wrapped in my cloak again. As I was handed into the chariot the Diary banged and half lurched out of my pocket.

I was already in the chariot and, momentarily, fully awake. Zerd had discovered *this book*! I sprang to intercept him with an anguished cry. He turned it over, amused, looked at the cover, said, 'Well, well, No. 8. High Quality Paper Account Book, eh?'

He tucked it back in my pocket.

'Where are we all going?' We were swinging into motion. Oh, *familiarity*; the sounds of men and birds on the march. We passed the dark gardens on one side, the white steps on the other, and on each step a Southern sentry lay dead.

'You have declared war by doing that.'

'It was time.'

Presently we were joined by other regiments. We must be complete now, a vast army, though small by Southern standards.

'We've been ready organised for some time now.'

'This road isn't taking us through the Town. Are we going to follow the river? Surely they'll find it easy to follow us?'

'It's quicker through the hills. It'll do them no good to follow us—they have a reasonably large force here but they won't want to have to face us in the hills, with us above them. I'm making towards the coast—they'll try to head me off and get me between here and the Capital where they've got the rest of their force. Well, they have a navy on the beaches but who knows, perhaps we can deal with that if we don't allow ourselves to be trapped between navy and army. Are you cold?'

'It is chilly . . .'

'It'll be chillier soon.' He wrapped a fur rug round me, folding it under my chin. Then he set a leather bottle of wine to my lips, and then made me eat meat and two apples. It was a narrow, high-slung chariot, a racing chariot and very draughty, drawn by a brace of birds unusually trained as a team, but I think he would have preferred to ride and was grateful to him for staying with me.

'Is your wife the princess in another chariot?'

'No—my wife is no longer of use to me.'

I shivered beside him.

'You're colder?'

'Depressed—' I didn't say horrified, and thought I was being tactful; then realised that Lara's disappearance was something I'd often willed.

'Depressed? Because my wife has been left behind at the Court? There's no need to be depressed, I should think she'll come to neither harm nor good.' He started to pick his teeth with a dagger. The chariot jolted high and I hoped he'd cut his tongue. At once I cheered up. The wish showed me I was throwing off the old, muzzy weakness of irrational gratitude.

Then I realised he was looking at me. 'When I said she was no longer of use to me—and she isn't, one doesn't need a decorative, high-born wife to be mistress of one's household and hostess at one's parties when the whole situation's about to dissolve with a burst into war—you thought I meant I'd got rid of her?'

I could only stare at him.

He said, watching me and the quirk at his mouth-corner deepening, 'That chase when you thought you'd found out something I would kill you for knowing—you found out something of a similar danger. You saw a dying woman, blue with poison, and heard her blame me. You remembered the illness of your friend, the hostage Smahil, on the hot plains?'

Indeed, I had been picturing the pink princess Lara, blue as Smahil and that discarded mistress had been.

'I saw no connection,' I began to say, but it came out in a whisper. 'You may have poisoned her—but the surgeon said Smahil's illness came from a bite, like a snake's—'

'Then let it rest,' he said, continuing to pick his teeth. 'No, I did not poison Smahil. But it is strange that you did not think so.'

I realised that a real threat had passed over me. This only confirmed all that I've guessed. With a bite or scratch, accidental or vicious, he can loose his own deadly poison through the system of the other and higher form of human being.

The air became bright within itself. There were still cold stars in the cold sky. We were in the hills. All the trees were coniferous and the rocks were enamelled with lichens like those on the rocks I studied so often below the tower. The shadows were brooding black and spicy. There were all our numberless, rough, savage sounds to help wake the waking forest, up here—the Hai, Hai of men to animals, barks of birds glad or irritated to be on the march again, squeals of wheels, whipcracks, hundreds of grunted conversations, beat of boots and sandals, etc., etc. We were moving fast. There was hardly a road, but the climb was easy, the rocks mainly huge and flat. We had hardly any baggage-train compared to former days. It was also rather astonishing how comparatively many men we had lost during the months of continuous brawling and rioting in the Capital.

I suppose I shall always think of the Northern army as 'we'. I've been part of them so often, and so many intense months at a time, through so many dangers, and I understand them so well. Nevertheless they are my hereditary enemies, and the enemies of that beautiful ultimate privacy, Atlan.

We passed waterfalls and could occasionally hear birdsong between all the rest of the row.

Half-way through the morning we were handed more meat, and soup. Zerd left me for a while and rode about seeing to an awful lot of things and visiting every part of the line. I seized the opportunity to scribble in this, though it came out rather jolted.

I was feeling very alive. Now it was warmer, but I realised for the first time that I was wearing nothing under the fur rug and my cloak but a little shift. Yet within the fur my thighs against each other were warm and smooth and reminded each other of their life.

Mid-evening we camped without tents. Neither are there any wine-girls, jugglers, dancers or musicians. Only Isad had killed a rodent that day, spearing it from his saddle, and he made a ghirza from half of a hard, hairy gourd with a long arm and strings of rodent-gut which he'd dried in a few hours.

Zerd, I (still rug-wrapped like a convalescent) and the commanders sat round a fragrant fire—the fuel was dried dung the men had been gathering—and Isad sang to his rather flat-toned ghirza, love songs which are the rage at the Court we've just left.

> The sickle of his smile
> Cut me to my middle—
> Made my heart lurch a mile—
> Explain me now that riddle.

Zerd watched me, I knew that he wanted the ceaseless love lyrics with their hypnotic tunes to beat their way past what he thinks my unnatural frigidity—and as a matter of fact, when I looked at his dark face his white fierce smile in it did seem the shape of a sickle . . .

The dark spirit of his nearness flows to me, laps me and enfolds me, the tide of his wanting me and his consciousness of myself is strong enough to overflow his own body and lap me warm. With two fingers he touched the cut across my cheek, made by the bat-wing in the vaults. He asked me what it was, his tingling breath not leaving it while I told him. He holds my bowl to my lips, his eyes waiting for mine to come up and meet his. Yes, he wants me. He should have taken me when I was confused with gratitude. Now that I am properly alive again, the very invigoration of his own presence is making me strong enough to ignore him.

I am a spectator to life—I always feel like an interloper, an impostor posing as a human being. I think that even had I not spent my formative years enclosed in the tower, I would always have felt like this. It is invigorating and exhilarating to be with someone like Zerd—someone who is very firmly rooted in life, someone to whom my whole inner mind, should he ever discover it, would seem abnormal—and who is, in spite of his liveness, someone who is aware of all the tricks human beings employ.

Zerd is human evil.

He is not ab-human, nor sub-human, nor even super-human. Any strong intelligent man could equal his feats of strength and brain. His ruthlessness is the root of human selfishness. He is elemental man—his skin is the same sort of thing as the highly developed fangs of some primitive races, atavistic remnants of the earlier life of the world, signs which more civilised artificial man has long since thrown off.

I went to the chariot to sleep. He wanted me to stay with him under the trees. When I was in the chariot I had a nightmare. I woke and lay looking up. The whispers seemed too loud and well-formed to be wind in the foliage. Before dawn Zerd appeared, he said he'd seen I was awake and we could talk to pass the time. We did not talk much, I pretended to be sleepy and he stroked my hair and held me cradled against him, but as soon as he appeared the whispers had gone. His is so actual a nature that the unreal can't be sustained near him—he comes, haunts go.

With him I get the feeling I am safe from the rest of life—but am in peril from him. He is handsome, desired by every woman, feared by soldiers, popular with mankind. Continents do shake at his tread.

A chilly, grey-skied day—when the sky can be seen.

The forests are thicker and more like jungle, with fantastic undergrowth, difficult, ridged ground and conical boulders difficult to find a way between, stony ice-cold streams that have to be forded.

Zerd has given me a shirt of his, and trousers far too big, absurd and flapping, which I've had to tie at the ankles with odd bits of cord. He hooted with laughter at me and then after that whenever I caught him looking at me he gave me an oddly tender smile. That pleases me so much that I have to remind myself he is good at that sort of thing.

Every now and then we catch a glimpse of the great mountain of the Capital—it is vomiting violent fire.

Unforgivable pain. I opened my eyes. Night. Pain in my leg, exquisite pain which I've never suffered before.

I was lying awake under the thick trees some way from the campfire. In my sleep I had thrown off my rug and should have been chilly in the night air, but instead I thought my leg was burning. Had some unnatural spark from the fairly distant fire set me alight without anyone noticing?

I tried to move my leg. I couldn't.

There are two of the worst kinds of nightmare I've had in my real life—the monster you cannot kill, every time you think you've managed it he appears again, and now the limb with the awful heaviness you cannot control. I am rather proud of the fact that even at that moment I was actually managing to think this, though my head was muzzy as though pain were a drink of which I had had too much.

'Zerd,' I whimpered, 'Zerd.' I clenched my teeth. I thought I was about to faint.

An arm groped to me from the darkness. 'Floss-hair?'

'Zerd,' I was hanging on to the name and it was difficult to remember other words to say. 'I think my leg is on fire.'

There was a spattering of sparks, a flare of flame, and he was holding a torch behind me. By its light we looked for my leg. I met only two narrow eyes, I believe they were reddish, and eyes were rather the last thing I'd expected. Before I did faint from the pain, I saw just enough more by the torchlight to show me a giant snake, very sinuously thick and with its coils stretched way out among the farther trees, lying there intently swallowing my leg, edging itself up by its teeth.

When I came to, I was in Zerd's arms. He was soothing, calming my shuddering. 'Don't move, it'll hurt worse.'

'Please, please get it off me.'

'It has thousands of tiny teeth, sloping backwards like a shark's—your leg would be a pulp covered bone if I pulled the snake off, even after killing it. But I'll kill it. Keep very still.'

This (I had another thought) would teach me to sleep out of the range of the pickets. My leg was swallowed up to just below the knee. If the snake got to the top of my thigh its teeth wouldn't be strong enough to get farther, it would just lie there digesting my leg inside it, I wouldn't be free till my leg had rotted right off—Zerd was now stooping with an axe. The snake was too busy eating me to notice. He brought the axe down on the snake about twelve inches below where he judged my foot to be. The snake, shocked, dug all its teeth in. I screamed. Two commanders and three sentries appeared all in a hurry. 'Keep back,' grunted Zerd. I presume they did, watching in horror, but I didn't look at them. Zerd was hacking at the snake which in its death agonies began a series of horrible jerks and kicks and thrashings which in their completely wild abandon were far more dangerous even than the deliberate squeezing-coils of such a snake would be when alive. The pain was terrible. I screamed again and again. I think I heard other people arriving and Isad sending them away again. Blood spurted everywhere.

It lay dead, still twitching like a death-convulsed eel, scores of times bigger than the ones I used to cut up at HQ. Zerd slit it down the sides from its jaw hinges, eased off its teeth, extricated my leg. It would in every way be silly to try and describe the pain. Having lifted me into the chariot and ordered everyone to leave us alone, he soothed unguents on to my leg, finally bound it again and again.

'My trousers which were so loose on you before will have to be slit now to enclose this bandaging,' he said matter-of-factly.

I was sobbing.

'Oh thank you, thank you. No one has ever been so wonderful to me. You have saved my life so many times, and it was so horrible. Will you ever forgive me that I was going to kill you, or have you already forgiven me out of your generosity?' I have never been so completely sincere, like a child saved from a terrible nightmare by a nurse to whom it knows it was unforgivable the very day before, and knows its unworthiness—no, I have felt like this one other time since childhood, when I met the grey-robed priest in the merchant's house.

'*Were* you?'

'Going to kill you—oh, not of course since I arrived in Southernland, it was all really too much for me right from the beginning but I was very grimly determined—'

'To assassinate me?'

The astonished laughter in his voice made me realise he didn't know, it was *new* to him.

'Didn't Ooldra tell you?'

'Why should she have?'

'When I was discovered in your room by Lara and I had to run—and it turned out Ooldra, whom I thought was helping me to kill you for my mother (didn't you know that was the only reason I was let out of the tower?) Ooldra wanted to betray me, she was going to you to tell you I meant to kill you, and she had witnesses to prove it. So I had to escape, one of the very narrowest escapes I've ever had—' My leg, deadened by the unguents, throbbed as though it were leaping a yard at each throb. It was all too much for me. I remembered vividly that night which had been the cause of delivering me into the governor's hands—the horror of my lovely Ooldra's revealed hate for me and for my mother, her arranging for my death and Zerd's by getting me to kill Zerd and then informing on me. But I hadn't killed Zerd, so she'd had to content herself with gloating over my death only, and I'd had to get away. 'Didn't Ooldra tell you, after all, that I'd been working to assassinate you ever since you let me join your army as one of the hostages?'

'You have no idea how much this interests me,' he said—unnecessarily, I should have thought. 'So you were playing the mythical heroine, who lures her country's desecrator to bed so that she can stab him? Poor little innocent on the altar of your mother's hate and patriotism. But you played your part very well at times—it was easy to think you a high-born lightskirt like your companion hostages. How sad it was all wasted, and I was interested in you only when you showed that other side of your personality—what I've come to realise is the real side of it. I suppose I saw it only when your acting was wearing thin—I exasperated you often, didn't I, and you threw

caution to the winds. *Very* reckless of you, and you new to
life. I was the first man you ever saw.'

I remembered Smahil in the Capital mentioning Ooldra's
'disappearance'. I pictured her, realising I'd escaped, not
bothering to tell on me but abandoning me to the dangers
of the South and embarking on her own journey back to
my mother's land. 'So Ooldra never told you?'

'She didn't get the chance. As soon as I found you
missing she was killed for failing to keep you. After all,
wasn't she supposed to be your nurse and companion?'

That took my breath away.

He'd searched for me that very night after I ran from
him—I'd been nowhere to be found. Had he been enraged
at Ooldra for failing to keep an eye on me? He had treated
her, *Ooldra*, like the servant no one else had ever thought
her, and had had her executed.

Ooldra was dead.

Ooldra is dead—So *that* is the haunt!

Ooldra's ghost, following me with its long hate, her
whispers in my ears—

'Turns out an even better thing I had her executed, now
that I know she was going to inform on your nefarious
activities. If word of all that had reached my princess,
you'd have been done for. But I never liked your Ooldra
being around.'

'She hated you.'

'Years before, she'd thrown herself at my head and
I'd—spurned her. Yes, that's the word, because the whole
scene did become quite melodramatic. But I don't like
cat-faced females.' He started whistling.

'I didn't think she was sexy enough to throw herself at
anyone,' I said. 'She was cold and high above the world—'

'Didn't you know she was your father's mistress?'

'Oh, yes, she told me on the last night but that still
doesn't mean—'

'And they have several children, whose backs were
branded before they were turned out on the world to

high-born foster parents who never quite realised how they got the children——'

I had never forgotten the tiny brand on my lover's back, I had known it so well.

Eng came to ask Zerd to confer round the camp-fire with the other commanders.

My loneliness gushed upon my being.

Now it is clear why I am so open to the haunt.

That time of magnetic flaming in the middle of the cold squalor, the obscenity of Terez, the violence, the bewildered near-hate, the yearning to all the delirious strength and tenderness in him—and he my father's son, my father the high priest's and Ooldra's—

Horror, corroding horror, revulsion from oneself and the beloved (if Smahil was 'the beloved')—a weight of guilt whose possible weight was hitherto unguessed; and beneath it all a kind of pride, for it really is a wicked sin one has committed: incest, very obscure and sinful; not many people have done so. My leg throbs and the whispers crowd on me. 'Zerd,' I whimper, 'Zerd.' And horribly it is repeated, a repetition clogging the air so that he cannot hear the original. Small insidious whispers, clogging air, thicker—thicker . . . Nearer, nearer, from all sides, I couldn't hear any *human* speech though the campfire conference was so near. Then he came, and dawn.

The army moved on.

Shall I ever be happy again?

'Bandits on the Golds' left flank, sir,' said the officer reporting.

We were driven there at once, for Zerd's bird was being groomed somewhere else.

I lay back in the fur, hardly watching anything we passed, too weak with different kinds of pain. I realised that Smahil is somewhere about in the 18th Foot. At the thought of meeting him any possible minute, by some accident, my stomach did not turn over as it should. But my knees went weak, and that made me feel rotten.

Presently we met the deputation of bandits.

They were a ragged, motley, dirty, picturesque group and they were fully confident in their own hard ruffianly flamboyance even though they were meeting the military man most famed for brilliance in the known world.

They wore big coloured sashes and most of their clothes were striped, fringed and tasselled. (And stuck full of weapons.) They were in appalling condition (the weapons were the only thing they wore immaculate) but because the original material and design of the clothes had been impressive they didn't seem to realise they'd changed. Some were on foot, some astride muscular skewbald ponies with fierce eyes, showy but insufficient obviously unnecessary harness, and so short their riders' feet nearly dragged on the rocks to either side.

When they saw Zerd they all saluted without waiting to be informed it was him. You could tell they were proud to have recognised him. Their salute was a wild, syncopated arm movement, each man made it separately, they hadn't been trained as a unit.

'I greet you,' said Zerd, getting out of the chariot.

Then there was a lot of talking I couldn't hear. Zerd sent someone for wine and the bandits politely drank a lot of it to show they didn't dislike it.

Finally Zerd came back. He ignored me and talked to Clor, Isad and Eng. Huddled near them, I made out that it is very tricky for an army to get anywhere near the Capital as the sentinel mountain and several others are *raining* fire nearly all the time, and so are quite a few mountains on the way to the coast. It is annoying of Southernland's mountains to all start their eruption-period now, but the bandits say everyone knows the great Southern magicians are working against him and the eruptions are the result. Zerd naturally laughs at that as he doesn't

believe in magic, also he says it'll make it rather awkward
for the even larger Southern army, and it will obviously be
coming to guerrilla warfare and he thinks he can beat
them at that. Well, the bandits say tactfully, it's well
known your army isn't worthy of you, and raw troops have
never before been known to be much good at guerrilla
tactics. And they offered their own services. They said
they are hereditary enemies of the Southern army and
would ask nothing more than to have the satisfaction of
hindering them.

'It's too easy,' growled Clor. 'They don't ask for metals,
goods or women. It's a trap. They want to report our plans
to the blasted South.'

'They've invited myself and commanders to a feast in
their stronghold, to discuss with their chief.'

'Let's risk offending them by refusing,' Clor urged
gloomily. 'While they're getting us drunk their main force
will fall on ours with the help of the Southerners who can't
be far behind now.'

But of course they went over to join the bandits.

One on a skewbald started forward and they all followed
him. As he was about to climb the cliff-slope behind me
he looked at me and called to the General.

'And your lady-wife, too!'

The General cocked an amused eyebrow at me, remembering me, not aiming the amusement for me to share.
'The lady is not my wife.'

I expected the bandit to ride on past but for a couple of
moments more he stared, which embarrassed me and I
smiled at him and shifted in my furs to give an order to
the chariot driver. I heard the bandit say in that cere-
monious-naïve way they have, 'She is your lady-mistress?
You must bring her to honour our chief's trough.' (As I
later found, they have troughs instead of tables.) I turned
and saw the bandit staring at the top of my cloak left
revealed by the fur.

'She is incapacitated for the ride by a leg only just beginning to heal,' Zerd said, not denying that I was his lady-mistress.

'I will esteem it an honour if you will let me drive her chariot,' said this courteous and hospitable bandit. 'It is a beautiful narrow chariot, and I can easily drive it here. I know these rocks and boulders as well as I know my girlfriend's bottom.'

Zerd didn't bother to say more. The driver got off the chariot-perch on to which the bandit bounded, a foot-bandit took his vacated saddle, and we moved up the perilous joggy ascent, the General's and commanders' marvellous birds making as light work of it as the skewbalds used all their lives to it, but making a lot of fuss and flapping their wings with that ugly tearing sound.

The bandit drove expertly but very carelessly, keeping the reins in one hand and turning round to show me something he'd been fishing for in his sash.

What he held was a piece of ragged cloth, exactly matching cloth and colour of my cloak.

'You reckernise this?' he said.

'You must be Kond.' He looked rather different now. The young man who'd torn my cloak that slaughter-morning in the rain had been thinner and crazier-eyed, with dirt-thick hair plastered to his skull. He was still ragged and dirty, but dry, and with a different air, of dangerous well-fed flamboyance.

'Ha,' he said, 'little did I realise I was being succoured and rescued by the General's mistress. No wonder you wouldn't come to the hills with me, eh? And now here you are after all.'

I was mildly amused by his conversation though I didn't bother to answer. I hardly felt nervous even about his driving. If at this reckless speed we overturned and I fell, helpless with my bandaged leg, and cracked my head on a rock, it would put an end to various things. For one thing,

the cold. I wasn't in the state of mind to be exhilarated by
the unnecessary cold. Not much farther up than the main
army, but on rocky ridges bare to the winds except for
stunted trees twisted almost parallel with the ground, the
cold numbed my jaw but pained my leg and spiked my
eyeballs. The bandits wore decrepit clothes but several
layers of them, though far less than I'd've needed.

'I kept this bit o' stuff,' he shouted, waving it at me as
we lurched terribly, 'in case you ever came, to prove to
you it was still me.'

'You thought I'd be gratified to find I'd saved such a
handsome bandit?'

He laughed uproariously as if I'd said something very
witty, and for a moment devoted his attention to tucking
the piece back in his sash.

In spite of this driving, we were still wheels-down when
we reached the great squat opening. The ponies were led
away. I was helped out of the chariot. The new warmth
was badly irritating my leg and I also had a fit of sneezing.
I didn't notice many details till I was in the great cavern.

Not tightly, respectfully, Kond carried me to a big
carved chair with a pelt across it. Zerd and the commanders were being greeted by a horrible man. He was very
big, with skin like leather, muscles like springs, and very
cold, dark-blue eyes. He wore a black bearskin slung over
one shoulder and belted with a wide studded weapon-
band, over shaggy ponyskin trews. He was so scarred that
at first his agate-studded dull-metal bracelets seemed just
more scars, his skin was so coruscated. He had a clear
pleasant voice, rather light. This was Ael, the bandit chief.

We all sat in front of an elaborately carved trough full of
bubbling stew, and dipped in. I didn't eat much because I
didn't like getting my fingers so messy. I'd been seated
too far from Zerd and Ael to hear much unless I made an
effort. I didn't bother. I watched night come on outside
the cavern entrance. A woman brought us mulled wine

and I asked if I could have milk instead. She nodded but didn't come back with it for me. There were dark openings round the rocky walls, they must lead to inner caves, and the roof was never more than seven feet high but in some places it got so low one would have to stoop. Under the low parts pallets had been set for sleeping. There were other troughs and groups in the cavern but the bandits didn't make too much noise—when they got noisy enough to disturb their chief's conversation with Zerd, Ael looked up and across at them and that was enough, except that once they were absorbed in the wrestling of two of their comrades and didn't see him and so fast one hardly realised what was happening he seized a spear from beside him and launched it at them. With powerful straight force it went straight through the fleshy part of a man's arm and he yelped and hurried to the women's end of the cavern. After that it was very quiet for a while, but Ael allowed a reasonable buzz of noise everywhere. Also, there were dogs tumbling and barking round the fires. I saw only one or two oldish children, I suppose the rest were down the women's end, where I couldn't make out much more than dark moving forms against the glow of cooking-fires.

There were only stars to be watched outside now. Part of the time I watched Ael, though each second I was frightened he'd notice. But neither he nor Zerd looked my way at all. The bandit chief's deep blue eyes were colder and more analytic than I'd ever seen even the pale eyes of the few sadists I've met.

'No wine for you?' asked Kond.

'Oh, hi. No, I asked a woman for milk instead and she promised to bring it but hasn't turned up since.'

'Milk? Feel sick?'

'A little—and a headache,' I said.

He got up and strolled purposefully away. When he came back he was accompanied by the sullen-eyed woman bearing a jug. She set this down before me and went again. Of course, in addition to showing her she must obey, he would not have performed the feminine task of carrying it himself. I drank from the jug-lip. The milk was hot and had a thick surface of rather smoky cream.

'Thank you. Is it safe to leave your chief's conference to fetch milk for a girl?'

'I know all they're saying, though it'll take the evening. Besides, one must be polite to the guest-of-honour's mistress.'

'Oh—Well, if you're depending on that—you'd better lay off looking after my comfort, I'm not the General's mistress, only I was arrested by his Southern sentries the night he left, so he brought me with him.'

'I'll still look after you,' he said sweetly. 'Didn't you cleverly save my life, and you only a baby and thinking me ungrateful at times, which I never was, but I just wanted to kill that bastard my jailer, and your sweet nature wouldn't allow it. It's a nature must be obvious to everyone, and I wouldn't believe the General hadn't taken advantage of you except I remembered your leg.' He directed a sympathetic regard on it. 'Drink up. How's your poor little head? By the way, what were you arrested for?'

'Trespassing.'

He gave a hoot and a splutter of laughter, went 'Haw-haw' and slapped his thigh. 'Ah, you're a one, you are. You're good at being in the wrong place at the right time.'

I remembered he'd thought I was a trespasser when I first discovered him in the Temple prison grounds.

Ael was honouring these guests to whom he was offering his martial support. Women now bore to us bowls of fresh-roast bear hams, a rare delicacy which impressed on us the valour and might of Ael's bandits. As a further gesture, he summoned a man whom he referred to as his taster, a golden-skinned slave they'd captured once. I could guess from my knowledge of Zerd's casual everyday life that he thought a taster in a bandit tribe ridiculously ostentatious. 'All the men dislike him because he's a yaller-skin and finicky at avoiding fights, but good with the women,' said Ael, amused by his double mastery: his rough, tough men and his civilised slave. The taster gave a demure smile as he approached the ham; this was his moment. A piece of the toughest ham had been set aside for him (his function was merely nominal). Almost before his adam's apple had bobbed up again after he swallowed, he let out a screech and clasped his abdomen. He screeched again, fell to the rock floor, writhed, disturbing a few filthy goatskin rugs, and died with froth on his lips.

Ael gave a happy tenor giggle like a child's.

'I told you the men disliked him.' He picked up a ham and started to eat it. Eng gave an involuntary movement. 'Oh, no, they knew which he'd be given,' Ael said. 'There's no danger. It's a case of the poison *meant* for the taster.'

The body was left before us till we'd finished eating and it was time for the entertainment. A comely girl came forward. She carried a shut basket and was accompanied by two fierce-looking adolescent boys with primitive tambourines. She had red hair in two very long plaits which went down the neck of her tunic and appeared with her ankles from the other end. The boys sat cross-legged and started to sway their bodies and instruments; she stood, swaying in time, opened her basket and took out a thin green-and-yellow snake. Although snakes were something which still made me shiver, I was fascinated by the things she did with this one. Finally she encouraged it to crawl up one of her nostrils and reappear out of her mouth.

She was clapped and Zerd threw her a brooch, so then the commanders threw her things too. I wanted to give her something but was wearing no jewellery at all.

Now it was time to go. The men rose and clasped each other's arms. It was arranged that Zerd should travel on towards the coast, getting his army as best he could between the volcanoes, and the bandits would wait only for the Southern army, to harry it for all they were worth, and follow it hindering it from every direction and giving Zerd time to reach the coast and deal with the Southern navy there.

The whole point was that the bandits expect a jolly good whack in Atlan, which under no circumstances would they get from their own government. I shan't be able to help laughing if after all this trouble everyone breaks through into Atlan and finds it a miserable place with no resources or wealth.

I hadn't realised how warm and comfortable this one evening had made me until I realised it was time to return to the cold, painful, jogging travelling.

'You're going to have to travel at speed, General,' said Kond.

'I think I can manage that,' Zerd replied.

'What about this young lady?' said Kond. 'I understand you brought her with you out of kindness. It won't half be a hard journey for such a young lady with such a sore leg.'

Zerd looked suspiciously at Kond. Yet he couldn't deny it. 'I don't deny it,' he said impatiently.

'It'll have time to heal up proper if she stays the few days with us before we come on to join you,' Kond said. 'Where with you it may never heal, what a shame it would be and all, and complications might even get it.'

'Cija?' Zerd said angrily, he knew what I'd reply. 'Do you feel you need to stay?'

'It would be an unexpected delight,' I said, 'not to have to travel like this.'

'It would be very kind,' Zerd said, turning to Ael, 'if you would keep her till her leg is nearer healing. I shall emphasise that I want her returned to me. She's not for sale,' he half-indicated Kond.

'She will be well treated,' Ael assured him.

I was *furious* at being talked of as a slave. Not for sale!

He might be trying to keep me safe while I was left alone here, by making them think me his property, or more likely just meant to keep me for himself, but I am damned well not a slave, never have been, and never will be. There's no need to accord me the respect he'd given his damn forest princess, whose blood was probably many times worse than mine.

The bandits and Northerners took ceremonial, cordial, temporary-leave of each other. Zerd came over to talk to me, which at least is an improvement, there was a time when he'd just have left without another look at me.

'You aren't nervous at staying?' he said. 'No,' I said, though I was a little.

'Probably you should be,' he said, with a saturnine glance, but that was only to upset me. 'Do you want me to leave anything with you?'

'The clothes I'm wearing, if you can spare them.'

'I think so.' He seemed at a loss, but didn't once mention my pain and hope it would be helped.

'Goodbye, Your Mightiness.'

'We'll be meeting again in a couple of weeks, Floss-hair.'

He and his commanders went out escorted by Ael and others.

I saw the wind meet their cloaks as they went out past the entrance and into the cold, roaring, icy-starred, black night. Kond was one of the escort.

While I waited for Ael and Kond to return and deal with me I just lay back in the big chair. The fires in the huge low cavern were now glowing to death. The dogs had stopped barking so much and were growling over bones and scratching for fleas. People were lying down on the pallets. I myself thought I already had some fleas. The smell of this place was pretty strong but it was rather comforting—I suppose if the temperature outside were less cold the smell inside would be actually horrid. But

even all those fires only warm the place in bits—it is full of
cold islands and draughts.

Finally I did ask a passing woman if there were any
fountain-rooms. She stared resentfully and said I'd have to
be satisfied with the communal pits about the ravine.
'What if I want to wash?' I said. 'Wash!' she repeated. 'I've
a bad leg,' I said. 'The ointments'll need washing off and
renewing every so often. Don't you wash your men's
wounds?' 'I suppose you can have a bowl of boiled water
every now and then,' she said, in the same voice the other
woman said I could have milk.

Later I heard, 'She's fell asleep, poor little soul, don't it
just show how she needs the rest.'

'Kond . . .' I murmured.

'Kond's here,' he said soapily, then I heard his chuckle.
Obviously one of those people whose own behaviour-
patterns strike them as very funny. 'You'll have to sleep in
my bed—there aren't any spares at the moment—but it's
good and wide.' Having blinked awake, the first thing my
eyes met were two very cold eyes. I was looking past
Kond, bending over me, to Ael who was leaning against
his high-backed chair and regarding me for the first time.
'You have no objection, chief, eh?' inquired Kond.

'It depends what you can trust her to tell the General.
And you can't cut out her tongue, unless you can think of
some reason to account for such an accident.'

'Ah, then,' said Kond. 'I don't mean her no harm to cut
her tongue out because of. There, baby, Kond will carry
you safe to bed now. Tell the Dragon if you like, if he
don't have an innocent mind enough to take it on the chin,
well I can only say he won't win many battles if he don't
never believe what he's told.'

When he'd laid me on the pallet, lain down beside me
without removing even his boots, and dragged the pelts
and rugs up over us, he did start pulling me towards him
but I acted sleepier even than I was. He threw a heavy

arm over me and I was content for about ten minutes thinking he'd dozed, then he was caressing my breast in an almost unexceptional, friendly, courteous way. I started and said, 'Oh, look, I thought you——' 'All right, darling,' he said goodnaturedly, desisting. He tugged me closer, grunted a few times, burrowed his unshaven head on my shoulder and was soon snoring into my neck.

It was only one new set of snores added to a dozen others. We were surrounded to either side, to our feet and heads by other pallets with sleepers over which Kond, stooping because of the low roof, had stepped nimbly when bearing me here. I could smell the boots of the man sleeping behind us—if he thrust with them during some nightmare, my head might be done for. There was just enough firelight left to play over the roof and show me, as I lay on my back staring up, a very pornographic drawing (though not badly-done, and lively) recently made by passing a candle under the roof and letting the carbon line more blackly the stale-smoke-black rock. I continued, however, to stare straight up as, if I looked to either side, I was embarrassed by similar scenes on the pallets. I did not mean to shut my eyes till I was very tired, for fear of the whispers. My mind wandered back to Kaselm and his offer of safety in the vaults which I'd rejected as a life of crime and dirt. And now . . . Oh, well, it was only for a few days and was better than hard, fast travelling among bitterly cold hills without a road and with a leg which gave me dizzy pains. Kaselm—during all my time of distrust (I'd become almost proud that I never trusted anyone) his 'deep game' had been kindness. But *now* I was again alone, and ill too, which I'd never before been, it might interfere with my small but hitherto sufficient resourcefulness.

No whispers came. I don't suppose Ooldra could have borne it in that sort of hole crowded with tough humanity.

*   *   *

At once I knew it was all right, somehow, I wasn't frightened even when I was wakened by something heavy bounding on me and something hot, wet and harsh on my face. It was a dog, admittedly a puppy, but it wasn't going to be much good at hunting bears if it was always that friendly to strangers. I got my hands out from under the bedclothes and it, and patted it awkwardly, and when it snuffled too much at me (perhaps, after all, it thought I was some kind of prey in a burrow) I hit it away so deliberately that it went. Just as well—its teeth were already well-developed.

It was morning, if I could trust the faint colourless light just percolating to here. I was still surrounded by snores. I'd wakened stiff and tried to shift but discovered I was pinned down. Besides Kond's head on my shoulder, there was his heavy arm across my ribcage and some time in the night he'd flung one leg over me as if he'd been dreaming of straddling a horse. Luckily it was my OK leg his was across.

I wondered how long ago dawn had been, and when the tribe woke. I hadn't been lying awake long when I heard a clatter and saw the sentries coming in from outside (of course I didn't know then who they were). Because of the roof-dip where I was I could only see their legs.

A little later the whole cavern seemed to be waking up. Some had heard the sentries come in, they stirred, that woke others. Underneath all the roof-dips in the cavern, the islands of pallets, people were waking, then rising. It didn't take them long to get up, they'd all slept fully clothed.

Kond gave a series of grunts, like those he'd gone to sleep with, and then nuzzled his head about on my neck. 'Do you mind?' I said. 'Your bristles aren't exactly soft.'

'Urr . . . rr?'

He opened his eyes, looked blearily up at me from my shoulder, flashed a grin, brought up a hand and pulled my hair, suddenly caught me a hefty whack as he pushed out his elbows, he stretched and gaped a yawn.

'Well, how did you sleep, angel-face?'

'I now have my full quota of fleas.'

'S'right, big, hairy fleas they are here. You'll be interested when you catches your first.'

'Oh, I'm already fascinated, don't worry.'

'Can you walk to breakfast?'

'I can limp if you help me and don't mind walking slowly.'

'We better start now then, or everyone'll've wolfed our share.'

He swung from under the covers, rose, held down a hand for me. I got up awkwardly, remembering at the last moment not to bang my head. Stooping, we made our way over the pallets, occasionally standing on bits of prone figures who soon let us know about it, till we could stand upright and saw bandits converging on the new-filled troughs beside the new-lit fires. The women served, and would have their meal later on what the men left. A very few other women were eating with the men, but none of the older or very young ones.

Kond and I sat where we had last night. I was rather put-off to find the same kind of stew in the trough again.

'Where's Ael?'

'He's served in his own room.'

'Room?'

'He has a private cave, one of the smaller ones off this.'

'Do you have this stew for breakfast, midday and dinner?'

'Doncha like it then?'

'It's all right but don't you get bored with it?'

'Oh, you won't get bored with it,' he cheerfully assured me, so for fear of sounding neurotic I didn't say I already was.

Now the men around the cavern were rising, wiping the backs of their arms across their mouths, taking spears from stacks and gathering together. Kond began the same procedure.

'Where are you going?' It hadn't occurred to me I might be left alone on my first day.

'Day's hunting—some hunting animals, some waiting above the pass for travellers.'

I felt a stiffness of distaste. 'And what shall I do?'

'I'll call a woman to see to you.' He was already striding away.

'Make it a nice woman,' I begged hastily catching at his sleeve. He turned to grin down at me. 'What you want a *nice* one for? You're nervous, aincha?'

I tried to think of an answer and the pause was enough to make him grin more broadly than ever as he went away. He liked me being nervous of his everyday life.

In a few minutes he was back with a middle-aged woman, handsome but incredibly weatherbeaten and pockmarked. However, that didn't put off the bandits; I'd already noticed her at breakfast, how many men smacked her as she served them and teased her just in order to be able to crow in delight over her monosyllabic replies as if they were hard-won compliments. I'd have preferred someone much smaller and gentler, but Kond was already saying, 'Well, see you.' About to dash away, he looked at the woman, winked at me, came back, lifted me up by clasping me in both arms and kissed me on the mouth. Ael appeared and everyone left noisily.

The woman and I were left facing each other. I felt at a disadvantage as I'd just flopped untidily into a chair again when Kond let me go.

'I understand you're going to help me. It's very kind of you,' I said, trying the craven approach though I knew perfectly well she had to obey Kond. 'But before you bathe my leg hadn't you better get your breakfast?' The other women were getting theirs.

'I can fix myself up a tasty broth later,' she said. 'I'll do you now.'

While she was unwinding my bandages and bathing the sticky painful mess underneath, she said, 'I'm Golra.'

'I'm Cija. Don't call me Mistress.' She'd shown no signs of doing so, so perhaps that was rather hopeful of me. She just grunted and next time she spoke started right off calling me Lady. I felt she didn't want to accept my insincere, nervous, alien intimacy.

It was a horrid day, full of the usual pain and a lot of dreary empty spaces. Before the noon-meal I managed to sleep a little. The whole day I hardly moved from the same chair. After I'd been shown where they were, I had to drag myself to the communal pits above the ravine. They were pretty sickening but the beastly numbing cold kept down the smell and at least there are separate pits for the sexes. In the afternoon I noticed definitely how all the women ignored me except for a group who seemed actively to dislike me. What seemed a whole age after the morning, I was sewing some deer-hide I'd begged as something to do from Golra, the men walked in.

Immediately the cavern's atmosphere lit and became charged with life. The women patted their hair and ran to and fro very industriously, as if they hadn't been dawdling all day; the men threw down their spears, kicked their dogs, also any children who got in the way, and bawled for something to drink.

I found myself shrinking.

I've lived with an army, off and on, for two years—I've even masqueraded as a boy for months—but I can't lose a kind of shock at them, especially if there are a sudden lot of them. Two years ago I thought there was no such thing as a man, that they were extinct from a feminine planet. They are a bit overpowering in the mass, surely anyone would admit that.

Through all the hoarse din, Kond appeared at my side. A girl was hopping along beside him, trying to get wine safely into his mug as he walked, and when she'd succeeded he drank and hit out at her and she affectionately bit his arm and giggled and raced away.

'Have some,' he said, sitting beside me.

I drank from his mug which he held to my lips. 'Thanks. Did you have a good day?'

'The usual rodents—' he spat on the rugs—'no travellers, and not a sign of the Southern army. But they can't be even a day behind yours. Our scouts'll probably find them tonight.'

He called for a girl who came and shaved him. That couldn't happen more than twice a week. He kept moving his head and talking about the hunting, but when she cut him he cursed and threatened that if it happened again she'd be done for. He asked if I'd had a good day and I nodded, but when the girl had gone and he was feeling his new chin, I said, 'Golra's all right, but some of the women seem to dislike me. One of them is the woman you made give me milk last night; do you suppose she resented it?'

'Ho,' he said deeply.

'Is she stirring them up?'

'No, they all disliked you before that.'

'But—how?' I began, alarmed. 'Because you're with me,' he said. 'I'm too tactful to tell you they think you are actually mine, but there it is. They're Dalig's women, and the women-friends of Dalig's women.'

'Well, who's Dalig?'

I got Kond's scowl in all its unshaven grimness, unmasked by stubble.

'He's the dirty bastard who used to be under me—since I was away in that mucking priest-ridden prison he's become Ael's second-in-command.'

'And everyone knows you hate each other?'

'One day soon it'll be him or me for good and all.'

He brooded, pulling his lip.

'Point Dalig out to me,' I invited, feeling as though I were humouring him.

He got behind my ear and directed my line of vision to a tall man, younger than I'd expected, wearing a leather jerkin on which bosses of metal had been sewn to serve as armour, but some of them were now hanging uselessly by threads, he had greasy hair to his shoulders, probably it had once been red, and at some time his nose had almost all been sheared off. Now there was a sort of nothing there, a white-scarred nothing, and his lips had had a few little rubies set in them.

'That makes it very rough when he kisses,' growled Kond. 'But they seem to bloody well like it enough.'

'Have you fought yet?'

'Only once seriously—but they pulled us apart as I was about to do him.'

'If you did, you'd be second-in-command again?'

'You said it.' He kicked a passing dog. 'Would I!'

After brooding some more, he suddenly turned round and said, 'What's your name?'

'Cija.'

'Cija—Funny I never knew it. I often wondered what it was, remembering you and the way you helped me and then yanked yourself away.'

I started up, embarrassed (though he could have asked my name a whole day earlier if he'd really often wanted to know it; still he had kept the bit of cloth and a man of this type and used to this life would be too much for me to handle unless he were kept at arm's length) and I forgot I'd a bad leg and he started up with his arm round me. 'Want me to take you somewhere?'

'I'd forgotten my leg—I'd like to ask Golra if there's such a thing here as a hairbrush.'

I dunno, they may have one—you can borrow my comb.'

Perhaps he was too naïve to know he'd worried me, perhaps he thought I wanted to make sure the General got me. Funny how people always think I'm his.

Kond's comb I received gingerly. It had been in one of

his scabbards, with a saw-edged knife, and had dirt thick between the teeth. It was wooden and rather warped and the teeth so widely spaced quite big knots would be between them. Still, I wouldn't get a cleaner one here. He pulled it out of my hand, roughly unwound my hair and started dragging the comb from root to end of each strand. This was a community so based on the system of woman's subservience that for him to do this publicly wasn't at all demeaning, just showed he wanted to.

'Ow! Ow!' and 'Ow!'

Behind me I heard him laughing into my hair, then he stuffed some into his mouth and said it tasted nice. His senseless crudity was getting on my nerves. 'Let go, barbarian.'

'Barbarian? What's that, eh?' I'd been ashamed of using such a corny, feminine, petulant word so I just growled, 'Oh, never *mind*,' and then saw Dalig coming over. He stood in front of us and threw back his head, his thumbs in his hipbelt, and laughed. I could see all the other faces in the cavern turning to watch with three little dark circles in each, two wide eyes and an expectant mouth.

'Kond the maidservant! None of the women can get the tangles out as well as Kond!' hooted the noseless bandit.

It was just a way of challenging, and Kond showed he appreciated that and wasn't going to waste time. He stood up, bashed his fist into Dalig's eye while he drew his knife with the other. Dalig got his leg behind the crook of Kond's and tried to crash him down but was pulled down with him and fell jarringly for a moment on the rock as Kond slipped from beneath him. Kond kicked him in the belly, which wasn't as effective as it sounds because of the metal-sewn jerkin, and then threw himself on him, trying to pin down his arms. Dalig got away and we all settled down to watch a good dirty fight.

I realised later than everyone else that it was matter-of-factly a fight to the death.

They both had knives out. Kond at one point managed
to hold off Dalig's stab and at the same time get Dalig's
weapon-belt unbuckled and sling it away, but at once he
was off balance and Dalig nearly got Kond's arm twisted
up behind his back—Kond swung over Dalig's shoulder,
chopped with the side of his hand hard on Dalig's adam's-
apple—Dalig coughed and got kicked, got his hand on
Kond's knife-wrist, twisted, roared as he pulled him over
(it was the first sound either had made with their voices)
and was tripped himself. They rolled over top to toe, each
gripping the other's knife-wrist with a spectacular-tendoned
arm, each trying to kick the other's head in. As a fight
there was not much future in this and the audience began
to yell.

Somehow one of the rugs had got bundled in between
them and a flap of it caught at Kond's eyes—Kond got his
knife-wrist free—so did Dalig, parried Kond's thrust, got
his ankles hooked round Kond's neck, lay heavily on him,
jerked, slashed at his throat. Blood appeared on Kond's
shoulder, paused, then poured out. Dalig slashed again,
quickly, twice, and made a welling cross-hatching on Kond's
shoulder and neck but hadn't got any vein. Scrabbling
with their boots and legs, Kond managed to tip Dalig off
him and they were both on their feet.

Then they started circling each other, stiff-legged, wary-
armed, ready any instant to stab or dodge. Kond's arm and
side were red, gouts began to drip to the rugs and collect
in the rocky hollows. The dogs round the circle began to
sniff and pant and their masters held them back by their
collars.

Now and then one would stab, and cut or be parried;
soon both were decorated with thin slashes oozing red
bead-driblets, and part of Kond's tunic was in ribbons.

Presently each man's panting could be heard, loud and
uneven, and harsh as though it came from a throat of gravel.

Suddenly, just at that moment when everyone has been

expecting it just long enough for it to startle them when it does happen, Kond's knife-hand flashed in low and up, under the stiff hem of Dalig's jerkin. The decisive thrust had come and gone just like that. Dalig must have been a very brave man, I expected him to scream but he only gave a sort of 'Ug' and his eyes glazed at the shock of the final *defeat*—Kond meant to step away that instant, but one of the loose hanging bosses on Dalig's jerkin had got itself wedged in an interstice of Kond's tight, elaborate, metal bracelet. Staggering, lurching, his eyes glazing, blood everywhere and the bones of his face standing out like white stone, Dalig howled, brought his big-toothed knife held in both hands down with all his force on Kond's head, and fell sprawled in blood. Kond was Kond, young and new-shaven with two eyes and a firm mouth and unkempt brown hair, and then his two eyes were sliding apart from each other and his head had been split right down.

There was an immediate high keening of women, Ael who had been watching everything without a change of his eyes motioned with his hand, he had survived so many similar battles but more scarred than not; and they came and folded their sprawled limbs and the women wept over them and they carried them away and the women followed . . .

I was sick again and again and a hard hand held my forehead, the scars against my brow increasing my grief and my nausea.

I saved him once and he came to that.

The Southern army was reported by scouts to be on its way through the pass. Things were organised and ready for this, only the women had to be bade farewell . . .

'This little bitch won't half be an encumbrance, chief.'

'She's to be delivered to the Dragon. But I think she's had a relapse, feverish—someone take her direct to him.'

I don't understand. How can the pain in my leg make

my head, eyes and ears, and my arms and stomach sore
and aching and dizzy?

'I'm all right.'

'You'll be no good in guerrilla warfare—and if you stay
here it'll mean bad blood with the Dragon. Better if you
get to him dead than we say we kept you.'

He spared two men to ride fast with me, and told them
to feed me well and keep me warm, or run the risk of
being executed if they delivered a corpse to the Northern
Dragon. If they rode hard, allowing for the detour to avoid
the Southerners, it would take little over a day and night
to catch up with our army. I was wrapped in furs and
finally Ael himself lifted me into a light wicker chariot
which would go fast but jolt terribly. His eyes went over
me as if checking on me, then rested briefly on mine.
They held for a few moments, but without a hint of
expression, then there was a 'Hai, hai!' and we sprang
forward. I wondered muzzily if he blamed me for the
killing of both his commanders, but surely he is too intelligent not to know better. It was in the air, it would have
happened any time.

I think I was delirious a lot of that journey. There were
only stars and a wind, sleet in my face, thick whispering
and more and more, then red flashes and when everything
was clearer I realised that we had halted above a plain on
which the delirium was actualised, there were black figures everywhere and behind that the mountain spurting
flame and the river on the plain winding between the
combatants, some splashing in the fords, and reflecting
the eruption as though it were a stream of lava.

'Is this a battle between the Southerners and Northerners?' I asked.

They said, Yes, it was, but indeed I could see that for
myself.

'But I thought we'd reach him before the Southerners
would—'

'We was delayed a few hours by the sleet, it was so thick for so long—but this must be the Southern army that was in the Capital.'

You stay here,' they said. 'You'll be all right. They won't come up here—just stay put.' They were itching to be in the battle, and they ran down the slope, becoming black silhouettes as they went distant from me in the warm air, then tinged with red reflection as they neared the river which in its turn reflected the towering eruption which seemed even nearer than it was. Now and then some black flakes would float towards us, but it was very occasional. I couldn't hear much of the rumble and thunder because of the din of the battle. One of my escort plunged into the ford at the hill's foot and at once became merged with the fighters there—the other caught a spear through chest and back almost before he'd got there, and staggered a few feet, then pitched on his face.

They'd left me with a leather bottle of gullet-warming, stomach-warming rum, bread and cheese, fresh fruit and rodent-steak which had been roasted that morning and was reasonably tender.

I made a good meal, to keep my mind off my position, but I found that the combination of food, warm air and urgent excitement had me feeling strong and well. I no longer felt a trace of sickness or delirium. I pushed back the furs and felt my leg. It ached but must be healing. It was suicide to stay stuck in a chariot, waiting—especially when one was perfectly strong—I got out and fell on the ground at once, I was weak from the days before.

I picked myself up, grazed in several places. My head went dizzy and there seemed confused black and yellow spots in my eyes—then I saw the fighting below me again, gritted my teeth and felt better than before.

Yes, I was really in an ideal position. This was what I'd

wanted all along. Quite alone, free of captors and forcible escorts, and everyone too busy to take any notice of me.

I was light-headed, thought I was walking at one angle and found myself walking at another—lost balance several times, and bumped into boulders I thought I'd avoid by many inches—but my mental confidence made up for that and slowly I made my way round the hill above the battle at which I hardly looked, till at last I'd skirted it. I couldn't see it at all round the hill's bend, and if I climbed down now and trekked in a straight line towards the volcano, I'd miss the battle altogether.

I sat on a flat stone, cushy with pink moss, or maybe it was just glowing pink in this light, and said to myself, 'But *why* do I want to get to the volcano?'

'That's a good question, Cija.'

There was a long, smug pause.

'Then answer it.'

'Oh. Well, because the city's behind it, beside it actually from where I am, and I can search through the city for my grey priest.'

'Is he there?'

'I don't know where else he'd be. He must have taken refuge there with those underground movements we're always hearing about—and at least it would be terrible not even to *try* to find him. He's the only person who'll know how to deal with Ooldra, if anyone knows he knows. Don't you realise, Cija, I must get rid of these whispers or I'll have them all my life.'

I'd sobered by the time, at red twilight, I reached the city and found the masses of frightened evacuees milling out.

Some of the roads were clogged with wagons; others were deserted. I learnt that the streets nearest the mountain were paved with red-hot lava, but the outer parts of the city were safe and most people were staying there, except for the many families who'd left in case the eruption became even more violent and engulfed the city. The eruption had lasted a long while and almost everybody thought it was giving signs of cooling down.

But also there were looting deserters and wounded of both armies—panic had spread among the citizens. Families who would have stayed were leaving because their neighbours were gone and they felt insecure.

As I penetrated the city, often having to try several roads before I could find one where I wouldn't be trampled by the streams of traffic in the opposite direction, I found chaos, all trades and normal life at a standstill.

Animals were wandering about, abandoned by their owners, already fierce with starvation. They fought and snarled on window-sills, roofs and cobbles. A small, fluffy cat, a domestic pet, was standing guard before a heap of rubbish. I approached. The cat's belly went down, its head up, and it screamed a threat.

I decided that the first place to try to get a lead on the priest—I knew by now it was pretty impossible, but here I was—was the merchant's house where I first met my priest. Someone there might have an idea where I could go for news of where to look.

I thought I'd remembered well enough how to get there, but when I reached the alley I was impeded by a flux of people all surging the other way—I managed to get against the wall and work myself along. The dusk was heavy with floating flakes and there was a red glare over people's faces. Everyone was grimy and paid no attention to anyone but themselves. I was limping but my leg hurt only when it was jogged.

I reached the merchant's house. The door was wide open. I ran up the shallow steps, through the passage, into the inner room. There was no one there, only a disorder of clothes and objects as if the family had left hurriedly. The knocker shaped like a little man warming his hands had been wrenched off the door but they had forgotten it after all, it lay on the floor in the folds of a child's dress. To make sure, I ran down into the cellar and then through every room in the house; but it was empty of life, except for the scuffling of an indignant rat across the floor as I entered the bedroom it had thought safe at last.

I limped out again and forced my way into the alley.

I caught at people's sleeves, aprons, trying to ask them if they knew where the merchant had gone, but they paid no notice to me. Then I was nearly squashed against the wall as a family passed with a heavily laden donkey and a young goat which made a pathetic row, its udder was huge with long-overdue milk. I caught at a fat woman who looked motherly—'Please, could you just tell me if you know where the peat merchant went?' but she jostled me heavily aside.

I saw it was useless. Dejected, I stood watching them all pass with their single-minded faces and bundles of gear. Families with wailing children, a keen-eyed pedlar in grey rags, a band of gutter women clutching belongings but obviously more interested in breaking into the various deserted inns about, singing raucously. This was getting worse. I decided I'd better try once more while there was still a chance of asking families who'd lived locally and would know the answer.

'Does anyone know where the peat merchant who used to live here has gone?'

My voice was nearly lost and might as well have been completely drowned—and then the pedlar turned round, and said, 'Sorry, I'm a stranger here myself.'

'Oh, what a *useless*—' I could have hit the man for turning round and raising my hopes for that.

He forced his way back to my side. 'Why do you want to know?'

'Oh, I might as well tell you—' I thought that as he was a pedlar he might not be fond enough of the law to tell on me—'A priest, one of the old régime, those who wear grey leather, he used to come here—'

'You just come back to the city? I hate to tell you, but he's probably been dead months, they've been killing them off—'

'No, I happen to know he was alive early last week at least—' I remembered his deep-sea eyes and his everything-face and how his presence cleansed and undemandingly made one not only whole but wholesome. Unconsciously I used his own phrasing. 'But where he is now I dare say they know only in the Land Beyond the Rain-gusts.'

His eyes narrowed.

'Why do you want to find him again?'

And then I was alert too, bravo, Cija the beautiful spy. 'I'm sorry, I'd prefer not to tell you till you tell me why you want to know why—'

'Mine was a normal query from a pedlar,' he said. 'But you seem to be hiding a guilty secret.'

I looked at him in alarm. He half-smiled.

'He described you to me—I couldn't mistake you,' said this pedlar, his accent losing its roughness. 'You're even wearing the same cloak he described you as wearing the day you engineered the escape.'

'He glimpsed me then?' I cried eagerly. 'And he knows *he* was the prisoner for whose sake it was done—he heard me call to Kond to release him—did he also recognise me—did he say he'd seen me before, as a page?—'

'A page?' The pedlar, quizzical, pushed back his hood a little to scratch his head of thick, long, pallid-gold hair. 'Well, everything's possible—and all that old man knows, they maybe realise in the Land Beyond the—'

'You've seen him recently? Where is he?'

'There is an inn with a big, brass sign in the 8th Winding Street from the 7th Bridge—wait, if I can find some charcoal I'll sketch you a map—'

'It's all right, I know this city very well. Thank you—

thank you very much—' We parted very briskly in our
opposite directions.

Now as I pushed my way on into the city I found that
many houses were on fire. At first I thought this due to
eruption-sparks. Then I saw how much looting was going
on—soldiers in Northern as many as Southern uniforms,
deserters, or wounded, but not too badly for this sport,
many of them drunk, too, roaring and firing empty houses
they'd emptied and, if they were Northern, also firing
inhabited houses to frighten out the occupants. One thing
interrupted all this jollity: if Southern and Northern met
looting the same house, they dropped all their plunder
and at once set on each other. There were camp-women
too—looting a confused city was better than watching
their men in battle. Going into houses in bands they were
efficiently rapacious. When they were with soldiers they
confined themselves more to receiving and sorting the stuff.

In the courtyard of a burning house, which a throng of
nuts in blackened Northern uniforms were busy ransacking,
a few women sat among piles of cloth, food, furniture and
jewellery, sorting it into baskets and laundry-bins and
shoeboxes and in fact any old thing. Needless to say, I was
hurrying all I could, limping so fast it was a dragging hop.
Each time I passed one nasty place I came to another, but
something about one of these women caught me and made
me look again.

She was sitting, greedily stuffing cheap gauds into a
biscuit-box. She wore patched dilapidated clothes. A man's
sweat-rag had been holding up her hair but slipped and
the long, black hair was all round her shoulders. Her face
was smoke-streaked, her glorious bones showing more
sharply than before, but it was easy to recognise the
Beauty—except that at first I hadn't thought to connect
her with this avid slattern.

Well, of course, all this time men were shouting out at
me, or catching at me; I was seized and kissed a couple of

times and once chased, which was awkward with my leg, but he was drunk and fell down before I did.

With all this I was as dirty and dilapidated as everyone else. I was also limping more joggily, you can't keep up limping speed for long.

To avoid a group of Southerners roaring along ahead, I turned up a roofed alley. It was very dark and when I cannoned into something I was horribly shaken.

'Oi-oi,' said a man's voice echoing in the tunnel. 'Look where yer going, mate.'

I tried to go on, but found my wrists gripped. I twisted and stopped short, he was really holding hard.

'What do you think you're doing?'

'It's an old trick, mate. Bash into someone in a dark alley, pick each other up apologetic, and off you go with my pocketful.' He started to frisk me, patting my pockets which were as barren as a great-grandmother, then his hand went into my shirt. 'Well,' he said. 'This is more interesting than a couple of jewelled goblets, isn't it?' His other hand crawled up my neck, the underside of my chin, pinching the flesh there a little, and up over my mouth and nostrils. His hand smelt of metal and dirt and blood and warmth. It explored further. 'You have nice hair, too.'

'Please let me go,' I said calmly. 'I'm in a hurry to get somewhere. It's important to me—I'm not bluffing.'

'I like to be asked so nice. But you'll need company in this area.'

'Don't change your direction for me.' 'I weren't going nowhere special.'

We emerged into the red glare. Immediately we turned to assess each other, and grinned as we caught the other's eyes. He was a big man, quite young, with a short, shapeless beard of coarse, black hair. I'd a right to resent his suspicion of me—he had a sack over his shoulder and it was full of loot.

'Well, where are you going?' he said.

'The 8th Winding Street from the 7th Bridge.' I didn't mention the inn in case I wanted to get rid of him later. 'Thank you for your company,' I said circumspectly.

He was useful, for no one at all any longer annoyed me with him there beside me, and he didn't ask all the questions I'd expected either.

But we soon passed a tavern and he said, would I like a drink? When I said, 'No' he said, Well, he would and I might as well have one with him as wait thirsty.

'But I told you, I'm in a hurry. please come on—or if you're dying of thirst, I'll go on alone. Thanks for coming this far.'

He gave me an amused look and came, but I could tell he was getting sullen underneath. He was thinking what was there in this for him after all, and he'd also come far enough with me and scared off enough trouble for him to think I owed him something. I decided I'd like to get rid of him soon, or else talk him into genuine friendliness, but with the city and men in this mood I wasn't hopeful.

'Do you know who's winning on the plain?' I said.

'Blasted Northerners,' he growled. 'But if our lot can hang on long enough there'll be reinforcements coming up, whole new army from the Temple-Town.'

'I hope Ael and his hoodlums have done their work well,' I thought.

'How did you get your leg in that state?' he said. I said it had been mauled while I was in the hills, and he said I was lucky I had him with me.

'Any of these scoundrels could have made quick work of you by now,' he said virtuously. 'Well, here we are already at the 8th Winder. Which house do you want?'

'It's all right, thanks, I can find it myself.'

'I get it. Well, we'll part here then. Give us a goodbye kiss.' I didn't want him to get nasty about being dismissed so I stood on tiptoe and put only one arm round his neck.

Before I knew what was happening he'd taken the opportunity to grab me. He hauled me over the ruins of a broken gate and into a fitfully red and black courtyard.

'Please—please—'

'Ah, now it won't take long. Not a virgin, are you?'

I was furious at the way I'd let myself be tricked, but I had to admit it didn't seem the end of the world. It was anger and fear more than horror that made me fight—a good thing because I think horror is physically weakening unless one is lucky enough to go actually a bit mad with it.

'Please—' I kept saying, but he took no notice. I hooked an arm over his shoulder and got one of the goblets in his sack and tried to stun him with it, but he seized it from me and laid the sack aside. He was trying to pin me down and though he was strong I wriggled too much, though it was only this way and that, I couldn't get free.

'You're only delaying yourself,' he remarked through teeth clamped into a grin in his beard. 'Come on now, what's so unfriendly about you? Anyone would think I was doing you a bad turn instead of having saved you a lot of bother.' His hand came past my face and I bit it as hard as I could—he grunted and tried to shake me off, but I hung on. Finally he hit me with the flat of his hand across the side of my head—not hard, but enough so my head swam and my teeth unclenched. He took his hand away, streaming red-hot blood, and we continued the fight. 'Think of your sack,' I said. 'If anyone came in now it'd be theirs for the taking—' 'This is a chance I'd sooner not miss,' he said, which I suppose I should have taken as a compliment, only I knew I was streaked with grime and tattered.

At last he got me hands-fast. I couldn't kick because of my leg. He lay on top of me and kissed me thoroughly. The maddening thing was that I found my body warm and expectant and it believed it right to be held curved close with his. My humiliation was sharp, only in my head.

Damn it, you can't really call it a rape, can you, when you're enjoying it?

He was very competent though rather heavy and I didn't have any more chance to fight. I shivered under him but when I said, 'Please—' I think we both knew it meant the opposite from before. I was crying and then felt very drowsy. He was considerate enough and also by then perhaps fond enough of me to hold me in his arms for a while and as I looked up I realised that the very same flame-glows were skedaddling about among the black shadows of this high-fenced courtyard, and we had indeed lost very little time.

'Let me up,' I said. 'I have to get on.'

He rose with me, half-supporting me, and we neither of us bothered to look at each other. I wanted to get away as quickly as possible and he knew that and had had what he'd wanted, but as I stumbled out over the gate-wreckage he came up beside me and said, 'Here,' thrusting something at me.

I hit it furiously away, he knew damned well I wasn't a whore.

'No, take it,' he said roughly. 'You may need it the way you're going round in this city, you're asking for bother.' And he made off, striding briskly.

What he'd left for me was a little statue, transparent crystal, not very valuable at all, though its long semi-circular eyes were a massed iridescence of tiny points of crystal and jewels. It was heavy, and what made me keep it was the least valuable-looking thing about it—perfect and unwithered in the vacuum of the statue's inside was a real flower, not artificial, but a kind I'd never seen before. It had a lot of curved, folded petals like glossy but very soft silk, shading from completely pure white to drowningly deep blue, flat violet leaves, and a central petal folded right over and so fine it was like a bubble with purple veins in it. I couldn't imagine where he'd got this statuette, possibly some temple. I wrapped it with the Diary in my cloak, in the inside top pocket he'd never reached, and I hurried on up the glaring cacophonous street.

I came to the inn. It had not been deserted. In fact it was crowded to overflowing. I went in and sat down.

I looked round and wondered who to approach. The tapsters were all busy and would it be stupid to trust them?

There was talk of the eruption, the battle and the dangerous streets. Everyone knew it was the end of an era for the Capital. Presently a big man walked in from outside. He had only red wounds where his eyes had been and he was berserk angry with the world about it. He lurched straight to the long bar-counter and with his hand oblivious of cuts swept all the glass tumblers and metal tankards off it to the floor. One of the customers put a hand on his shoulder and he bellowed and turned on him. A free-for-all started, I'll never know how they do, people are just eager and being the very first is the only thing they don't like but if someone else will begin they're fine. The tapsters waded in, clonking everyone on the head with brooms and shoving them outside where the fight continued.

Someone came up to me. 'Out of here, girlie.'

'I was doing no harm—and I want to talk to the inn-master.'

'You all do. No, we've had enough.'

He hustled me to the door and felt the bulges in my cloak. 'Ho, what have we here?'

'Nothing of yours.'

'We have to make sure—' He gaped at the statuette. Then I was very glad I hadn't cringed and sworn innocence, which is always a temptation when one's been pushed around as much as I have. He at once leapt to the right conclusion (though actually the wrong one) and respectfully asked me to sit down again.

'I'm sorry, please forgive me, it's so easy to suspect the wrong people nowadays. Boss! There's a lady to see you.'

A burly man with a nice tough face appeared. The tapster said, 'She brought this, wanted to see you.'

The inn-master took it reverently and smiled at me. 'Thank you. We were sure it was lost forever, it was nowhere to be found. It seemed too much to hope that one of us had got hold of it, but here we are after all. This is marvellous. I see you've a bad leg. We'll boil some new bandages for it while you feed.'

'Is the priest here?'

'Which, love?'

'The old one—the one with a face like—'

He smiled at my inability to describe him and went away. Later he came back. 'He's in the cellar. Jeel, light her down.'

Jeel the tapster's candle threw huge descending shadows. The walls were dripping with slime when we'd gone down three twisting flights. I waited, desperately weary, while Jeel moved a chest and levered up the trapdoor it'd stood on. The perpendicular rusty iron ladder which led down inside the trapdoor was nasty work what with my leg, and Jeel unable to help much because of the candle, which wasn't very happy anyway in the damp, musty air, not that *we* loved it. Also the ladder swung a bit, it wasn't fixed at the bottom; I suppose this was so if anyone unwelcome climbed down if they could be given a violent series of swings from the top till they fell off.

At the bottom. Now we walked along a slimy stone passage, opened a well-oiled door and suddenly the air was better and it was warmer. My priest was sitting at a table with a good meal. There was a fire and ventilation from a revolving wall-screw, obviously the end of an air-well.

The priest didn't say anything, just grinned at me and that meant welcome and recognition of all that had previously passed between us.

'When you and the young lady's finished, the Boss says he thinks it a good idea if you come up,' said Jeel. 'It

wouldn't be very gay if you was stuck down here if any
earthquakes started. And there's such confusion up top,
you're as likely to be killed without any malice at all,
they've no time to recognise you if you're in disguise,
which you are.'

'Earthquakes!' I said. 'It's only an eruption.'

'Well, I don't know about the city,' said Jeel, but earthquakes on the plains are giving the armies bother, that's
the latest. You can't very well fight a battle when the
battlefield's splitting up under your feet and besides, divid-
ing all the companies.' He left.

'Feed, child,' said the priest. I watched him as I obeyed.
He was making a hearty meal, using both hands, and was
wearing black and grey rags like any layman. 'I have to
thank you for many things,' he said.

'Not so many—I came to ask a favour—'

It's a small hope, I said to myself, but while he listened
I told him all about Ooldra—my sin with her son, my
brother Smahil, the whispers, the lot. 'Is there anything
can be done?'

'It seems she hated you so much, and was with you so
long, that she stays now she is dead, bound by a link of
malignant concentration. And you were laid open. It is
more terrible that he is her son than your father's. But you
have many things to expiate and nullify. Apparently your
birth was in every way very inauspicious. Evil and good
are balancing each other on a hair-fine quivering equi-
librium; if one gets too great, it will overbalance the
other. You have to fight harder than most people. But I
dedicate you to absolving your birth prophecy in a bigger
way than revenge on Zerd for little ravages. Do you accept
this?'

'What must I do?'

'Warn Atlan. So far all attempts have failed—but a
small, lone girl may have a better chance of slipping

through the coast-watch, and you already seem to be good at survival. Can you swim?'

'Quite well.'

'I will give you your instructions later,' he said calmly. 'Now put out all the candles but one. And stay close to me and quite quiet.' His voice became very gentle, as if he were about to weep over something. 'Close your eyes.'

Immediately I was in blackness, no light of candle or fire seemed to penetrate my lids. For a while I heard him breathing steadily but as if under strain—then that sound went. Suddenly I was afraid in emptiness, I wanted to open my eyes to see if he were still there but they were not mine to open, they were heavy and cold as all my muscles.

Then, after dark emptiness in which I had forgotten movement, I did feel something stirring. And it was in me, but not mine. Some coldness was moving in me. At first it was vaguely pleasant, this stirring, and I was in the darkness which I realised was myself, or at least my consciousness, and it was vast, though I couldn't feel all of it at the same time.

Now the movement which was not me was a fast turmoil, it was beginning to thrash wildly, sending waves of me against myself. I tried to cry out but my mouth was too far away. Then I realised that its agony was far, far worse than mine, that it was being torn out of me.

I could hear the priest's voice far away and above, but each word was not a sound, it was a weight. They were falling like sledgehammers and the thing in me was squirming wildly to avoid them.

'Ooldra—' said the priest in conclusion. She knew she had been recognised to her central essence. The other words had been each commanding and terrible, and besides all together had formed a pattern from which there was only one way out. She gave a cry, half a scream, and it was the most passionate, desolate sound I've ever heard.

It was not a sound from a human throat, it was stripped of all memory of humanity. It was harsh with despair, but despair still passionate, as it faced into the total loss. The chill that ran up my spine I welcomed: it told me I was still in the world.

I saw the flames and felt my body.

'I love you, Highest God,' I said aloud from the love that was in me, that had grown from that endless glimpse of the agony of evil.

'And the agony of evil,' said the priest, 'is the light of the Highest God seen by those that have rejected him though he is in their selves. He is still in their self, but they are too shrivelled to bear it.'

It seemed a long time later, after we had rested, that we took the one candle and were climbing up the way I had come. I was remembering my own little God, my Cousin in Divinity, as I clung to the swaying ladder, and thanking him for making it that statuette the man had given me instead of anything else in his sack. I was thinking of all sorts of little things—a twisted nail in the wall, the slanting candle flame, a strand of hair in my eyes—just as I had when I was riding in the carriage with my mother and Ooldra, going to do away with our enemy.

As they bathed my leg in the inn's back-room, the huge thought lulled me. Just like that he had said, 'Warn Atlan' —and that was why I had been spared through so much.

Should I ever see inside of that last memory of the World as it was created, that last stronghold of Divine peace, which had sealed itself anciently and remained sealed while the rest of the World multiplied in mortal turmoil, each petty nastiness contributing to the high mass-meaning evil?

The battle was over.

Yes, the Southern reniforcements had arrived from the

Temple-Town, but they were like a stag with a puma on its back, the brigands in small bands from first to last had not let up worrying and decimating them, and hardly one had been caught in return. The battlefield had heaved and cracked: nearly whole platoons had disappeared at a time, according to the survivors. These were swarming into the city. In every doorway, on every pavement and in the gutters they were resting, tending each others' wounds, looting, and continuing the battle without any organisation. The surviving officers were faced with a superhuman task in gathering them together let alone controlling them, and many officers, particularly Southerners who had not so much to lose, were shrugging their shoulders and letting go.

My priest and I bade the inn farewell and thanks, were given knives and hurried out into the chaos with our cloak-hoods well down over our faces. The air was very hot now.

We steadily made towards the plain, which with luck we could cross. We'd then be safely on our way to the coast.

'If we can always keep a little ahead of the war—' I said hopefully.

'This World is doomed to war,' he said cheerfully, slapping out sparks which had caught his cloak. 'It will end in war, having been in war ever since the gods were tempted by the sight of the daughters of men, and fell. I had always thought that a good thing!—but remain deeply fond of my Cousin, especially now I know he's a real World-god and by his nature implicated right up to the nose in the affairs of this World and no other.

The priest hadn't yet told me what to do to get from the coast actually *into* Atlan—he said he'd tell me when we were out of the city. It was urgent that no one have the slightest chance of overhearing. At last, Atlan to be entered—Certainly the end of an era.

The priest said, 'The Earth-Serpent has entered the

lists: in Heaven's timeless War with Hell, the Earth gods, those who loved men and fell and became one with this World, and are drunk with the dark Earth, and yet though they fell from Heaven are not Evil, for Earth has its own rightness as it has its own centre of gravity—those gods were not till now in the War, but they are in essence war-gods—and their strong blind-sighted offspring the Serpent will bring earth-war to the Land Beyond the Rain-gusts, and pierce its Heavenliness with the powerful scales of his own mortality, and thenceforth the earth will be all of Earth.'

Presently we came to a square where Northerners were lying in untidy rows. Their wounds were being tended by overworked surgeons who seemed to have lost most of their instruments and anaesthetics—beside them dog-tired officers, still in blood-caked uniforms, held candles and tried not to drop tallow on the patients whose wounds were being dug at with penknives sterilised by being passed through candle-flame.

Suddenly we were startled by a sort of hoarse choking cry behind us over the steady groans and moans.

'Cija!'

I turned. An officer, nearly unrecognisable under blood and weariness and dirt and smoke-black, leapt towards me and suddenly I was clasped tight to him, my nose squashed on buttons.

'Cija!'

'Smahil, please, Smahil—' I disengaged myself with a strength of revulsion.

'Gods, I haven't seen you since the day we left here a season ago—have you been here all the time? What's happened? Your leg—Tell me everything—Have you been all right all this time? Why couldn't you join me?'

'I didn't want to, Smahil.'

Something in my tone stopped him and made him look at me. There was a pause; then he said, 'You bitch', softly.

'Ah, no, Smahil—Listen—Smahil—'

I had forgotten the priest who stood waiting while I told Smahil all I'd discovered.

'You see now? We're brother and sister—'

'So what? It only makes it more interesting.'

His tone and manner were off-hand, his eyes glittering in his pale face. I could tell I'd made him furiously angry about something.

'So you want to get back to your demon lover and you're seizing any excuse to leave the only person who's ever been any good for you—bravo, it's even a virtuous excuse and you've always been hot on virtue—'

'You know there's nothing between him and me—'

'So I'm your moony Ooldra's son, so the High Priest's my father, so OK this is a shock to me, I always knew I was a foster-child but this is a shock to me—and all you can do is leave me. You hate me because we've made love, you never want to touch me again, it's all over your face and the way you're acting—'

Yes, I did hate him then. All right. No, I disliked him—but I wanted to tell him how he's always *owned* me, how at times he drove me frantic with that, and most important how although even the haunt of his mother was at last dead (though he wouldn't understand that) and so we were out of danger if we did continue in our sin, I was starting on a high mission and had to leave him. But he gave me no chance to say all this.

'By everything in you, Cija, I hope one day, one day but it will only be after many more years, you'll realise how immature you are. You've never even loved, have you? Have you? Your torrid emotional life has been confined to a bird and a little serving-girl—and a girlish fascination for the big, bad General.'

'I love him,' I said in a low, vehement voice, indicating the priest who was wandering from us, moving his feet in a little sort of tap-dance, tactfully paying no more attention to us, but looking at the wounded for whom only surgery could do anything.

'That elderly labourer? I suppose you think he looks fatherly. I've never seen such a lecherous, sly face—'

'It's wonderful, a *total* face—'

'See that shack, planks slanted against the wall over there? You'll find an orderly boiling soup in there. I'll be with you soon.'

'No, Smahil—'

About to walk away, he turned back, his brows down, whole face edgy.

Our eyes met. He caught me to him. 'We'll discuss it tonight—little sister. Go on, and don't worry, Don't worry. I've always know, what's best for you—I'll look after you. Off you go.'

'Smahil,' I was desperately worried, but for a moment wanted to touch my finger to his scar, then drew back for it was newly opened, 'I'm not staying with you. I'm going with my friend there—'

'Oh, are you?' His eyes glittered, but with even more impatience than anger. 'That's soon put a stop to.' He strode to the priest, who was stooping over a casualty, ran his sword through him and without waiting to watch him collapse said to me 'Get some soup inside you till I come', and walked away to continue with his duty.

I ran to the priest, crouched by him, lifted his head from the chest of the wounded man who moaned faintly for water.

My priest was quite dead. His face was still his in every way except that the twinkle in his eye had already become opaque.

So who now would show me the way to Atlan?

t I had pledged myself to that, and soon I was on the irts of the plain. Emerging from the crowded city, t and eyes numb, I met the shambles of the plain and realised only then that I had seen nothing as I traversed the streets.

The plain looked like the heaving chest of a prone giant, but this was not because the earthquake was still continuing. The ground at the edges of the great brand-new gaping fissures was still trembling, and every now and then a clod would drop thundering to the bottom—otherwise the movement came from thousands of crawling or upright men and animals, helping each other out of the fissures, giving a shifting appearance to the edges of the several immense mounds which hadn't existed last time I was here.

The row was terrible, screams of wounded men, and frightened animals which careered around increasing the numbers of the wounded, and the cries of those caught in the cracks.

Large black sky-birds were already wheeling above it all, uttering harsh cries, and increasingly landing on mounds and settling down to gorge.

Enormous grave-pits were being dug, and corpses tipped in: other units were building pyres of corpses and firing them, which smelt horrible.

I noted an odd disturbance and went nearer. Then I saw that some people were watching, some feebly dragging themselves out of the area of a fight between two great birds, riderless, the elaborate harness awry on their bodies like a signature of man's attempt to subjugate such elemental force: it was not the birds but the harness which looked ridiculous.

They had obviously met after the excitement of the battle and something had slashed them mutually into one of those characteristic rages. Unlike fights between other species of bird, there would have been very little ogling or fighting shy; they would have darted right in at each other with immediate savagery. Horrid murder-eager barks, thick blood and big, curved feathers hit the air.

I don't think I was watching so much as I stood in that

thin ring of spectators, I was waiting. I had known it
would be, even before I recognised the one-eyed, black
bird—the other was a speckled grey with half its crest torn
off—and I stood there, wind in my hair and clothes,
various aspects of the death-smell everywhere, the blood
coursing through my veins while I stood—For yes, all
comes to that blood, to me: I had been given the statuette by what seemed the luckiest coincidence, and now
that I was about to start on a journey it was really about
time I sank my fear of the bird—and here it was. It would
be very useful, when it had done with this fight.

The rapid wings rasped, the feathers came, the hooked
beaks thrust in and tore out after a brief stay, the spurs
were in danger of becoming locked but they were intelligent fighters. I was annoyed at the thought that they
would tear each other to pieces. But Ums was not badly
damaged, and the grey already becoming exhausted. He
had been pierced in many places; and with a guttural
squeak he sank to the ground, a heap of blood and feathers.
Ums in a sort of dainty paroxysm did a little dance on him,
occasionally bending to sink his beak in him, and then
gradually quietened and presently stood still, staring with
his one eye out over the battlefield.

So I began to walk to him.

A Southern NCO caught at me. 'No, miss—not over
there. Just because he's stopped a moment don't mean
he's not still dangerous. If you're looking for someone—'

'No. It's all right. He's my bird.'

'Oh? I seem to remember there was our commander Iro
riding him—no sign of him now. But even if you haven't
made a mistake, miss, don't think he can be approached
now. He won't know you, and if he did it wouldn't make
no difference,' he said ominously.

The bird stood like an arch-beaked, two-legged, black
monolith, giant against the wheeling, croaking, red sky,
the horizon low, flat and distant between his legs.

I continued to approach him. At first I had a low feeling of loss—oh, yes—Lel—Iro dead—but really, Lel had long since ceased to be any of my business. And there'll always be someone to succeed Iro. I continued to approach. The blind eye was grey, the staring eye red with the frozen triumph of the animal, where a human would be merely exhausted. When they had given him to me, before each new meeting was a little more and a little more a giving of myself to him, they'd told me he'd lost that eye in a fight over a female. Well, that female was long since forgotten, and now I am approaching him to take up again that fierce loneliness between us.

He sensed the approach—the eye in a swift bird-movement cocked my way; for a moment I felt panic, I felt that he is far too elementally an earth creature to have been sent to me to help Atlan, leave him alone, go on your way, stop taking every coincidence as a personal tribute—

He stared and then stalked towards me. It was different from the mad, rushing scamper he's always used before. His eye glowed into mine. He uttered a series of short, quick, staccato barks. Then he thrust his head under my arm and crooned and crooned and crooned.

The Southern NCO looked at me in amazement and awe.

I put my foot in the stirrup, having pulled it straight, and was in the saddle.

I had hardly to twitch the reins before, with that complete almost pre-understanding which has always existed between us, he had turned in the direction I wanted.

He picked his way, claws spread, over the mangled dead, separate arms and ears, horses' nostrils, smeared together, the flotsam of every battlefield.

Behind us the funeral fires churned up russet-purple into the sky.

— IV —

THE POSSESSION

As we left the environs of the City behind us and came among the high, harsh, black pines, I think we were pursued by animals like big pumas. It was strange. They were never near enough for me to know what exactly they were, and whether they were after us or busy with each other. I thought even that it might be one swift one, as we didn't see more than one at a time, but it would have to be in such different places so quickly. I don't know if Ums noticed, he didn't turn, only his crest was laid back. Then in a burst of eruption-light I saw three big pumas bounding at us. In some lights they seemed silver, in some glaring golden. I was not sure if they were really white like mine in the mountains. Later we went among many trees, and didn't see them again.

We slept against each other, way past where the town gathers in the hoop of the lazy, slavering moors. On the long journey from here to the coast, there would be no more civilisation. I did not know what I could do when we reached the coast; meanwhile it was enough to get there. The night was full of sounds of wilderness. The wind screamed through the stark, purple grasses. Ums was very warm. We had eaten a good meal; I'd cooked the lizard, nearly three feet long, which he'd killed. I'd had to stamp

188

out the embers, the wind would have carried them everywhere in an instant like dangerous seeds. It had been hard
work keeping the fire from blowing out or getting too big.
We had fallen back easily into the old way of his taking
half the raw meat of his kill, letting me take the rest for
my cooking. Actually I always take less than half, as he
needs more, though like all magnificent fighting animals
he is lean and can exist on a minimum.

Somehow I'd thought I'd never have another nightmare
after Ooldra's exorcism. Yet there was a sense of warning
which made me sulky.

I suddenly started awake; the warning receded and
there was only stillness flowing into and into and into the
bowl of the night, and the thin, high kreeep-kreeep, kreeep-
kreeep of the crickets was the pattern on the side of the
bowl.

Dawn is falling into the night.

I close my eyes and hear the sough of the wind across the
plains. The soughing of the wind lives here. A man could
be born and live and die here, and every minute of his
life hear the regular beat, the distant roar, the show-
owowoow of the wind.

There are not and will be no farms, cottages, huts, bridges.
The plain stretches to every side, bright gold, trees
ignoring their shadows, taut menace behind every line of
tall grass, tiny animals and large insects before our feet,
somewhere over there the sea, there mountains (always
mountains) with their blue, white, grey, mauve and purple shades suggesting valleys of firs and high, stark slopes
with scree and caves and huge, warm, unfriendly, shaggy
bears.

The early morning sky was a kind of yellow. And the
sun, like a white hole in the yellow, pouring out light . . .

I remembered the Superlativity teaches that the sun is the glory of thousands of pure souls all shining together.

I knew that speed was necessary, and once we found the river all we'd have to do would be to follow it South and East, so I was glad when we came upon a sort of network of shallow streams running all together over a vast expanse of pebbles, each pebble glinting whether or not under water, the water blue and a clean white skull here and there, where some animal had breathed its last by the water—there were no other kinds of bones, they must all have been carted away by scavengers for their marrow.

We went all together towards the river—Ums and I, the little streams plinkling busily, the many small, shrill, blue birds overhead. I halted Ums with my knees. By our path a lone blue rock rose higher than my head; a spring gushed from it in a great hurry to join the others. It was little, and I waited a long time till the thin trickle would cup fully to the brink of my hands. I drank, then waited another while for full hands, then bent forward over Ums' head and got him to drink. He slurped sideways to avoid cutting me, but it was not enough and we got acrid milk from spurge plants later.

Ums objected to the little blue birds. They twittered and swooped in patterns low above our heads. I was enjoying this prettiness and did not realise it was irking his everready rage till he rose up, stretching his neck so I had to cling, and gave as long a hoarsebellow as he could sustain. They fled for a little way, then they were back again and beneath us the streams in the same joyous haste.

The pebbles and streams became a river over the bank of a rise. We rose too; we had come out of a dip in the plain, and the sky and river were turbulent with dark grey and dark white, and the wind meets us like a curling, turning, curling, spurling sea-edge all waves and patterns and he breasts it and its blast strikes us and does not slay and the wind parts and runs past us like a river.

My hair and clothes follow the backwards rider's-lean of my body. My Cousin! What it is to ride one with a creature whose each savage stride is part of a rhythm like the swiftened, terrible rhythm of the mountains growing.

The wind's force against my breast, against us, is so great that at first I am lost in wind, my six senses aware only of wind, then the force of our motion into it is more highly active.

And the rhythm continues with each savage stride.

Later the wilderness became less sullen. Armadillos scurried in the scrubby undergrowth. Over there long ripple after long ripple makes it seem as if the tall, saffron grasslands are gliding towards us, but it is only wind scudding the thousands of feathery grass-heads against the flanks of the herds grazing in it. There are boar, grunting, hacking, turning bloodshot pratically useless eyes here and there; the wind is ours inasmuch as it does not tell their disgusting nostrils of us. There, majestic as unhurried swimmers, dark and shambling on the horizon, mammoth: the leader's tusks are growing at such a back-curve that in a few more years they will have got his own eyes—perhaps he will have been able to keep their points at bay by filing them on bark. There are lumbering, trundling, giant ground sloth, desiccating foliage.

These great bulks, in their own element, would have crushed me with terror before even noticing me, had I been alone. Now I was a lord of the wilderness, for I rode one of their lords, one of the swiftest, fiercest and strongest, and he was my loyal companion; he would let nothing happen to me.

Several times we saved time by crossing loops of the river, now broad and swift and shining, blue enclosed between its high, rocky, flowering banks. Ums trod daintily down these, in places nearly perpendicular, then stepped without stride-change into the swift blue where it gurgled at the bank-foot. Often, still without altering rhythm, I would find him swimming under me; a broad spear-head wake following us across the noisy, glittering, blue and white currents. Once there came a disturbance: I thought we were approaching one of those periodic whirlypools which had suddenly appeared before us; but it was approaching us, and presently the head slid up out at us. It came at us, longer than Ums' own, and grinning with ruthless conceit. I thought, 'What can be done? Ums is not in his element, smaller than this thing, and hampered by me.'

This was a river-snake, an amphibian with a long, glaucous body merging into tail (competently thrashing water) and covered, I now saw, with a starring of yellow warts. These constellations nestled in the wrinkles of a skin which must be far too thick even for Ums' beak to pierce easily— and the beak it would have to be, for his claws were underwater. He continued to swim towards the reptile which continued to bear down on us. It took no notice of me, except that there may have been slight amusement and contempt in the huge, gold-speckled, oval eyes fixed on Ums. Here was a creature which allowed men to ride it! Its long snout writhed, revealing diseased gums edged with bone, a single, circular tooth. A sort of ululating shriek of anticipated triumph echoed over the river; Ums made no sound but continued straight at the onslaught, lifted and thrust his neck, sank his beak between those two eyes which went glassy amazed and offended—there was a blood-spout—Ums uttered several barks, started a wide detour just in time to avoid even the first of the convulsions as the tail was so far away it took a few minutes for the news it was dying to reach it, and we elegantly climbed up the farther bank, leaving behind us the now purple river.

When we reached bushes half hidden under wild vines,

it was high time I dismounted. My leg was stiff of course, also sore, but obviously on the mend and all the better for being forgotten a while. I ate a great deal—found gold sloes near, also huckleberries which I was hungry enough to eat though it's a nuisance, continual seed-spitting. It wasn't really a filling meal, still less for Ums, but we also found a nest deserted among reeds—four largish oval eggs, three to him and one to me (a little raw egg goes a long way for me) which we pierced and sucked.

After all this, and running water too, I lay down under a fragrant vine-tangle in which gauzy insects skittered round—of course I never tether him.

I wrote quite a while in this book and was astonished when a chilly feeling made me look up and out and I saw how low the sun was in the sky. I leapt up, clutching Diary and pencil dangling on its tape (nearly frayed through in places now) and looked for Ums. He was in sight— actually I shouldn't think he'd ever let me out of his sight, which is both possessive and protective, especially in a place like this—and though I didn't like to call and attract I don't know what monster's attention, he soon looked up, saw me standing watching him, and came at once. He extended to me a claw with a rather mangled lizard, but I showed him it was to be his and he swallowed it and I mounted.

Dusk fell around us like the drifting settling of un-numbered tiny mauve motes.

I'm such a fine heroine, so fit to save almost-lost causes. Never underestimate the army.

Soon, in the dusk, I came upon a Southern encampment, just settling down for the night and all heads turning startled as I, equally startled, spurred Ums right through them, spattering the sparks of the fire they were just in the process of lighting.

Well, I thought as we settled back into a steady canter, that's done it. How often does a girl on a Northern bird ride through their camp and on? But I was on them so suddenly in this dark, wooded country, I didn't have enough warning to skirt such a sizeable camp. There's no sound of pursuit. They must have decided to let me go—I'm only one, and not even a soldier. That'll teach me to think myself so far ahead that I can afford to relax. Of course, they must know more about this terrain than I can—which river-loops to miss, for instance. I had a head-start when I set off but I might well have ruined everything.

Later still I was hunched in thought on Ums lolloping along under a starry sky, when I became aware that his crest was rising and he was giving low throat-snarls. Almost at once I heard a whirr, felt something yank me off the saddle. I cried out. The lasso dragged me on the ground, though one foot (luckily the good one) was still entangled in the stirrup and Ums was rearing and would soon be charging in the opposite direction.

Then four men on ponies approached from the dark trees, zig-zagged towards him so he didn't know where to charge, and though he was soon fighting hard they managed to get my foot from the stirrup incidentally to muzzling him. By the rope on the muzzle they dragged him to a nearby tree to which they tethered him. He went on barking and striking muzzle and claws into the tough bark, making short dashes as far as he could.

I was picked up and immediately swung at my dark companions. But with a low guffaw someone caught my arm and held it away.

'What is this?' I said. 'Can't a traveller go a few miles even in the wilderness, without interference?'

'Bring a brand over and let's see what we've got,' said someone. 'Sounds like a youngster or a girl.'

A brand was brought, which told me there must be a fire well hidden behind the trees. It was thrust nearly in my face. I winced and blinked. The glare lit not only my face but theirs—

'Bandits!' I said. 'What *is* this?'

'By the Dugs of my Mother, if it's not that whey-faced lady-girl, the one the Northern Dragon left with us and Kond got killed with,' said a jovial man with lank plaits.

'What're you doing here, love?'

'We thought you was a lone Southerner, that's why we treated you this way. Sorry. Your leg all right?'

'Perhaps she is working for them. Why else should she be riding round here?'

'Use your nut. To join the Dragon when he arrives.'

'A right devil of a bird she got hold of, didn't she?'

I said, 'The Dragon? Is he coming?'

'Be here tomorrow morning, I should think, yes. Didn't you know, then? There's a Southern camp, maybe you sniffed them, over the rise; they want to reach the coast and warn their navy to be ready before the main Southern and Northern forces have time to get there—half the navy's supposed to be in the middle of careening right now, which'll be a right old hitch for them—they don't know we've been trailing them all day. We're gonna fall on them tonight when they're snoring their sweet dreams.'

'Well,' I said reluctantly, 'they no longer think they're quite alone. They saw me—' I didn't say I'd galloped right among them.

'Ah, don't worry, it's a nuisance but don't think you've bitched it all. Just, it'll mean a fight sooner and not so easy. Though actually I'd've thought they'd be after you before now. They're a slow lot. Or perhaps they thought you was coming to join a camp they'd not guessed of—so maybe they've got scouts out now, sniffing for us.'

'I've brought a lot of trouble—' I said feebly.

'Don't mean a thing to us, darling. Near half of us were against falling on them asleep, but howled down by the rest. In a case like so, the chief lets the vote decide it, d'y'see. Now we've won after all—makes a better fight if they're all awake. I'll just tell all our lot to be ready—they

don't need it. We're always ready enough for anything.'
The man with plaits made off behind the trees.

I turned to another bandit, whose gold ear-rings in the shape of nude couples cast a glimmer on his face.

'Do you mind giving me back my bird?' I said humbly. 'I'm on a private mission—got to get somewhere in a hurry—'

'Private mission in *this* kind o' land, eh? Oh, well, maybe you know what you think you're talking about. But how you can ride that demon at the best of times I dunno. And now you're here you may as well get a bite— we'll attend to your demon, too, if you like—and then watch the fight or make off again, whichever you like. If you leave us now you may only ride straight into the arms of their scouts.'

He led me down a dip, behind the screen of trees, and I was in a hollow lit by several fires whose argent wood-smoke was lost long before it could top the surrounding foliage. There was not much noise, but nobody was falling over himself to keep silent. My teeth watered as I was sat down and was given a hunk of roast festooned with strip-sliced onions. A few hungry curious hyaenas stared with pale eyes from among the boles at the top of the further slope—Ael and his new second-in-command were holding a conversation with each other as they urinated against a tree-trunk over there, and the man with plaits waited civilly till they had finished and turned to him, rebuckling their belts.

I supposed their attention was being drawn, among other things, to me but I was too busy eating to watch.

'Not having milk?'

I turned round and there they were watching me, but not grinning or looking pleasant.

I didn't know what on earth to say so I shrugged and went on eating, getting rather smeared with fatty gravy.

They lowered themselves on to the long flattened grass,

which served as a thick straw mat, the second-in-command to my left and Ael to my right.

Ael reached a brawny scar-patterned arm ended by a dagger, sliced off a roast-hunk, and bent to gnaw it. 'You've come a little late,' he said, not looking at me. 'The Dragon's already asked for you—I said I sent her on to you, with two of my men. Their bodies were found on the battlefield, and the chariot she should have been in was discovered empty on the hillside with the remains of a hefty meal beside it, he told me. This is a great pity, I said politely. But the Dragon said, She can't be dead. Who would have kidnapped her, I said reasonably, and yet not yet contacted you for the ransom. We decided perhaps they, or she, or both, were killed just before they could. He was angry and distrait. His two brows became one bar, and that black. But I said my rascals must have died defending you, and because we need each other he took that, and there was no schism because of the betrayed trust.' He wiped his mouth along the harsh back of his arm. 'He will not think to find you with us any more,' he said.

'So you aren't keeping me here to give to him, since he doesn't expect it? I can journey on after this—this kind hospitality?' I said gladly . . . 'Bustling little bitch,' said the second without any particular malice.

'To go where, in this wilderness?' said Ael, his composed voice and look quite opposite to the sudden action of his body as he hurled a bone across the glade and hit a hyaenodon which yowled affrontedly and limped away whining. Ael giggled a little.

I was trying to think quickly of an answer which would acquit me of trying to get to the coast to warn the Southern navy, when there was a completely unexpected burst of howls out of the darkness and the Southerners who had found our position and crept up were upon us. They must have dealt with the sentry.

In a flash I was alone at the cooking-fire, staring bemused at hunks of deserted roast. Every bandit had seized his sawedged knife and chopper-ended spear, and sprung forming an instantaneous mêlée. The glade suddenly rang with the clash and gurgling shouts. The hyaenas stared in amazement from the distance to which they'd retreated, but presently ran down and began tugging away the meat farthest from the fight. The foliage swayed with disturbed birds, but I couldn't hear their rustling above the din.

I got up, stuffing meat and onions into my hood and getting a long-lidded pitcher of rum hooked by its handle through my belt. I hurried over to Ums and untethered him. (He'd already been unmuzzled to be fed.) I mounted.

About to ride him up the bank, I paused.

The fighting bands were about the same size. The bandits fought like devils, it was their trade, unmindful of themselves as long as they could hew down the opponent in as short a time as it could all be over. But many of the Southerners were mounted, and though ever ready with their arms the bandits had not had time to unhobble their ponies.

I spurred Ums back to the scene.

I had only a knife, given me at the priest's inn, but this I brought slicing down on any Southern anatomy I could see. All my usual hesitancy and squeamishness was submerged by my long hate for the uncleanness of the Southern civilisation. I sliced for the child-wives buried alive, for the artificial vegetables, for the gentle priests murdered. I had no time to be appalled by the butchery I was causing—I was dodging the next stroke and causing more. Ums needed no second bidding. He was the reason I could venture thus and stay protected by his height and ferocity. He reared and clawed and butted with that horrible hook on the end of his beak. He clawed down only those whom I chose. The bandits redoubled their battle-exultant yells. I had never been in any battle. The lid of the pitcher at my side broke open and swung clattering on its hinge while the rum gushed out over the Southerners on foot. Ums pulled down a horse, a stallion whose eyes and nostrils flared vermilion as he side-feinted to get Ums' throat with his noble big yellow teeth, but the beak was too quick, it ripped into his lung and he rolled over on his rider.

My first battle was over. Remaining Southerners skulked away to their awkwardly large camp. Bandits jeered after them.

Over, the slashing maiming, the orgasmic slaying, the throbbing, reasonless, dark life in the womb of an earth-goddess. I looked at my hands and wrists and they were bloody, the hilt of my knife slimy and its blade disgusting.

Between my legs the bird quivered and barked. This it had helped me to. Could I be cleansed?

Ael walked to my side. He stood there, his head not much below the level of mine. He took my knife, of which nervelessly my fingers let him relieve me, wiped it methodically with the tall grass near, handed it back to me. His deep blue eyes did not move from mine.

'Never leave a blade to rust,' he said in his light high voice.

'You think I deserve killer's lessons?'

'You are new to me,' he said. 'I've not known a woman slay so well, and yet you're a woman.'

I looked the few inches through the muzzy dusk to the depths of his eyes.

'You are kind to notice me at last,' I said. I felt a triple uncleanness, gentle and languid and welcoming, Ums' and my own and his, yet everything was really the same.

'You're a child,' Ael mused. 'I wondered why Zerd valued you. Yet you've much to learn. I will teach you. You've found yourself freedom, a fine mount, and done much on your own. You hate the military and government of this country as much as we do. Do you hate the Northern military too? No one shall give you back. Among us

you are safe, with the lawlessness we maintain strictly.
Postpone whatever reason it is you want to reach the
coast. We'll get there. I'll teach you the two arts—love
and war,' the bandit chief reached up his coruscated arm
for me to take and so dismount.

I kneed Ums, who at once lolloped into motion, up over
the rim and on into the night.

Two days later we reached the coast. The river became
more impetuous as I became more cautious—then the
surge and boom and surge was clearly heard, resolved
from the low sibilant pounding it had lately been in my
ears—then finally I saw a horizon of shimmering flatness.
Blue, grey, silver—a cloud of spume, battering the rocks
between which our foaming river thrust itself. I was seeing
again the sea. I have not seen the sea since my childhood.

For years, and years (seventeen years, I watched the sea
in its numberless moods. I watched it blue and flat; I
watched it mauve and crawling, slightly wrinkled, like an
ancient crocodile; I watched it crawl away and leave a
wavy-ribbed stretch of purple ooze, dotted, pitted with
debris unidentifiable through distance; I watched its smile
lilt glittering under the glittering sun; I watched it, a
robust sighing wraith, under a mezzanine sky of wheeling,
mewing, suntouched birds, under rose or green or crimson or gold sunset, under twilight, under eclipsing dusk,
under black night and night drowning stars in the intent
mirror-eye of its darling; I watched it huge and gusty,
white and blue, uproarious with winds; I watched it foaming on beaches overhung by trees, beaches which climbed
swiftly to become mountainous slopes; occasionally I saw
tiny figures race along the white shores, or into the sucking,
swift blue laced with white aureoles and high-flung, quivering mists of foam—they dragged in wriggling-silver-
glinting-heavy nets, but I could not see more than their
tininess, and I thought them females. I was not so placed

that it was possible for me to see any harbour, any boats, or ships of trade. The city's bay was behind the nearest mountain. I watched the sea grey, shiny under drizzle; grey, churning under heavy rain; I watched it black, rising and howling, its foam rearing high and whirling in funnels, lashed by storms. But always I was high above it, safe, untouched, its virile smell, the details of its action far below me and totally inaccessible.

Since then I had met the harbour-mouth of a great river, crowded with shipping and lined by wharfs, but now I had come upon the ground floor of the shore; I looked cautiously round, but could see no coastguard, let alone sign that I had come anywhere near the careening navy. I left Ums and advanced between the rocks; there were stiff star-shaped flowers on them. A sort of tortoise-spider, big and red and as though covered with shell, scuttled away sideways. I passed the rocks, taking off my sandals because of all the little green rock-pools, in which I glimpsed lovely moving things, or perhaps they were just still and water-swayed, and presently fine gritty sand spurted between my toes. I kicked away a tangling ribbon of rubbery green, then the sand was sticky and crumbly, and then recurring flat wavelets hissed up and away and up and licked my toes.

I had reached this—this great new experience, and I had no idea what to do.

My brother had killed my priest before I could be told what must be done—and all I know is that Atlan must be warned that the world is after her like a pack of belling, baying, tongue-lolling hounds, and that her vacuum is no longer of use.

I didn't dare light a fire and despaired of finding any real vegetation—but Ums displayed unexpected resourcefulness. From what instinct or sense I know not, he waded out into the waves till they reached his breast, and stared intently

into them with his one eye, beak poised ready. Suddenly
it flashed down—and came up with a furious, desperate,
silver fish, fat and jumping galvanically except in the middle where it was pinioned. Ums laid it on the sand and
skewered it before it could leap away.

I chopped off its head, which was staring with a reproachful and hardly yet glassy eye, and its green, strong, frilly
tail, and removed its spine, etc., while Ums fished for
more.

I didn't really fancy raw fish. But fresh water was near
to hand of course (the river) and luckily several of the fish
turned out to be carrying roe.

I crouched, picking at raw fish with scale-silvered fingers,
while Ums, having already golloped his, stood with wide-
spread legs, menacing profile lifted in each direction for
an indefinite period of time, changing with a short jerky
bird-movement, a giant black silhouette between me and
that close primeval sea, which divided us from that continent which has lain apart from the world since the gods
fell.

Cold winds were beginning to flow in and across the
shore. I shivered bitterly, rinsed my fingers and mouth
and looked round for somewhere to sleep.

The sand was too flat. It was cold, also anything could
find us there unprotected. Scouts from the Southern Advance maybe, or their navy which couldn't be far distant
from here. A rock pool seemed the only likely shelter. But
over there was a cliff, its sides argent with guano, already
tinged with richness as the sun began to set. There were
no sea-birds on its summit now, it couldn't be the season,
but it looked friendly, easy to scale, though very little
vegetation and that scrubby. Surely there'd be a cave-
niche of some kind where we could huddle. I led Ums to
the cliff and we started to climb. It was easy, but we found
nothing and I was beginning to despair when, nearly at
the top, a flight of sunset-coloured butterfies fluttered out,

disturbed by our approach, and we saw they'd come from a small murky opening between bastions of honey rock.

I wondered if we could get in there. I found that I could, and that it was big enough inside, though only just, for both of us. But how could I get Ums through the opening? He stood on the ledge outside, looking through at me; then extended his head on its neck, then his breast—he was now in a straight line, and his legs came through fairly easily. He looked smug and nuzzled my shoulder, thereby nicking my already travelworn cloak. How we were to get away quickly if we had to I didn't know, but never mind, eh? Here we were and we settled down to sleep in the cramped gloom, I with my head twisted uncomfortably but eagerly so I could watch the sunset.

'Gosh!' I said. Ums, realising from my tone that I'd not seen danger, did not raise his gaze.

From this height, though blurred by the sunset, there was visible a mass, curvilinear, of uncertain colour, not very high but of endless length, beaming dazzling upon the horizon as though the sun itself were burning forth from it as it sank lower into its heart.

I don't know what woke me. There seemed no sound above that of the sea—even the winds had cessated. There was a sharp awareness in the air—or a communication from the air to me of the sense of becoming aware. Ums, unusual in a highly alert brute of prey, was still asleep. I was reminded of the night last autumn when I woke and found a huge shining puma, and Ums still asleep . . .

I looked out of the opening and saw a brilliant star, then another and another. They were tiny and cold, but once your eyes were used to picking them out you realised they were everywhere. The sea heaved under them. I could no longer see that miraculous distant coastline, unless it were that faint radiance far out, as it were a diffusion of starlight hemming the waves, I looked down below me—and saw dim figures walking towards the shore.

They made no sound on the sand, they carried no light. Were they Southern scouts? Navals? Or bandits?

But yes, they had a light with them. Or rather—always just behind one of them. They were all men, about a dozen, all barefoot as far as I could see, and the leader left a golden aureole on the sand after each footstep. This glow lingered, too faint to do more than throw shadows on the ankle-bones of those following, until the leader took his next step. This obviously could not be an artificial light— for one thing it served no purpose down there, not even lighting the way; for another, it could not be a signal, and was rather dangerous than otherwise, as these days in these parts any light shown by a small party is unwise; also, it seemed too soft to be artificial. Yet a man whose bare feet were attended by haloes was surely too good to be true.

I watched them, my breath bated. I could make out that they were walking gravely but without signs of search or flight, straight towards the shore, not in single file nor two by two but in an orderly way not at all straggling, their heads uncovered. There was nothing remarkable about their clothes, which were townsmen's plain tunics and leggings, except for the leader whom I realised with a sort of calm shock was wearing rags. I half expected them all to walk straight on into the sea, but just before the spurling of the first froth-creamed wavelets glistering their points licking on the sand, the company stopped and seated themselves cross-legged in a circle.

I was agog to see what would happen next, though surely they'd do no more than talk a while at least, and I couldn't hope to hear, but now behind me Ums stirred and coughed.

I don't think they heard, but *he* was awake. He thrust his yawning head past me, grew still as he saw men below.

'Quiet, Ums,' I muttered. 'They're too many of us.' Really I only wanted to be able to go on watching them, but instinctively placatory I thought of the reason most likely to appeal to him. But he had stiffened, apparently, with malevolence. Throwing his usual creature-of-the-wild-sense to the chill winds, he scrambled out with surprising speed, and started down the slope barking.

The men rose and faced him. They seemed full of consternation. They made no move to find weapons; it was as though here, on the edge of things, they had expected no trouble, certainly not a furious Northern bird with which they could not speak.

I raced down after the creature.

'Ums! Ums!' Finally I called to the men, 'Scatter! He's not bluffing!'

They scattered, still gazing with fascination at his rapid approach, except the leader who stood there still. As Ums rushed to him, and I too raced nearer, we saw his keen grey eyes, glittering with a starlight of their own, a movement lambent. Ums did not falter, but rushed right up to him, then stopped with his beak within a few inches of the man's chest.

'Pedlar!' I said.

This seemingly scornful greeting brought home to me that I did not know his name, but that I ought perhaps to have said 'Lord!'

However, he didn't seem to mind. Ignoring Ums, who still stood as though transfixed, he put his hands behind his back and strolled over to me. He looked quizzical.

'The little girl of the City riot! You've come a long way. Is your leg better? Did you find the priest?'

'Perfectly better, thank you. I took the bandages off finally yesterday.'

I stood and looked at him. His thick strands of pallid-gold hair stirred in the breeze. His rags, also, stirred, showing the hard horney muscles. Who was this man who had travelled the ways of the South disguised as a pedlar, while I myself was making my immense but rambling Journey? The others were coming back. They regarded us and Ums with curiosity. 'What is she?' asked a slender boy with a toss of sunfire hair.

'A friend of the old grey priest's,' said the pedlar.

'He sent me to warn Atlan,' I said. I could tell these people were his real companions, that there was no need to be silent before them. 'So of course I came to the coast, but as far as I know nothing else is possible now—he was killed before he could instruct me.'

They grew very grave and drew closer together round me, though not one uttered any exclamation.

'Who was the murderer?'

'My brother,' I said and there was a silence. They studied me—I felt it was consideringly. Did they think me unfit, unbalanced, or outright one of an enemy syndicate?

'He did not realise what he did,' I said in a low voice.

'Of what do you intend to warn Atlan?'

I hesitated. At first I thought he was being sardonic because of my unworthiness.

'Of the coming invasion—behind her centuries-old silence she can have no inkling that at last the outside world has forged its spearhead. She may even have forgotten any other methods of defence.'

'You think she needs to be notified to prepare?'

'Of course—'

'Have you all been busy evolving new lungs?' asked the boy.

'More or less. The Northerners have discovered a way to air-flood even such a huge vacuum.'

The pedlar stood by, the wild breezes caressing him. The boy stared. He was only about thirteen, straight and tall but still with young, sloped shoulders and a hollow at the top of the back of his neck. To him, and I think some of the others too, my statement was news. But it was typical of them that there were no moans nor even exclamations.

'The Northerners are those led by the one called the Dragon, aren't they?' said the boy.

'Yes,' I said, which couldn't reassure him.

'Does your brother know you've come here?' asked another.

'He has no idea,' I muttered.

'Sit down,' the pedlar ordered. I did and so did everyone else.

'Have you any food?' I couldn't stop myself asking eagerly. 'And can you release my bird now—he'll do no harm.'

'Are you sure?' asked the pedlar, smiling grimly at me, but before I could work out how seriously he meant it and how to answer he'd sort of carelessly snapped his fingers in Ums' face and Ums gave a long shiver. He turned his burning eye for a long time on the pedlar, then to me. This decided him. Moving as if each great muscle were throwing off the recent bewildering indignity, he came to me and stood just behind me. Then he began a series of grunts and snarling coughs.

I was glad the pedlar didn't start to speak through this, get fed up, and petrify him again. He started to gather large shells—there were so many he hardly had to move, though I'd noticed very few before—and he fished about in each with his dagger, and without fail each yielded a whelk or an oyster or something. Another volunteered to fish, catching them in his hands, chilly work at the best of times. I thought of offering Ums' services but didn't know how he'd behave. However, the fisher seemed to have as good luck as the pedlar. The others sat around talking in low voices, then fell to on the meal. It was raw though, because of course sending fire-smoke up in the sky was out of the question.

The pedlar sat friendly beside me, but I was rather afraid of him.

Also, I noticed that my arms as I ate were rather grubby, with a sort of mottled grey effect which I myself thought quite attractive, but which he probably wouldn't. I haven't washed properly for ages, since the night I escaped from Court with Kaselm, but I could imagine the pedlar thinking 'Ho. She had plenty of opportunity to wash in rivers and things on the way here, even if she was in a hurry. Ho.' Or words to that effect.

'If,' he said after a while, 'you ever got there, how would you set about warning their leaders?'

'I'd have to find the nearest city of course. After that it'd be easy.'

'You have infinite resource, obviously.'

'I have led a very unusual life, full of desperate ventures,' I said expansively. 'I've had to accomplish a lot and generally I've succeeded in—Well, in muddling through,' I amended more honestly.

He gave a laugh, a sort of brief peal, a definite Ha ha! 'You've come from what? Apparently you're completely alone, no family, no guardians? And where have you aimed your life— before you were directed into the Atlan adventure?'

'I think,' I said slowly, 'I wanted always to come to Atlan. The first time I heard the word I felt a singing, here, for which the voice that spoke it couldn't have been responsible. Did you know that she can be seen from this coast, if you get high up, say on that cliff? I never thought of that possibility, that though she's outside the world she's visible, rather like that prehistoric phenomenon the moon—I couldn't see much, it was sunset, but she is long and low and blazing—'

'I know,' he said and put a hard honey-coloured arm round my shoulders. 'And I see that we really shall have to take you there.'

'T-take me—there—?'

'Surely such an ingenious lady has guessed that we belong there?'

'I didn't realise properly—'

I paused, then suddenly bombarded him with questions—no doubts. 'How did you get out? Were you born this side? Have you any means of repulsing an army?'

'We have our method of getting In and Out. We have an army of our own—but it's not huge and has had no practice. Every man in it is, of course, an Atlantean—and courage and intelligence so universal must help an army tremendously. But we have seen no action whatsoever—our fathers, our fathers' fathers' fathers have seen none—and every one of us has a rooted repugnance for blood-spurting.'

'But have you no advanced weapons?'

'Advanced weapons?'

'You are so highly developed that you could devise your vacuum—have you no chemicals, like the Southerners, who can throw into the air a gas which immediately ignites as of itself, and just—just burns up everything near?'

I realised that everyone else had stopped talking. They were simply all staring at me. The boy regarded me without fear, but with terror and distaste. His eyes were gold, even in the night.

'The future Emperor of Atlan,' said the pedlar, indicating him. 'I am His Momentity's regent until he reaches puberty.'

I regarded the future Emperor almost with irritation. 'His Momentity must forgive my nasty story. Some might regard swift fire as better than the forms of poison they release in a mist of disease. But of course these are expensive, elaborate weapons—they've been reserving them all as a special gift for you, because they were so sure your scientists would have provided you with even more elaborate ones.'

'We have no scientists.'

How could I believe this? Yet after the first impact, it did fit with my long idea of Atlan as an earthly paradise.

'But the whole world regards Atlan as synonymous for the most advanced possible warfare!'

This they took differently. Some felt distaste, the pedlar-regent looked amused but of course it was an old story to him, the boy-emperor looked almost flattered for a moment. 'Then perhaps they'll handle us carefully!' he suggested.

'Yes,' I agreed. 'With more care and more cruelty.' 'And the Dragon, too, is on our track,' he said.

My fingers curled in to my palms. I found them sticky. I shivered, but was only mildly shocked to find my fear voluptuous.

Now they talked. I found out my pedlar, The High Regent himself of Atlan, is named Juzd and had spent the last half-year in Southernland. What he'd found about the world's designs on his own continent had got the Atlantean leaders extremely worried. (I thought that was putting it mildly, myself.) But now he was due to return, and these lords had come to the mainland to meet him and escort him back. It was typical of their innate trust and innocence, undisturbed for centuries, that even the Emperor had been allowed to come. But what Juzd had told them of the latest developments had divided them a little. The majority were inclined to think they should take a sortie and go and deal with some of these small bands of enemies wandering towards them.

I said, 'May I say I happen to know that's an excellent idea? You have no weapons but your trick of freezing anybody by looking into their eyes should come in most useful.'

'No weapons?' they said. If they weren't Atlanteans I'd have said they scoffed. They drew from the folds of their tunics and cloaks short spears tipped with the vital parts of sting-rays which were dead but still electrically charged, also small shields composed of the whole shells of turtles. I felt a fool. As I've learnt, as soon as one realises the innocence of Altlanteans, one must be careful not to think of them as children,

'Beloved,' said Juzd to me, 'you are little and tired. Lie down to sleep. Tomorrow we shall show you the way to Atlan and you will go there with your bird, which we will allow to enter to be with you. You have no need to warn anyone of anything any more now, but you will be happy in safety.'

Atlan at last! Offered to me. 'But don't you need my help for battle?' I said. 'There are few of you, you need every one you can get, even against small parties for they are used to battle, and my bird too is fine for—'

'We don't need you,' Juzd said. I don't know why I believed him. 'And you need at last a refuge. How often have you rested in safety in the last few years?'

I was waked before dawn. We gathered the usual food, and sat cross-legged on the sand to eat it. Juzd and I sat together.

I looked at these men who were embarking on a warlike adventure. None of them seemed excited or pleased (though calm and fearless) not even the boy. As future Emperor, he was surely to have gone to safety with me, but he had insisted on staying. This, however, wasn't from a desire to make his first kill and become a man, but because he must be actively present when his land was threatened. Anyway, I was amazed when they gave in to him. They didn't seem to realise they might lose him. Smahil would have said, Perhaps they didn't much care.

I thought of how I feel about battles and bloodshed. It sickens me, to be sure, but that is a mixture of conscience and reaction; I'm always as eager as anything beforehand except when I'm afraid for myself or friends. Normal natural cruelty doesn't horrify me in the least, I'm quite at home with it, though then again I'm different from the

Atlanteans in the opposite way: I'm more inclined to squeamishness and resentment.

'Have you, who seem to know so much, ever met the Dragon?' Juzd asked. I said circumspectly, 'As a matter of fact, yes, once or twice', and he said he hadn't got that far and what was he like?

I said, 'At any rate, in spite of his brilliance and ruthlessness, he is more human than the Southern government. That's strange, actually, as only his father (who was a great General himself) was what we call human. He seems to have been a more haughty and aristocratic leader than his son, who stoops to various tricks to gain quite petty ends incidental to his campaigns—from marrying anyone susceptible enough not to recognise his greed for advancement, to telling quite silly lies.'

'That is what comes of a union with a lower species,' Juzd observed. 'His mother was one of those big bluish females from the North, I've heard.'

'And I bet, though he took after her, he was always pretty arrogant with her,' I said. Suddenly I imagined Zerd as a horrible little scaly boy, and I didn't know whether to laugh or what. Then I thought of him, at the Court of his father's king, daring everyone to snigger at him because of his skin, the nobles, the ladies, ladymaidens, and his own brothers and sisters who even if illegitimate must all have been better-born.

'When higher mates with lower,' Juzd said slowly, 'there is always a fall. The lower is never raised to the higher's level, but pulls down. Just as when the gods saw the fascination of Earth and mated with Earth's daughters, just as when man commits sodomy.' He looked at me till I wondered if he thought my relationship with Ums, gift from Zerd, too intense. I felt like saying, Oh we're just good friends.

But I know that even to be with Ums is bad for me.

If one loves everything, saving only war and cruelty and

inside-out mockeries of realities, one is right from heaven's point of view; love everything, as I incline to do, having come from the tower where I had nothing to love except the sky—love *everything* (but it must be *love*) and one is *right* for the spinning, dark, self-sufficient Earth. Those are the thoughts the bird-demon infused me with.

Juzd looked at me with all the grey keenness of his eyes: he seemed to know what I ws thinking.

He said, 'There are Three Deeps passing through this World (though their Beginnings and Endings are in other Places). They are Hell, Earth and Heaven. And as we also pass through the world, we pass through them. At first they seem to intermingle; but at last there come lives when our sensitivities are sharpened and the Three Deeps hit us separately. And then every man must choose: whether he belongs to Good, Evil or the Earth.'

'I choose the Earth,' I said.

He smiled, but already sadly. 'Think well, Beloved; for remember that in The End the Earth, the hot mystic One Element, will also have to choose to whom its mysticism is directed. There can be Three for a while, but then there must be One. It is dangerous to serve Earth, though good for a while, for at The End all your service to Earth may be taken by Hell.'

'Can't you see Earth serving Heaven?'

He shrugged.

'Or Heaven and Hell serving Earth?'

'In The End, that would be blasphemy, Beloved,' he said.

Soon it was high time for me to get going and leave them grimly but calmly to it. Juzd asked if I can swim—said he hadn't asked before as the priest'd hardly have sent me if I couldn't, but might as well make sure. And could Ums? I said, 'Certainly.'

I said goodbye to them all and mounted Ums. I was so

happy to be going to Atlan, but I did have qualms at leaving Juzd. Dawn was coming up. We must be there by full light. I turned and watched the dull thud and roar of the surf and waves on the shining grey beach. Each wave was decapitated by the back-curling spray of the wave before it. Ums plunged in.

When I next looked back the shore was a thin line, even the cliff.

I was drenched. Ums had nothing to carry but the saddle, myself, the Diary and a bag of provisions, but I insisted he stop once or twice on the rocks if only for me to wring the sea out of my clothes. A haze soon rose on the spurling vision line, a gold-green haze this time, but it would take ages to reach her.

There was no danger of missing the important rock. It was the last, before us a vast empty expanse, and it jutting up shiny dark in its strange convolutions continually washed over by the waves.

We landed, slipping a little, for the waves were strong and there was not much of a ledge. I dismounted and led Ums to the leeward side of the main jut. It was—well, I wanted to cry at the things I think about him sometimes, he followed me without question, when I rode him straight out and out into the sea he made no demur at all.

As I regarded the side of the jut I felt misgiving, though. The door was certainly well hid. I would have sworn it was solid rock. But I lifted aside a strand of seaweed and finally found the knob; it was even better disguised than I'd been told, as some little creature had hooked its shell on it. It clung there while I twisted the knob and lo and behold there was a harsh rasp and a cavity appeared dark green. Not without timidity Ums and I scrambled through— and stopped halfway. There was nothing there, beyond a short down-slope of hollowed rock—nothing but green sea, with fish passing. Where was the tunnel I'd been promised? Had it been demolished since they'd traversed it? Ums whickered and tried to nudge me out.

But I noticed there was no water at all on the floor of the short downward rock tunnel which faced directly into the sea which reached above its roof. I went down in, ready to run as soon as I met water—I came to the end of the rock and stepped right into the sea, above me and to every side. I stood breathing and dry, yet when I looked down I nearly screamed. Passing just beneath my feet, in the endless depth was a huge white shark, twisting, belly and corpse-mouth up. Then at last I realised that I was in a transparent undersea tunnel—walls, roof and floor transparent. I went back up and led Ums firmly in; I showed him how I could walk safe in the sea, and coaxed him, and he came shivering with his eyes a fixed glare. I shut the door after us as I had been told. We were alone, in a submerged green existence.

I led him slowly. Though I knew that if there were a breach anywhere in the tunnel it would be full of water, I had a horrid feeling each time I put a foot down. I don't know why the air was so good, as there could be no ventilation, but though it wasn't exactly fresh it wasn't at all unpleasant. Also I realised how thick the glass must be (if it were glass) to withstand—well, centuries of sword-fish, giant squid, sharks sharpening their teeth, and con-gers bashing themselves against it every now and then, though I suppose most of the local fish knew by now to swim above or under it. Yet it was as clear as though it were a fraction of an inch thin, there was no distortion.

When he was more confident, I mounted him. I've no idea how many miles we travelled under the sea, but he galloped as only a powerful bird can.

We were a long way under. Up above the day must be getting strong, but the green down here became only a little more translucent.

Funnily enough, though the undersea journey must

have taken a whole day and night and near all the next day too, it didn't seem too long. It was such a new experience. The food held out, for we stinted ourselves. There were oysters, crab, fish of various kinds—but though it was well packed it wasn't very enjoyable, as it was all raw. There were two leather bottles of fresh water. I had to drink from the bottles' lips, and Ums had to plunge his beak in and slurp.

Every so often in the side of the tunnel was an ordinary-looking latrine, which must however have flushed into the sea by a series of air-locks or something. They were screened off on three sides from the rest of the tunnel, but on the other side fish could look in all they liked. I couldn't help feeling silly. Ums couldn't use these, and I felt guilty, but presumed Juzd had known what he was doing when he let him come, and perhaps the tunnel was cleaned sometimes. When the green grew very dark, and I felt very tired, I judged it was night. I simply lay on the hard transparent floor, Ums roosting beside me, and I went to sleep in the middle of a large school of silver fish.

Parts of the tunnel were obscured on the outside with anemones suckered to it or with growths of coral through which tiny fish loitered. In places, we travelled under a roof of ribbon-like weeds, blue and green and rosy, whose streamers fluttered.

We witnessed innumerable pursuits, some of which ended in disaster. Once a gigantic octopus rushed eagerly at us, poor thing, and wouldn't give up for ages, swimming alongside and launching dashing attacks, immense oval eyes going cross-eyed over his or her horrid orange beak, arms waving galvanically in all directions and occasionally getting a grip round some of the tunnel. He or she must have been awfully puzzled. Ums, who had by now quite got the hang of the situation, was amused and raised his head and nodded it in a jeering triumphant way. Finally the octopus, from sheer frustration, loosed a cloud of murky inky stuff and made off.

Later a school of big fish like dolphins went past high up, playing with each other delightfully and not at all ponderously in spite of their size. Several of them had protuberances from their bellies which I couldn't understand. Then I saw they were embryos, already partly emerged, tail first, so that in the few weeks before birth they could learn to swim.

Even when huge active creatures passed, I couldn't hear the sound of the water, and if it hadn't been for Ums I should have got a feeling of deafness. We were by now going fast, lost in contemplation of this all-enveloping subterranean world through which we tore, though we might have been ghosts for all the difficulty we suffered. My legs got tired riding, especially the convalescent one, but I am used to long treks and Ums is so powerful it's practically impossible to tire him.

The tunnel passed into a wider tunnel outside a vast subterranean cavern. It rapidly became dark, a murky gloom—a real gloom, with a quality of melancholia more than claustrophobia. For the first few yards I could see spires of rock in the weirdest shapes, surrealistic under and behind the water, fish passing amongst them like jewels in a moving pattern, shapes like butterfies, fins flowing, till one could not tell which were fins and which plants—but in the dark we walked onwards, only our brains ordering us to trust. Presently pale eyes began to appear, to watch us, to flash or drift past or zip towards us—I could have sworn they were right in the tunnel with us, separated from us only by darkness.

The slope upwards was so imperceptible I never knew when it began. But when we got out of the cavern, the light was an incredibly purer green, like the liquid skin of baby apples, and it couldn't have been just the sudden contrast that made it seem so.

The floating jewels about us now had all an upward curve, fish and plants and the indeterminates somewhere or other between the two, all streaming up or with fins or crests or ribbons pointing or swaying up, as though the creatures of this level were here because they wanted to get even higher. A shoal of tiny fish, each no bigger than a glinting, but nearly transparent pink fingernail, but each with a long dorsal fin and tail like a length of net, passed up in a cloud to every side of us, above and below, and must have taken about five minutes to get left behind even though we were moving through it all the time.

The element became a visual carillon of sliding flakes of liquid crystal—here was every shade and tone of blue, light violet, green—as we went higher and higher so some of the blues became silvery, the greens nearly cream. Yellow beams began to pour down, sharp or diffused—the ascent was steeper, yet we were almost running.

Without warning I was dazzled. We rose into a light at first shockingly brilliant; then realised it was simply the light of day above the sea. Instantly I looked eagerly ahead. There it was—before me a great swelling cliff-line, mounting in mighty undulations to the sky, hiding the interior of the island-continent. It was clothed with trees diversely the shape of fountains, and all gave a rich gleaming, glowing effect, as though each seventh or eighth leaf must be a brighter emerald, silver or gold than all the other normal leaves. These glowing foliages moved a little, back and forth and almost all together, as though there were a small but strong wind up here, and streaks of burnished colour which must be birds darted among them. I wished I could hear the wind and birds and waves— suddenly the silence seemed terrible, which had not crushed me all those hours in the sea. Yes, a wind—for I looked about me and the waves on the surface of the sea were choppy, blowing inshore alongside me with all their white manes tossing and spurling; sleek silver flanks dived and looped amongst them: dolphins, whose undersides I had been watching from below a few minutes before.

Directly ahead, at the beach, I could not look. It sparkled and shot rays of light as though chunks of meteor recently fallen from the sun lay on it.

A bare raft of black rock thrust out from the hillside. The tunnel, in which we felt baked as the day beat on the glass-substance, curved round and went right under the rock before plunging again under the surface. The rock's tepid shadow fell over us—but there was no one on it. I realised it must have been a look-out post, where the tunnel rose bearing its helplessly revealed occupants for inspection, but so long had the safety of the Atlanteans lasted, they no longer manned this post.

A few more furlongs under water—and a blank door lay before us. With sudden panic I caught at the handle, but it opened at once. There was no lock I could see. The door was low, Ums had to bend his head. We emerged on to a beach, difficult and uneven, blinding to look at. It was covered with huge reflecting crystals: so intense that rainbows shimmered over some of them. So, unobserved, we entered Atlan.

Ums made no sound, but he was quivering at this emergence. Before starting inland, I stood and looked back. Only sea. I advanced to the edge, the waves licked my toes. I leaned forward—and fell at once. I gasped but no air reached my lungs. I should have heard my own crow for breath, but it hardly reached me. Ums seized my cloak in his beak and pulled me on to the crystals again before the cloth ripped.

So the dolphins out there were playing a game of catch-as-catch-can with danger: there was no air above the surface for them to breathe.

No wonder there were no sea-birds above the waves. I didn't know how high the vacuum extended, but even so there was a risk of plunging heavily, unsupported by atmosphere, for any unwary bird. Atlan to herself—her own species, insulated, no migrations to and from the shores of the world.

But as I learnt later, on other parts of the coast the atmosphere starts a little further back for the convenience of fishermen.

So we rose and went inland, treading carefully over the rocking crystals, avoiding their sharp points and corners, their lights playing on our faces.

There was no hurry, nor even a goal. This was the final leisure—for I had to warn no one, I had no one to meet.

We started up the hillside. The trees were rarely thick enough to impede the light. Where they were, shadow lay like fragrant turquoise velvet on the turf. I could see the birds properly and Ums snorted angrily at them—though they took no notice of us. They flew low and had wonderful long crests and tails. Now I could hear them properly too, but was surprised. They gave shrill squawks, and seemed very busy about nothing. They reminded me in shape but not in fragile colour and dignity, of the vast shoal of tiny fish we had passed.

Presently flowering trees began to intersperse the others— gradually the others gave way altogether, and everywhere one looked there were masses of bloom. I caught a glimpse of the first living creature, other than birds, that I'd seen in Atlan: two very long eyes glowed out at me, they were large liquid eyes like a gazelle's but almost alarmingly unnatural in their length, they curved right round the sides of the face which now emerged from the shadows, and reached nearly to the ears. No, the face did not emerge, it was in fact retreating (though without apparent fear) but it was striped in grey and black and took time to be realised. The swish-therefore-flash of her golden mane and tail showed her to me just as she retreated right amongst the flowering trees. A thin, striped mare—a tiny, ungainly, striped, gold-tailed creature moved with her, tottering on its new legs, without removing its head from under her belly.

We came under the edge of the trees, and looked out over a wide blue meadow which ran downhill to another belt of trees, dark trees this time, though only their tops showed. The sun was lower—we had already been in Atlan several hours. We had seen insects, glinting and hairy, but nothing further. We had eaten the last of our food in the tunnel—but what was there to eat here? Nevertheless I was not hungry.

As we went out into the meadow—it was so steep we needed to brace ourselves not to run downhill—I saw it was completely ankle-deep with blue flowers of a type unknown to me, yet strangely familiar. They were many thousands like the one I had found in the statuette given me by that ruffian—it must have lain in its own tiny vacuum to be a sacred memory for the exiled colonists, unwithered since before the Great Scaling so many centuries ago . . .

Now I could smell them and no longer behind crystal, they were fresh and fragrant, and soft on my legs . . .

Ums' droppings reeked among the flowers. Some were crushed irreparably. Suddenly I was guilty, I was ashamed. I felt an alien bringing crudity: I had no right to pretend I took joy in the ways of Atlan for I was bringing this into her. Yet what had I done really? Surely there was slaughter and excretion here—there were animals.

Many meadows, hillsides, cliffs, woods, later it was twilight, though not chilly. The sky was violet as those flower-petals: graded from blue to purple, and a colourless light lingered on the edge of navy clouds.

A waterfall fell from a great height, a cliff in a wood. The torrent did not sparkle much in this light. It gurgled, gushed, plashed, sent up a fume, at its foot and all down its length, over rocks and boulders of pure crystal. Lichens and moss lay atop some of them—a rich shadow lay on the boulders beneath those with the mat of plant-life. There were orchids in the waterfall, flowers such as I had seen in the jungle-forests of the Dragon's March (strange how I used now the name the Southerners had given him). The twilight advanced, deepened, intensified over this wild richness which gave me a sense of—well, yes, of such a richness of wildness that though it would not be unwholesome it might prove perilous.

Here now there was a tangling of great leaves and blossoms, less than half-seen in the twilight but their smells heavy. They made sounds of movement too, though I could feel no wind. But it was as though they were fringed and tasselled and swaying. My bird began to grunt, he made a hack with his beak at anything that impeded him no matter how little. Occasionally great trees, spreadfoliaged like pyramids, loomed before us; they seemed dead black, as though no light at all could strike response from them. Yet this was no thick forest. There was no undergrowth, only grass and clumps of ferns. Here and there we were open to the sky that glimmered violet upon us; white flowers resting on the turf were like reflected stars.

Occasionally we saw the starlit froth of cool blue and white water, or heard its skinkling on stones. Also, under the sky, I could see that the air was stencilled by streams of moths and winged beetles and flies—each stream was making in the same direction, ours but more to the right. They must be what made the noise against the leaves. Also there was a buzzing from the flies.

Now winding to us, faint echoing as though separated from us by so many trees, so much wood-life, all of which was absorbing its share, came a melody, a kind of potent wailing, as if from some kind of pipe.

I caught my breath. Ums tossed his head, he coughed;

if he had not been a bird he would have slavered. The roots of my hair felt like quicksilver. I ran forward—now we were going in the same direction as the insect-patterns, but when I had turned I didn't know. The turf tingled when my feet touched it, or perhaps vice versa. The pipe soared louder, then made a sort of low ululating noise.

Good heavens, I thought, how can one instrument make sounds like that? Then I realised they were other sounds—grouped around the pipe, probably in motion—there were squeaks, twitterings, chirruping and yapping. Then abruptly a bellow rose above the rest; it grew and reverberated from a roar to a yawl and sank away in something like a sob. The realisation that it had in its own way accompanied the rise and wail of the pipe did nothing to soothe the prickle of my scalp. What were we advancing to? I hastened on—I couldn't turn back, yet I went on with a pulsing eagerness, a kind of loving terror.

We were there. Through the blonde low-hanging foliage animals played with an incessant delicacy. Their hooves, their claws, their paws, huge or tiny—the touch of each was delicate on the glowing sward. A delightful urgency was in the air. Continuous movement, the joyous playing, the swaying unmathematical lines, they mingled, dancing and chasing in and out of the groves of trees, gambolling, they obeyed the leaping ululation. Our friends the winged insects flittered and zoomed above our heads. A lion reared on his hind-legs, roared to the pipe, passed a stag, weaved among a line of swans, his eyes and mane fire-amber. There was a goat, just an ordinary-looking brown and white goat with a goat-smell, who moved zigzag through a crowd of animals like ant-eaters which looped about his thin, cleft hooves. So they danced seemingly without knowledge that they would be enemies, hereditary enemies again when this night was over; that instead of partners in an enchanted dance, they would be hunters and hunted. The earth seemed suddenly to glow with an intensity which melted its visual solidity. I could see under it little lizards with scales like lit emeralds and rubies and amethysts, spread claws, flicker of vermilion tongue, a dart to here and a stare from oblong eyes and another dart to there. There were worms, naked and pale as pink silk, beetles, baby spiders hardly visible and swarming blue blotched, hairy spiders, labyrinths of grass- and flower-roots.

No animal seemed to notice me. If they saw me, I was just another of the creatures all around them with whom they did not habitually mingle.

Where the music throbbed most, the dancing was deepest. But I caught glimpses, rarely, of the piper between their movement. His pipe was long and twined with green; insects were clustered, quivering on it. He was seated on a knoll and naked, his smooth, yellowish skin reflecting no light from stars nor glowing earth, umber nipples hardly rising or falling on the wide chest, but his cheeks ballooned a bit, so making his narrow, dreaming, black eyes even more slanting. He had straight, black hair to his waist. I think his eyebrows continued out each in an arc beyond the sides of his head, as though they were the antennae of a moth.

Hung about his shoulders, like a shepherd, he carried a little gazelle-thing with spots and smudgy horns.

Ums beside me edged forward. His splayed talons gripped nervily on the turf and threw black shadows on the glittering insects and lizards beneath.

I saw at what his one eye was glaring. A female bird, a little smaller than himself, white with an uneven edging of grey-blue on her wings. She had bluish eyes and a bluish crest, half raised in ecstasy. Her crest and spurs were smaller, her tail shorter than his.

She'd not yet noticed him.

He left me, moved forward to her. He seemed so black in that tender pulsing, rainbow radiance. The eager strength in him was not going to be controlled. I realised, though merely with surprise, that he did not regard her as a specially enchanting creature, worthy to be a me of his own kind—she was a female. He was going to take her.

She saw him. She came towards him, her silvery-rose claws—she was altogether a fairy-tale bird—gripping the turf. She was about to pass him, with a sort of impersonal lovingness, to change her dance to pass him as he had (she believed) specially come to pass her. Her steps, like those of all the other animals, were timed to the pipe which only excited Ums. He moved forward without grace, or with the grace only of power, not to pass but to meet. She found her way blocked, accepted this as part of it all and side-stepped to loop round him. He emitted a hoarse, impatient, brief protest, and again barred her way. His crest rose jerkily, disturbed a heavy red cluster of berries big as grapes and a cloud of humming gnats rose unsettled from it. She stared with wonder, the beginning of alarm, at his head.

Ums' wings lifted, shut down, lifted. The rasp hit the music as the warbling bellows of the larger animals had not. The animals near turned and regarded him as though he had made an unpleasant noise in church. The female passaged away again, as though nervous to dissociate herself as soon as possible from this intruder.

Ums followed, before her at every turn, he had no intention of letting her get away and his wings fell and rasped up more rapidly. His bird-of-prey red eye gleamed. It was like a hot coal. A topaz-striped tiger, horribly long and lean, pacing near with a flock of stately-happy flamingoes all together, turned and stiffened and began to lash his tail from side to side.

The female, still in time to the music, tried to escape behind the goat. She was nervous but calm. Ums followed. The goat, following the condemnatory dislike which was spreading among the animals—heads everywhere were turning—butted and bleated, no more than a hint to 'get away'. Ums, hot coal still fixed glowering on the female, lifted a foot and raked his claws down the side of the goat's head, at the same time shoving him away.

Blood dripped steaming; where it fell, the turf dimmed and then became opaque.

The female at last faced him again. He thrust his neck over hers, a rough fore-play, a way of getting control. He moved behind her and she turned awkwardly, brought her lovely wing up and flapped it in his face, a warning. At this insult, this added playing-coy after all the rest, he let out a harsh, deep squawk of fury, seized the wing in his beak and dragged her over to the side of the dance. She went perforce, uttering bewildered pain-moans, white and blue feathers drifting everywhere. Ums clawed aside a peacock in the way; other feathers were added to the drift.

The dance had all but stopped. They were animals again; Ums' squawk was answered by the challenges of lion, tiger, a big bull with a yellow arc of horns, the shrill belligerent cries of foxes and rodents. The smell of the blood had broken the pipe-spell. There was tail-lashing, uncertain growls which would soon be certain, but no longer singing. Eyes fixed glaring on Ums who pushed the female behind him and stood poised ready with eager arrogance. Eyes from the peacock's tail lay staring on the grass.

A cold little wind rustled. I realised the pipe had stopped. I glanced round, saw in the night on the knoll the man standing naked, the pipe dangling in one hand, the other up caressing the little whimpering gazelle about his shoulders. His narrow eyes were not clearly to be seen, it was all much darker without the earth-light, but I think they were watchful on the ring round Ums—then he turned full to me. I met his gaze with curiosity and a readiness, he the shepherd of his creatures and I of mine which were having an argument as creatures will. My look was turned back into me. His was of disgust, complete. Then, as though he dismissed me, he was gone.

A dark blue bird with red crest up, and plumage edged with red, left the ring of animals and approached my black bird. The other animals, I thought, would leave it at that, their bird spokesman for all their wrath, single combat, diatryma v. diatryma.

The few circled each other for a few tense-wary moments, but Ums was a born fighter even among such a savage race as his own—he belonged to that separate species Fighter just as Ael did, and the sergeant with pale eyes, and Zerd who had given me this one—and he soon put an end to the ogling, darted in and sank his hooked beak in the other's neck. The blue bird was not a Fighter. He squealed with pain and defiance, and lashed out but missed. He had courage. But Ums was still unscathed when the blue's blood spurted out. Every dark nostril widened, there was a low growl, swish-swash as the lion's tail beat in the grass and up like a stiff springy rope on his own flanks.

The blue got up a foot.

Gods, I thought, don't let Ums lose his other eye.

The blue had had his say, for incompetent it was proving. This was to be no single combat, Ums was no honourable foe, he was an intruder. The tiger sprang almost before the lion did. Their teeth and claws dug in simultaneously. Ums was brought to his knees, to his belly, leg twisted. Low growls thrummed the air. More animals joined, ignoring the blue bird which staggered to the female. They watched a moment, then went away into the trees. The smaller creatures scampered away too—some turned in the wood and looked back at Ums being eaten alive.

But nothing, even with Ums' powerful heart, could have survived long under that onslaught of beasts. As I drew my knife, which I did almost immediately for though I knew it was useless and death, I could not leave him who had taken me through so much, I realised there was no need; there was no longer quivering, tossing of the Fighter dying fighting under the rending suffocation. The beasts fed gurgling and tearing. A grey wolf lifted his wolf-head to the stars and howled. A little marsupial, with rat-teeth and running on hind-legs, darted in and came back with a curved black wing like a shield, which often it had been to me, or like an exotic lady's-fan except that it gouted crimson at the stump. In a deep smear on the turf all patterned with the prints of hooves and claws and pads and paws, a single stirrup lay. The rowelled spur, which I'd so rarely used, glinted. My instep ached as it remembered how often it had fitted over that metal bar, now lying loose, its frayed strap no longer proud and taut.

I stumbled on among the trees. I looked up. In the starlight rain slanted like ghirza strings across the hills. I didn't know where I was going, only to get away as far as I could from the scene of Ums' death, which seemed the ultimate in the deaths of my companions, for really he had been the nearest to me, it was almost the death of part of myself, and I was newly *alone*.

Suddenly the sky itself became a waterfall, like the one I had seen earlier only greatly more vast. Thunder followed lightning. The trees wailed.

I did not call myself fanciful when it seemed to me the wind pursued me. I *was* a new germ introduced into Atlan, I had brought with me the air and thoughts of my world, without wishing ill I was ill.

My Atlan hated me.

The dark was complete, every now and then huge clouds made their sluggish way between Atlan and the stars. Or perhaps they were moving at a great rate: their size made them take so long to pass.

A hard wind rose straight before my feet, lifting my cloak. I paused. I could only just see, narrowing my eyes, the sheer precipice over which my toes thrust unsupported.

I drew back with a cry the wind hurled deafening in my own ears, and ran on to the left, and back into the wood.

I passed the wood, and came on to the loneliest hill-top I've ever known. Black wind rushed past me and on over the valley. Queer things turned as they too rushed past, leered at me and were gone before I properly saw them.

The beat of hooves galloping, galloping across the valley.

I myself came down on to the hard road. It wound away, spasmodically lightning-lit, and amongst the gallop of the horses I could hear the strain of axles, the creak of wood, the crack of whips. Chariots! I must crouch hidden to watch them pass—for in Atlan all were enemies to me who had given Atlan such love.

First riders dashed past on the dark-shine of the road, their flaxen hair free, for though they had pulled their cloak-hoods up over their heads, their speed had tugged them off again. Those were Atlanteans, and here were the chariots they escorted. There were no torches, but by star-gleam and lightning-slash I saw the fair men standing in the first chariots. My pedlar, Juzd the regent! But I hesitated to run forward. Dark men in the next chariots that streamed in hurtling line up the road. And one, standing mighty behind his driver, his face hidden behind the bronze helm that made the eyes narrow and the nose thin and straight, in the fitful light the gleam of a gold pelt over his wide shoulders.

I dashed out on the road even as the high-hub wheels blurred roaring past, the spray they made drenching me as much as the rain did.

'Wait! Stay!'

The wind tossed and tumbled my voice as though it were a plaything, a despised plaything.

A rider pulled his horse up plunging behind me. A hoof, fetlock hair swirling, just shaved my sodden hood. A voice cursed.

As more chariots passed, I could see now they were drawn by birds. I doubled over and retched.

'Well, who are you, what is it?' said the voice, still cursing.

'You are no Atlantean,' I babbled at once.

'Big surprise, eh? Yes, we've got through at last, us from the other side, and your regent with us, we're making for the capital by his invitation. You shut us out but you're glad enough to welcome us at need. Out of the way. Questions later. The whole continent can ask its questions later.'

'Is that your General, in the gold sheepskin?'

'One thing I'll say, you've sharp eyes to know it's sheepskin. Yes, he's all in style to ride into the Great City. A new Emperor must impress his people.'

'Emperor!'

The man chuckled. He held down a hand, I could locate it by the gleam of the finger-nails. 'Up you come. You sound comely enough. I'll see what an Atlan maid is like—and be the first of us to ride with one into our new HQ! It'll make up quite a bit for entering this Atlan on a dark, rainy night—for all we can see of her we might still be the other side of the ocean. I'll explain all on the way.'

I rode pillion, my arms gripped round his back, as we hastened on.

'Well, tell me it all.'

'What's your name?'

I wished he would cut the courting and get on with the story. 'That shall be the price of your tale.' He growled good-humouredly that we of Atlan set a high value on ourselves. 'Don't think just because you've been sealed away from us we'll think you rare. There'll be more than enough of you even for our needs for a while, till the rest of our army is shipped over and yours taught how to work with it. Or perhaps it'll take even longer—our Blue-Scales'n all may decide to keep the airlessness as they call it intact,

and we'll all come over through that there tunnel. I'd give
a lot to see our sergeant-major thinking a shark was coming at him!'

'But how did this start? The Dragon to be *emperor*—
What did he do to Juzd?'

'Ah, you've been hearing narky tales about him, even
away here? You're bemused. He wouldn't hurt a *fly*. Have
no fear, he's not come to lay Atlan to the sword. This is to
be our land, and we'll treat it well. No, it's the Southerners,
and the Northerners too, the Northerners that sent us on
what they thought would be a wild-goose chase and the
death of us all and our gallant Blue-loins, too, it's all them
that think it safe to be our enemies we're going to show—'

'But *how*—'

'It's a long story and I'll tell it when we're snug out of
this pesky downpour. But the end was, after fighting the
Southerners in the middle of their own earthquake, we
was all split up, regiment from regiment, and no time to
re-form. Ah, they seized their chance. Their reinforcements,
that wasn't split up at all, hunted us to the coast. They
hoped to crush us atwixt them and their navy. But we
went willing, too. Lads, says our Blue-Nose, we'll hope for
a trick or two on them yet, I know more'n they think, he
says. For by ill management their navy was more than half
careening when we gets to the coast, where they're having
a right good time with fires and drink and noise, and we
marches raggle-taggle up to them and says Very retiring
types, these navy types, eh—for one minute they're so
noisy it's ironic to say that, the next they're running for
their lives. Retiring as fast as they can. So we all holler
with laughter and lay into them. Then up comes this fair
gentleman and his little band. You are killing our enemies,
they say, as if we done it all just for them. Well, the
leader hangs back a bit, but the rest are right eager and
they all go in a huddle with our Blue-Chin. He tells them
what danger they're in, how the Southerners and the

Northern King and now the priest Kaselm at the head of
as deadly an army of wharf-rats and hole-dwellers as ever
was, are all coming against their precious Atlan, and how
each of them, the lot of them knows the secret that'll fill
the airlessness—which, as I understand, is a lie, none of
the Southerners knowing a mite of the secret—but how us
lot have nobly—well, valiantly and gallantly—been holding them off and how they all hate us, ah, even the
Northern King that sent us to get rid of us first on the
Southerners before he sent his favourites for the Atlan
pickings. (Didn't trust our Blue-Shins, he didn't, thought
he might have a go for the throne one of these days. And
now he's higher than him!) Ah, said these fair gentlemen,
you're a great General, you save us. My army's scattered,
says our merry Blue-Thighs, and me with no base to gather
the lads to and from. Use Atlan, they says, it's clear times
have changed and our secret is threatened on all sides,
and by all accounts you're a brilliant General and can lead
your army and ours and set all to rout. Ah, says our
Blue-Blood, but I'm to be of high rank. And their Emperor hisself, stuck gaping at him since he first sets eyes
on him, as clear a case of what they call hero-woship as
ever I'll see, says, You're the New Man, you're the New
World. You are my Emperor!'

Weak, I shuddered.

'So you see how you must welcome us,' said my host.
'There'll be no ravaging here, no screaming bonfires, no
little girls tossed on spears spitted through their nicest
parts—But justice, sweet, clear'n impartial.'

His stupendous stupid Momentity the boy with the
sunfire head, the noble, innocent Atlan counsellors—they
rode on gladly before us. The land, older and wiser than
its inhabitants, shuddered and wailed and rumbled in
great grief and great wrath at our passing.

*   *   *

We camped for the last hours of the night in a very damp dell at the foot of a hill on the far side of that valley. Every man had his own pack of food, most of it furnished, like the horses, by the Atlanteans as soon as they got through the tunnel—wherever the cache was I'd missed it—and my— host, captor, whatever he was—shared dried peas and meat with me, and then expected to roll me up with him in his blanket. 'No,' I said firmly. 'Atlan girls aren't like that. Why, I've not even seen you, and you've not seen me.'

'You sound sweet enough,' he said nicely.

Oh, this was so much the last kind of familiar dialogue I'd expected in Atlan! 'Well, I've not formed that opinion of you,' I said. I was going to refuse. I had business of my own. I didn't feel guilty over taking his food: he'd get plenty when he was the guest-conqueror in the Great City. But it seemed Atlan was no longer Atlan before I'd spent even a day there.

'Come and feel me,' he said persuasively. 'Beyond a bit of stubble, you'll find me fine. I'm twenty-nine, brown eyes, five foot ten—'

'Oh, you're spoiling all the mystery,' I said. I got up and wandered, ignoring his calls. Used to the lay-out of camps, I guessed where the General would be and presently found out I was right. Nobody took any notice of a cloaked figure wandering in the dark rain, Atlan's weeping sky. I saw him. He was talking with Juzd. I waited till Juzd left. I didn't want Juzd to see me again so soon, crawling *to* the Dragon.

He sprawled back against the bank, where a little over-hang made the rain sputter on to his boots, leaving his head to dry from the journey.

I went softly up to him. Through the drum and patter I said, 'Zerd.'

He leapt to his feet (nearly banging his head) sprang at me. and seized my wrist. He said, 'You!'

I was pleased.

'Yes, it's me—Emperor.'

'Juzd said a girl—You—What are you doing here? How do you know to call me that?'

'Oh,' I said lightly. 'I fell in with a man of your escort when your chariot passed me on the road, and he told me everything. Now I suggest you bring me in out of the rain.'

'I always said you'd make the best spy I ever—' He yanked me under the overhang. I sat down composedly, glad he couldn't see the smirk of delight I couldn't get off my mouth. He hunkered on his heels, staring full to my all-but-invisible profile.

'How long have you been here?'

'One day. I was just in time to see the old, real Atlan before you take over and turn her into a second North kingdom. Are you glad to see me?'

He started to grab, then let me go. He said uncertainly, 'You've changed. I always knew you would, yet now it's— You've disconcerted me Cija.' He was almost asking for sympathy. I held in my giggles: I knew they might go on and on. The hysteria was bubbling feverish in me. 'You're mine at last?'

'I'm yours at last.'

He took a deep breath. Still he did not grab. 'You've made me wait long enough,' he grumbled. 'What made you come to your senses?'

'It happened an hour ago. And I didn't decide. It happened. Even in Atlan, you pursue me. Or rather,' I said modestly, 'you come. It's no good holding it off. I think I must belong to you.'

'So you're a fatalist . . . This Atlan, from what you say you don't approve of my being given it? Mind you, it was a gift, I didn't take it.'

'I'm sure that wouldn't matter to you except when you're trying to impress someone like me. And *she*, not *it*.'

'Uh?'

'Atlan, she not—'

'You don't approve?'

I said slowly, 'You are a brilliant General, a meteor who will stay up, but ever moving, ever blazing. Your blaze is power; but you yourself are power-lust. I see you, old, then dead, never leaving the world, still at the head of a train of regiments whose marching feet and axles lift the earth and fill men's hearts with dread, and you at the head, a grinning death's head, lusting after power, marching after it.'

He peered at me for a few moments.

Then he said, 'Yes. You are right.'

And the half-smile did not quite reach his dark eyes.

'Nevertheless,' he said, 'you'll benefit as my Empress. You'll see. We'll have—'

'Empress?' I sort of squeaked rather without dignity.

All at once he was the one to take command of the situation as it dangled. With a hint of the old amusement in his voice he said, 'So you haven't come to me because of my new preferment? You meant to be my loving, loyal slave-girl? But surely you realised no one else would be my Empress?'

'You have two wives at least that I know of,' I said primly, an effort in itself as my heart was going like mad. It wasn't that I was so bowled over at the thought of being an empress, not even a princess or queen but an empress, and of Atlan—well, it wasn't *all* that—but mainly because I was to be his wife, the first one he had ever married without the ulterior motive of rising in the world.

He yawned loudly. 'Them? What, one princess in the Southern Court and the other in the Northern, both soon to be conquered by me? When one is an Emperor one can start over again as far as wives are concerned.'

I didn't really take to the sound of that plural. 'You really think I'm worthy of this honour?'

The sarcasm went right over his head. 'If,' he said

seriously, 'it had ever occurred to me (which of course it never did) to wish for some particular kind of a girl, you are what I would have wished for.'

'You'll look after me? And be with me? And not put me aside when someone greater comes by? But then, I suppose no one can be much higher than Empress of Atlan and Southernland and the North kingdom.'

'And you can't have forgotten you're a Goddess, too? I'll even have the gold-coin-floor of the Northern King transferred here for you.'

'Smahil said it must be mythical. He said gold is so soft they'd lose their imprint as soon as they were walked on and might as well not have been coins in the first place.'

He laughed. 'That up-and-coming young officer was far too smart. Gold coins are invariably made with an alloy that hardens them. Look—hail coming down outside.' He reached out into the shimmer and clatter, said, 'Open your mouth.' I thought of the wrath, the heart of Atlan pouring out its icy lament, its last passionate protest, but I let him feed me hailstones. It was good to be foolish with him, to forget the passion he had aroused for he would lift me high above it. Presently he said softly, 'Would you mind if I held you?'

So I discovered that Zerd's neck is eight kisses long.

He has won. It is all over, all defence, all despair, the purpose and the fighting done with. And I am held in the arms of the death's head, close to it, separated from its corruptness only by his body's and young soul's own ignorance of the corruptness time will break him to, separated from the corruption of earthly war itself only by time and his present ignorance and glory, the blaze of his beauty and arrogance and his body's no-knowledge and I love him.

EPILOGUE

WELL, here I am on the last pages, and I will have to go quickly. I am very nicely settled with everything I can ask for, gold floor and all, in the Palace of the great City built into the mountain (all the terraced streets and main buildings and open places make use of the natural bridges and caves, to say nothing of all the stalagmites and stalactites, and it is a white and blue-veined mountain) on the innermost island of all the concentric circles of land separated by narrow circles of sea which make up Atlan.

The courtyard of the Palace is a glass floor over a deep, green lake. When their masters are late in coming, or when an octopus passes underneath and disturbs them, the horses will strike with their diamond hooves on the courtyard. Their hooves are shod with crescents all of whole diamond—and when they snort and paw the ground the diamonds cut and groove the thick glass. It has been happening for years, the glass is grooved all over, and that is why nobody slips on it.

Yes, all the other lands we have known are subservient to us, and after the most elementary of campaigns. The Northern King's final humiliation is among the keenest of my husband's triumphs.

I insisted on accompanying him, as I've put up with so much while a hostage that campaigning seems nothing with the comforts of an empress, and we had some wonderful times together, though it all went so easily that we could hardly have been said to have had any adventures. I think the most memorable incident was seeing a scarecrow by the wayside dressed in the Superlativity's robes.

It was a shock when my mother came bustling to me. I'd almost forgotten her. 'Clever girl, to get him. You're not going to kill him though.' 'I wouldn't dream of it.' 'Good girl. I offer him my country—I presume he'll let me stay to rule as regent—on condition he deals with the High Priest. Your father is getting too much for me.' That old quarrel, that old striving for that little mastery, had been going on all the time! It was like the unending struggle we are told souls suffer in hell, trying over and over to get the drink which is always removed at the last instant and then with toil nearly gained again.

So at long last my little birth-land is famous and important, the base from which an eye is kept on Northkingdom.

And my birth-prophecy, about which all that fuss was made—I have helped to bring my country under stranger-rule—though, heaven knows, in a very quibbling way, one could say only by being married to the stranger.

I took the opportunity to visit my tower. The nurses were gone; in the old book-room, my books, which nobody ever knew I read and so learnt about men and women even while I believed men had vanished from the face of the earth—mouldy, my favourite pages stuck together with green spots; my Passage had fallen into rubble without my loving use and seemed far smaller than I remembered. I went to the end of it where I had seen the first man I ever saw, and stared out at the mountains again. In all my life mountains have been big. And these, which I watched all my childhood, seemed to symbolise the states of my freedom. The first, conical, terrible, the opening of my cage for my task; the second, about to lurch forward, Southernland; the third, insubstantial shapes and shades shifting, Atlan, the unknown goal.

When we settled home again here I was still telling myself I was terribly happy sometime before I became aware that Zerd was hardly ever with me any more, and that to let 'I am ever so full of joy' become a habit is as dulling as to let misery become a habit.

His desire for me is more spasmodic, but still as intense. I try to forget that too may not last. His desire is of course very satisfying, I mean for me. It satisfies me to be wanted, but I want more from him than this want of his which is a selfishness, the branch of his power-lust which includes me. Yes, he loved me. Well, he has me now. And, yes, he is now frequently unfaithful. There is a girl with pale gold hair—she has held out nearly a year. He is beginning to love her, she has provided him with the time.

Before I knew that the Southern way of making food chemical has been adopted in Atlan, it was too far gone to be stopped. I did try, but was looked upon as a crank. They said, 'Yes, yes,' politely, but it was useless. It would have been just the same if I had kept quiet, except that my stock with my subjects went down a little. I pleaded with Zerd and he laughed.

The Atlanteans are wild about all the new things we are showing them. They are intermarrying with us enthusiastically. Eagerly they helped, for industry, to silt up the plain where the animals danced to the pipe. The Northerners, lords every one of them, each with a household of idolising Atlanteans, have no need to work and so they spend their time hunting the unicorns which they discovered are fine to eat. They will soon be extinct.

I am Empress in Atlan. Two white pangolins play at my feet, a white peacock drifts across my lawn, a white unicorn waits in my stable. He has no name. I have never been able to name any other mount. The little girl who had adventures is over and done with; no mature balanced woman has been able to take her place. I am an observer, there is nothing active about me. I am neutral, perhaps negative.

I have reached the end of this book.

My nurse Glurbia's account-book is quite filled, with minute, cramped writing, even the margins have been used up. Now I shall start another diary—for I *must* always have such a private degree of my identity—but it will never be the same as this one.

However, the inmost kernel of my soul I *must* retain. All the rest of me belongs to him, my beloved, to him.

And he loves me sometimes.